Dedicated to my husband, who encouraged me at every turn.

LEFT *Turn*

The Women of Caprock

LANCY MCCALL

LEFT TURN

Contact Info: https://lancymccall.com

Cover Design by: Best Page Forward

ISBN: 978-1-958975-01-5 (paperback) 978-1-958975-00-8 (ebook)

Published by KruizeTech Press | Houston, Texas

LEFT *Turn*

The Women of Caprock

LANCY MCCALL

KruizeTech Press

Houston, Texas USA

Left turn — an unexpected turn of events.
—Urban Dictionary

Chapter 1

Traveling

ALEX CLOSED her laptop and moved away from the presenter's podium, pleased with the response from the audience. Today was the last day of her company's annual management conference in London. Caprock Enterprises operated in countries all over the world, and managers from those locations had all gathered this week to discuss next year's budget and long-term goals for the future. As the attendees stood and mingled, she easily picked out the women present. Only eight of eighty-four. But eight women in the room was more than last year. *And,* Alex thought, *no waiting in line for the restroom was always a plus.*

Jackie, the company's IT director, came up and helped her gather cords. Alex nodded her thanks as the slender woman handed her the last cable. Alex regularly worked with Jackie's department on projects involving the company's multiple financial systems, and the two of them had become friendly over the last two years. They'd spent a lot of time together this past week as Jackie had helped her put faces to the names of people she'd worked with via email and conference calls, but had never met in person.

"Right, then. Sounded positive. What do you think?" Jackie's crisp British accent sounded at odds against the backdrop of the Texas drawls permeating the room. While the people in the room represented numerous countries, almost half were from the U.S. and most of upper management were from Texas. They were in the oilfield industry, after all.

"I'm so happy I *finally* got to pitch this idea to the management team. I've been working on Frank for a solid year. Hearing the same message from you helped push him to act. Thanks for the support." Alex coiled the cable and stuffed it into her bag.

"Well, you weren't wrong. IT was struggling to keep up with all the requests coming in from different departments, and your idea of consolidating the handling of these initiatives into one overseeing department would make my life easier."

When Alex had first joined Caprock, the company had recently been reorganized, and she'd quickly learned that meant it was drastically *disorganized*. Each division was rushing to get its operations streamlined independently, with no coordination among any of them.

While they'd hired her to integrate the financial systems at the corporate level, her team's resounding success meant she'd received a growing number of requests to assist with efforts beyond their original purview. With the broader perspective, Alex realized how inefficiently the company had managed its improvement efforts by leaving those activities in the hands of the division managers. They needed something more centralized so they could pool resources and combine efforts.

Luckily, such an animal existed. A project management

office would help standardize how the divisions approached managing projects and coordinate efforts across the company. While she'd never worked in a PMO before, she knew several acquaintances who did, and had picked their brains on how they worked. She'd spent the last year researching what it would take to get one started for Caprock and documenting the benefits of doing so.

Alex's gaze skimmed over the mingling crowd again. "When I received the schedule, I worried about presenting on the last day, but I think the extra time worked in my favor. I pitched the concept here and there throughout the week before hitting them with the formal presentation today. And I'm encouraged by the feedback I just received. They actually paid attention and seemed interested in the idea. So, yeah, I feel pretty good right n—" Alex stopped abruptly as her boss approached.

Frank Lambert, her company's CFO, had decades of experience and a penchant for speaking only when he had something important to say.

"Ladies." Frank nodded at Jackie and focused on Alex. "Solid presentation, Alex. Jeff wants you to put together a proposal on this new project office you're touting. What's the acronym again?"

Alex froze at the mention of a proposal. Jeff Davis was the CEO of the company and her boss' boss. Had he just given the green light for her pet project? "It's called the PMO, short for project management office."

"Right. Let's use this opportunity to demonstrate the formal process we're advocating. While we're at it, use one of those project start-up documents you always tell me we should be using to get the ball rolling."

Her eyes gleamed and she couldn't contain the smile

that spread across her face. This was it. All that hard work was about to pay off. "When does he want the proposal by?" Alex asked.

"Yesterday, of course." Frank's grin flashed, then disappeared. "We've missed the first pass for the budget, so if you get the proposal done quickly—and everything sounds reasonable—we still may be able to stick it in before the final pass."

Wait, what? Alex plopped into the chair behind her. "Holy sh—" She caught herself. "You mean *this year's* budget? As in, get it up and running by January... like in three months?" Her elation faded as reality sank in. "I'm not sure I can pull all the numbers together before the final budget deadline."

"I have faith in you. You've been researching this for a while now. I'm sure you have more pieced together than you realize." Someone called his name from across the room, and he glanced over his shoulder. "Anyway, get with me early next week and we'll outline some rough ideas." He gave them a casual wave as he turned to go. "See you back in Houston."

"I don't know why you worried so much." Jackie smirked down at Alex, her tone droll. "Instead of hiding away in your hotel room last night refining your presentation, you could have been getting to know that chap at the bar... the one who couldn't keep his eyes off you. He was very disappointed when you left early."

Alex snorted. "Yeah, right. Like I *ever* have time for nonsense like that." She dismissed the memory of the guy trying to buy their drinks last night. Determined to focus on the present, Alex hopped up from the chair and stashed the rest of her stuff in her computer bag.

"Oh my gawd." Alex grimaced as she drew out the last word. Her Texas upbringing popped up at weird times. "I never expected them to approve it for this year. I was aiming for next year. I've got a ton of work to do. Geez, I'll have to start as soon as I get on the plane," she said as she glanced at her watch. "Speaking of, I better get goin' or I'll miss my flight. Catch you later, Jackie. Thank you so much for your help this week."

"No worries. Safe travels."

Thirty minutes later, as Alex jotted notes in her binder, her phone vibrated and the sound of "Radioactive" by Imagine Dragons filled the taxi's interior. Her mother's name glared at her from the screen. Alex debated answering the call, but didn't want to lose her train of thought. It wasn't that she had issues with her mom, but the woman lived in a different world from Alex. She was probably calling to discuss a new recipe or something the neighbors did. Those conversations were great for lazy Sunday afternoons, but right now, Alex was focused on work.

Alex dismissed the call and made a note to call her mother later. Realizing she was going to have to adjust her plans for the upcoming holidays to accommodate this last-minute change, she marked the reminder with a big asterisk. Her mom would be disappointed when she didn't come home. Again.

Alex winced and turned her thoughts back to the PMO. In her head, she did a little happy dance. *It's finally happening,* she thought. If she and her team could pull the numbers together and get it approved, she could be in charge of one of the most influential departments in the company next year. Accomplishing that before her thirtieth birthday would make the victory even sweeter.

As the cab approached the unloading lane at the airport, Alex gathered her papers, organized them into her bag, and prepared to disembark.

~

Years ago, Fin's agent had recommended the Heathrow VIP service and the privacy it granted him when flying out of London. His route this morning had been a series of handovers from one check-in point to another. The driver who'd picked him up at his hotel, the escort at the VIP drop-off point who'd led him to the VIP area, and the staff who'd made sure he was comfortable. He sipped his drink while the lounge butler reviewed his documents and performed the security screening within the luxury suite, a perk provided for those who used the service.

He needed to thank Addie again for this travel tip. The use of private hallways to walk through the airport, thereby avoiding the press, was a gift he appreciated every time. Thanks to social media and the propensity of fans to post live when they encountered him in public, the paparazzi seemed to have instant access to him. While he appreciated the fans, the constant threat of media hounds—who seemed to increasingly ignore personal boundaries—stressed him out more and more each year. Every time he started a new film, he wondered if this would be the one to break him and turn him into a hermit who hid away from the world.

Fin dreaded the long flight to Houston, but was excited about an upcoming break in the schedule following this weekend's activities. The pause was unusual on a promotional tour—something to do with the director's family—and Fin intended to take full advantage of the downtime. His first priority was rest and relaxation. He wanted a vacation and was determined to play tourist while in Texas. And while he was resting, he planned to dive into a manuscript forwarded to him by a friend. He and Addie had often discussed partnering together on a project over the years, and this might be the opportunity. But he needed to vet it first before presenting it to her.

His phone buzzed in his pocket and he smiled when he read his agent's name on the screen. "How do ye always ken when I'm thinking of ye, lassie?" he asked as he answered the call. His Scottish brogue had lightened over the years of working abroad, but tended to show up when he was relaxed.

"Humph," she snorted. "If that were true, we would never hang up. I bring the spice to your life."

He laughed. Lately, she was the only one who could make him laugh, this woman he thought of as a big sister. "Aye, that's likely true." He pictured her sitting in her LA office, her doe-like brown eyes concentrating on her computer screen and her wavy dark hair tucked behind the ear where she held the phone. And behind her, her latest lover rubbing her shoulders. Addie was never without company, and Los Angeles was full of young, virile men eager to knock about with a powerful Holly-wood agent.

"How was the VIP service? Still top-notch?"

"That's exactly what I had on my mind. This is the best travel tip I've ever received. All those years wearing disguises and dashing in late to avoid the paparazzi... what a waste. I wish I'd found it earlier. And why don't all airports have this kind of service?"

"Hmm... We've requested this service in your last two contracts. I'm going to add it as a standard perk going forward. I don't know why we didn't do that earlier."

"Thanks, love. How's your day going? How's Los Angeles?"

"Oh, the usual... spoiled, whiny clients who need their egos stroked. I wish I could find more like you, low on the melodrama and never causing trouble. You got any more family members interested in acting?" She laughed at her own joke.

Fin snorted at the notion of his brother trying to act his way out of anything as he noticed the lounge butler motioning to him. "Looks like it's time to go, lass. I'll let you know when I land in Houston. Cheers, love."

"Yep," Addie said as he disconnected and stood.

"Mr. McAlister," the man said, his name tag identifying him as George. He nodded to the buttoned-up woman standing next to him, "Helen will escort you to your flight. And thank you again for using our service."

"Thank *you*, George. Have a good one," Fin replied as he followed the austere Helen down a corridor marked "Departures." She led him outside, where a chauffeur loaded his belongings into a luxury sedan intended to take him straight to the plane.

Fin sighed, relieved that even this part of the journey through the airport protected him from being recognized and fawned over. The problem wasn't the fans, he reflected again, but the relentless reporters and paparazzi who made him crazy. The fans he could handle. They were only interested in interacting with him, not invading his private life and turning things upside down.

After exiting the car, Helen led him up a stairwell and through a door near his flight's gate. His step lightened at the upcoming vacation. All he had to do was survive the transatlantic flight and show up for a couple of meet-and-greets, then he was free to disappear. Hopefully, he'd be seated beside a Luddite who didn't follow social media or have a clue who he was.

ALEX SETTLED in to her first-class seat, a perk provided by her company for long flights like this one. At five feet, nine inches tall, she needed every bit of leg room she could get. She was athletic and slim, but had broad shoulders for a woman. Planes became crowded when sitting next to men in the habit of taking up all the space. The wide, roomy seats in first class meant she wouldn't have to explain proper etiquette to someone hogging the armrest or spreading his legs into her personal space.

Alex opened her laptop, eager to work on the proposal for the new PMO. Her fingers flew over the keyboard as she outlined the budget items she needed to pull together. She paused and reminded herself to appreciate this moment. Alex leaned back and closed her eyes, relishing that her dream project was finally getting some traction, and giving a nod of thanks to the universe for spacious seats on ten-hour flights.

"Excuse me, miss?" A deep, soft-spoken voice with a lovely Scottish accent caressed her ear. "That is my seat."

Alex's eyes sprang open as she replied, "Oh, I'm sorry... Am I in the wrong one?"

As she reached for her phone to double-check her ticket, he lifted his hand and responded, "No, you're fine. I didnae want to startle you when I stepped into the window seat. You looked comfortable and... maybe asleep."

Alex laughed as she swung her legs to the side, allowing the man room to move past her into the seat next to her. As he sat and made himself comfortable, she took in his fashionable attire. Her first impression had been that he fit the cliche of "tall, dark, and handsome," but as Alex swept her gaze over him, absorbing more details, she realized she had missed something vital. He was famous. Very famous. Her traveling companion for the next ten hours was none other than Scottish actor and Hollywood's latest A-list leading man, Finley McAlister.

Chapter 2

Conversations on a Plane

As the flight attendants gave the safety review, Alex considered how she should handle sitting with someone so famous. Just ignore him? Start up a conversation? Should she acknowledge she recognized him? Deciding to approach it the way she did every time she traveled, she pulled out the safety card and followed along, leaving it to her fellow passenger to set the ground rules. If he wanted privacy, she would give it to him. As fascinated as she was sitting next to a celebrity, she did have an urgent proposal she needed to put together.

Once the plane left the ground, the flight attendant brought their drinks. Alex had given her order earlier, but hadn't seen when the actor had done so. Possibly they already had his preferences on file. She was ignorant of all things related to celebrities.

As the woman reached across to hand Finley McAlister his drink, the plane hit a pocket of air and dipped. Alex whisked her laptop out of the way as he lunged forward and grabbed the cup. All three expressed sighs of relief at the averted disaster.

"Thanks," Alex said, as she accepted the napkins from the flight attendant and dabbed at the few drops that landed on her slacks. She looked at her fellow passenger and offered him a smile. "Quick moves on your part," she said.

He grinned back. "Aye, nothing like a drink-soaked laptop to get your trip off to a good start." He wiped a spot on the armrest and one on the drink tray she'd missed.

"Thanks," she said, nodding at the drink tray. "I'm actually ending my trip, but that still would have sucked. I'm headed home after a week of management meetings. And you? Business or pleasure?" She turned to face him.

He went motionless and stared into her eyes, as if trying to read her intent. Had she known what a brilliant blue his eyes were? He suddenly grinned and sat back in his seat.

"Both. A few days of work, then I'm on holiday for two weeks."

"Oh, yeah? Are you taking your vacation in the Houston area? Or flying on to somewhere else?"

He looked away from her to stare out the window and sighed. "I don't quite know. I would like to disappear and go off the grid, but I may not have the option. So I'm playing it by ear." He cleared his throat and turned back to her, the uncertainty in his eyes vanishing. "You are from Houston?"

The doubt in his voice before the change of subject surprised her. She'd expected a Hollywood actor to be full of confidence. "Yes. I grew up in West Texas, but have lived in Houston for many years now. I'm Alex," she said as she extended her hand to him.

He took her hand in his and raised an eyebrow. "Alex? Unusual for a woman."

The unexpected warmth of his hand sent an electric zing up her arm, distracting her. *What the heck was that?* she wondered.

She rubbed her fingers together and focused on his unspoken question. "Short for Alexis, but Alex fits me better. Also, particularly useful to have a man's name when working in a male-dominated field within a male-dominated industry." She smirked at the last bit, then asked, "And you are...?"

"Fin. And I understand how that would work to your advantage. What do you do for a living?"

So that's how we're playing this, Alex thought. *Focus on me and we don't have to acknowledge who you are.* With the rules of engagement set, Alex told him about her job as a project manager, throwing in a few stories about working in the sometimes "redneck" environment of oilfield manufacturing. She entertained him with stories of traveling as the only female in the group. He had a rich laugh, and she enjoyed bringing a grin to his face.

"I like your accent," he told her.

She gave him an affronted look, then played up her Texas drawl, "*Ah* have no idea to what y'all are *referrin'. Ah* do *nawt* have an accent." She burst into giggles, and he laughed with her. "Oh, man. You know, I tell people not everyone from Texas is a cowboy or an oil baron, but I was raised on a cattle ranch, rode horses, and rounded up cows. And now I work in the oilfield. I'm a walking cliché!" She rolled her eyes and threw her hands in the air.

He chuckled at her joke and asked, "You ride horses?"

"I did. It's been a while. How about you?"

"Aye. I love horses. I keep a few back home and ride as much as possible. Unfortunately, it's not as often as I would like," he added, his mouth turned down.

"Where is 'back home?' In Scotland?" she prompted. Again, he went still and narrowed his eyes at her, so she added, "Your brogue isn't as pronounced as some of my colleagues, but it still comes through."

Fin's shoulders relaxed. "Aye, in Scotland. I grew up near Aberdeen and still have a home there."

They traded stories from their childhoods. She learned he had an older brother and a younger sister with whom he'd shared many adventures exploring the countryside. He learned she had grown up an only child surrounded by an extended family made up of ranch hands, veterinarians, and other ranch-related workers. They laughed at each other's youthful adventures until the flight attendant interrupted them for the meal.

As they ate, Fin pointed to her laptop and asked if he had interrupted her work. His consideration touched Alex. "No, it's fine. You may not have noticed, but I'm an extrovert and like to talk to people. Maybe a tad too much," she added with a grin. "But not everyone wants to engage that way, so I keep it handy in case the passenger next to me would rather not converse."

"I'm curious. How do you determine if people want to talk? Or if they would prefer to sit quietly?"

She shrugged. "Tool of my trade. I work with everyone from the shop floor to the C-level executives. And *that* comes with a slew of varied environments, expertise, social norms, and personalities. It's critical to know how to read the room—to understand the atmosphere and keep every one of those diverse personalities focused on the endgame. Body language, terminology used, behavior patterns... a person communicates much of their inner thoughts without ever opening their mouth. It's my job to filter through the noise and decipher what's going on beyond what's being said."

He stared at her. She could see the wheels turning in his head, trying to remember what he had said and how he had behaved... wondering if she knew his secrets. She'd seen that startled look before when she'd described what she did. Fin squirmed in his seat and Alex sensed his discomfort growing.

"For instance, I pegged you as a 'sitting in silence type' so you surprised me by making small talk." She grinned at him and gave him a friendly wink, hoping to break the tension caused by her previous remark.

He burst out laughing. "Well, no one has ever accused me of being—what is it you Americans say?—a 'Chatty Cathy,' but you're easy to talk to." He paused long enough for Alex to wonder if he would say anything further, then added, "I'm an introvert by nature and have become protective of my privacy in recent years."

She nodded. "The Internet has made it easy to feel exposed. We should all pay more attention to our privacy. It's an excellent practice."

He ate a few bites as he pondered this.

The conversation turned to places each had visited and locations still on their bucket lists. The time passed pleasantly, and Alex realized they only had a few hours left on the flight. Strange how disappointing that was.

Fin stretched in his seat and watched Alex stand to retrieve her backpack from the overhead bin. She was tall for a woman and moved with a grace born of both athleticism and confidence. Her wavy blond hair swayed around her shoulders as she moved. He noticed several men and one woman likewise observing her physique and smiled in appreciation, wondering if she was aware of the effect she had on others. He doubted it.

As the captain announced the weather conditions for Houston, he closed his eyes and thought about the last nine hours. He felt so relaxed. Alex was delightful company, her sense of humor both witty and self-effacing. She didn't seem to know who he was, which meant he could let down his guard and be himself. He didn't have to mind what he said or watch for an unexpected camera pointing at him. He wanted that feeling to continue, an escape from reality for a little while longer.

From everything they discussed, he gathered Alex was single. She was a career woman who worked hard and lived fully. He wondered if she would be up to spending some time with him during his self-imposed retreat.

Paper rustled beside him, and he opened his eyes to see her looking at him while she opened a pack of pretzels. Before he could say anything, she asked, "Tired?"

"No, I was thinking how lovely this plane ride has been."

"Yeah, me too. You're a wonderful conversationalist."

"So... Since I've got time to kill while I'm in town, what should I do in Houston?"

"Oh, gosh, let me see... Houston is an international city and has all kinds of cuisines to choose from. And it might surprise you to learn that Houston has an impressive theater district. You can catch all kinds of performances—ballet, symphony. We also have museums, loads of history, and a great zoo..." She trailed off as Fin held up his hand.

"You misunderstand me. I meant what do *you* like to do in your spare time?" Fin appreciated her enthusiasm. She obviously loved her city.

"Oh, sorry," she said, "I play volleyball. I'm in a co-ed league during the week and then play on a women's team on the occasional weekend. When I'm not traveling, that is."

"Volleyball."

"Yes." She raised her eyebrow at him.

"Like beach volleyball?"

"Yes, in the co-ed league. We play fours... um, four people on a team. It's sand volleyball on a men's regulation net. After playing each week in the sand on the taller men's net, I feel like a superhero when I get in the gym on a women's net. Like I can block *anything* that comes near me." Her cheeks reddened as she tapered off. "Um, it's a load of fun." She pressed her lips together and looked away.

Her passion touched him, and her embarrassment over it endeared her to him. "I've played volleyball before. It is fun."

She looked at him and grinned. He stared into her stormy gray eyes, wondering why he felt so drawn to her? Was it the departure from his normal world that was attractive? Or the woman herself who intrigued him?

The captain interrupted their scrutiny of each other by announcing the imminent arrival at their gate and asking everyone to stay seated until it was time to disembark. Fin watched Alex give her head a tiny shake while she gathered her things and realized he wasn't ready to end their conversation. Something about this woman drew him to her. Perhaps it was because she didn't know who he was, or possibly it was simply Alex herself. Either way, he wanted to extend their time together.

Fin reached over and laid his hand on her arm. She jumped at his touch, and he hesitated. He cleared his throat. "Alex, I hope I'm not being too forward as we've just met, but would you like to have dinner with me while I'm in town?"

He watched as she sat back in her seat and stared at him. What was going through her head? Was he being too forward? He tried not to fidget as he waited for her response.

"Yes, Fin, I'd love to go to dinner with you. Let me give you my phone number so you can call me."

He reached for his phone. "And what day is your volley-ball league?" he asked casually, as he typed in her contact information.

"Um, let's see... right now, league nights are Tuesdays and Thursdays. Why do you want to know?"

The weight of her gaze burned into him as he continued to stare at his phone. "If dinner goes well, perhaps I can come watch you play volleyball?"

"What?" she squeaked.

He looked up and smiled. "My schedule is clear for two weeks and it's been a while since I've seen a good volleyball match. Even longer since I've played myself." He laughed to himself as he remembered the last match he had played with his siblings and cousins. The game ended up more of a free-for-all than an actual match, and they had all wound up in a muddy mess.

Fin waited for her answer.

~

He wants to go to volleyball with me?

Alex wasn't sure why a big-shot Hollywood actor would want to hang around with a bunch of average Joes. As she recalled his earlier statements about getting away and privacy becoming a priority, she wondered if he wanted to lose himself in normalcy. Okay, fine. He seemed nice enough, and she didn't get any creepy vibes from him. Why not let him have his "regular guy" time? Her friends wouldn't mind. He would only be in town for a little while, so why not live on the wild side?

"Sure," she told him. "Call me when your schedule allows, and we'll coordinate. You know, if you're interested in playing, people are always looking for subs for absent team members. We're easy that way."

His smile lit up his face. "Excellent. I'll call you this weekend and we'll go play volleyball. Then I'll take you out somewhere more formal on a separate night."

Alex's eyes widened, but before she could respond, the plane doors opened and everyone exited the plane. As they walked down the jetway, Fin donned a hat and dark glasses. Alex raised her eyebrow at him, but said nothing as they walked together in companionable silence to the baggage area. Occasionally, Alex looked his way, but Fin kept grinning and continued walking.

As they watched the conveyor belt bumping along spewing forth everyone's bags, Alex noticed the growing buzz in the crowd and spied a group of girls pointing at Fin. *Uh oh,* she thought, *his cover is about to get blown and he won't like that.* Her slate-blue suitcase approached, and she recognized an opportunity for escape. She dragged the bag off the carousel and turned her back to the crowd.

"Okay, this is me. It was nice to meet you, Fin. You have my number. Let me know when you're free. See ya!" she exclaimed, then spun and walked away before everything went awry.

Fin's "You too" reply followed her as she walked away,

his gaze burning into her back. She couldn't believe a movie star had asked her on a date, and she had said yes! While she'd never expected to hear from the man again, she thought it was a great story to tell her friends. They were going to lose their minds when she told them about meeting him.

Chapter 3

Friday Night

FIN WATCHED ALEX WALK AWAY. He had decided earlier to forego the celebrity treatment at the Houston airport, hoping to prolong his time with Alex, and had texted Addie earlier while still in flight so she could make adjustments as needed. Fin wasn't sure what had just happened, but ten hours of easy banter with an incredibly attractive woman had abruptly ended.

Before he could consider her hasty departure further, someone shrieked, "Oh my god, that's Finley McAlister!" He stiffened and assumed his Hollywood face, as Addie liked to call it. It was time to play celebrity. Thank goodness Alex had left before anyone spotted him. He smiled brighter.

Fin gripped the handle on his suitcase and looked for his driver, hoping he'd given Addie enough time to convey the change in plans. He spotted a man holding a sign with his travel pseudonym written on it. The fake name was a trick he'd learned long ago to avoid advertising his arrival. Nothing attracted fans like a guy holding up your name around the airport. Despite these precautions, his fans had spotted him.

Fin nodded to the driver in acknowledgment and motioned for him to stow the sign as he wandered over, his fans trailing after him.

Thirty minutes later, Fin sat safely ensconced in the backseat of the car arranged by his agent to take him to his hotel. Speaking of his friend and business partner, he sent her a text letting her know he had arrived. Before he could tuck his phone away, it buzzed with Addie's face appearing on the screen.

"What?" He laughed into the phone as he answered.

"You did good signing autographs at the airport," her smoky voice came over the line. Addie sounded sultry naturally, and her Mexican accent added to the exotic vibe.

Fin groaned. "You're kidding. I barely left there. How is it I've already made the news?"

"You are a star. People tweet. I scan for tweets about you. It's all a part of the service I deliver, pretty boy. Now, are you ready for tonight? Got all your luggage? Everything good?"

He smiled at her maternal attitude. "Yes, Mother. I can also wipe my own arse."

"Ha ha." Addie paused, then added, "Look, Fin, I am aware how much you hate these things, but tonight should be a quick in and out. All you have to do is show up, smile at the camera, and wave to the fans. You can sneak away after an acceptable amount of time. Luckily, the meet-and-greet is in the same hotel you are staying at, so escaping should be easy. You might squeeze in a nap beforehand if you're jet-lagged. Wouldn't want you to have any bruises from fatigue under those baby blues. Although given the hour, you better set an alarm if you sleep because you don't have much time before you have to make an appearance." She paused and waited for him to speak.

"I am fine. Truly."

"Okay. Now, about the rest of your week... I knew you wanted time off, so I researched some things for you to do around there—"

Fin interrupted her. "I've planned my week already."

"*¿Qué?*"

Fin smiled at the question and had a random thought that he knew more Spanish since Addie came into his life. "I met someone on the plane who's from here and had some ideas."

Silence greeted him. He waited. He discovered years ago he would always win the silent treatment contest with Addie. The woman could not contain herself.

"Was this local mystery person a woman?" she asked cautiously.

"Aye," he answered.

"Oh, Fin... you know they love your stardom."

"No, it's not like that. She didn't even recognize me. It was... it was lovely. I was just a regular guy on a business trip chatting with a stranger on a plane."

More silence. He pictured the gears spinning in her head. "You're making me very nervous right now."

"Don't worry. I am a grown man. Look, we're almost at the hotel. I'll buzz you later and let you know how everything went. Addie, it's okay. Cheers, love."

"Fin, I really—"

He disconnected and cut off whatever pearls of wisdom she would have thrown at him. Fin was beyond lucky to have found Addie. She was a guiding light who helped him navigate not only the legalities and responsibilities that came with his chosen profession, but also the politics and ugly social pressure that could make or break a career. He was certain he would have left the industry long ago without her by his side. But right now, this week... he wanted to fulfill his obligations for this latest project and disappear. He was tired. Tired from his work and tired of himself.

Fin laid his head against the headrest and thought about the woman from the plane. Alex. No, Alexis. He smiled as he remembered her exuberance. She seemed so confident in herself. And she was wrong about her name... Alexis fit her perfectly. He assumed she could fit in well as one of the boys, but there was no hiding she was all woman. He had covertly studied her during the flight. She had a natural attractiveness that caught your eye first, but her animated fervor and her easy laughter were what held your attention. And he was fairly certain she had no clue how captivating she was. The times Alex had gotten up to move around the cabin, Fin had noted how fit she looked and once, when she'd reached into the overhead compartment, her shirt had raised and given him an unexpected glimpse of a nicely defined stomach. He looked forward to spending more time with her. His brow furrowed. He needed to rearrange some things on his schedule so he could do exactly that.

Fin perused the calendar on his phone. The dinner tonight and the press junket tomorrow were "must attend" functions, but the other events Addie had lined up were extra "show up and be seen" gatherings he could blow off with no notice. He removed them and blocked tentative spots for evening activities with Alex. He would call her tomorrow and ask what time volleyball was, and then they could plan their second evening later.

~

ALEX PLOPPED the suitcase on her bed and tossed her coat on the chair in the corner. That poor thing only came out when she traveled, as the Houston climate was far too mild for a winter coat.

As she unzipped her bag to unpack, she stifled a yawn. She learned long ago to avoid that afternoon flight from the U.K. or else jet lag would disturb her rhythm for days until she acclimated. Unfortunately, her schedule this week meant the late flight was the only one that worked. And given today was Friday, she had a full weekend to recover. Besides, she couldn't grumble too much about the flight given the company she'd shared on the way home.

She finished unpacking her bag and was stowing it away in her closet when a voice she recognized called from the back of her house.

Alex wandered out to greet Eddie, her landlord. "Hello, you big ray of sunshine. Any trouble with Felix?"

"None, as usual. He probably thinks we all belong to him." He set her cat on the floor and held his arms open for a hug. When she stepped into his embrace and hugged him fiercely, he lifted her up and twirled her about.

"Well, now. It must have been a good trip. Usually when you arrive this late, you're dragging ass." He chuckled as he set her down.

"Great trip." She reached out to the cat, and Felix jumped up into her arms. "I got approvals all around on one project and looks like they're interested in my PMO idea. Oh, and..." she paused dramatically, "you will absolutely die when I tell you who I sat beside for ten hours flying home."

"Ooh, sounds like a story I need to hear. Let's save it for supper so Gabe can hear it as well. We knew you'd be getting home at a weird time, so he threw something together. Since you're not a fan of British cuisine, he's made a full-on Cajun meal that's waiting on you next door. Change into your comfy clothes, then come over and dish."

Alex's stomach rumbled at the thought of Gabe's famous seafood gumbo. "Oh man, sounds delicious. Give me five minutes and I'll be right over." Eddie's partner, Gabe, was the head chef at one of Houston's most prominent restaurants and Cajun food was his specialty.

Eddie left and Alex dumped Felix onto her bed, then hopped into the shower for a quick wash. She brushed her teeth and shoved on a t-shirt with sweatpants. On her way out the door, she picked up the bag containing the gifts she'd purchased for her two best friends.

Alex lived in the smaller, one-bedroom side of a duplex she shared with her landlord. Eddie, whom she'd met through work a few years ago, owned both their property and the one next door. The two properties together made up what he referred to as their compound. Both houses had been converted into duplexes. Eddie had redone the landscaping, adding a large paved area between and behind the houses, perfect for guest parking or outdoor social events. The covered parking area sported an upstairs apartment, which brought the number of living spaces on the lot to five.

Eddie and Gabe were the brothers she'd never had, and their social nature meant she met new and intriguing people at their many parties and gatherings. And the pair loved Felix, so when she traveled, they watched him for her. In return, she brought them mementos for their collections. Eddie loved ties, and Gabe had a collection of spoons. Every time she traveled, she tried to pick up another piece for each of them.

She knocked on their pristine white front door. Gabe opened the door and gave her a welcoming hug. He was such a contrast to his partner. Where Eddie was blond, lean, and flamboyant—both in his appearance and his personality—Gabe was tall, dark, and quiet. If you didn't know him, you might consider him menacing by his appearance alone. He looked strikingly similar to the actor who played the prisoner in the movie *The Green Mile*. But Gabe was the furthest thing from a baddie—he was a big, soft kitty cat.

She kissed his cheek and said, "A little birdie told me y'all have gumbo over here and I came to mooch."

"Funny. You will never be mooching in this house, Lexi Bear," he replied in his deep, resonant voice. "Come on in and sit down. You want wine? Or iced tea?"

As she sat at the table, Eddie's dog came over to greet her. Dixie, a rescue dog with mixed terrier origins, rose on her hind legs to stand against Alex's leg. Alex set the gift bag on the table, picked her up, and rubbed Dixie's head, nodding at the wine bottle Gabe held. "Wine, please." She had learned over the years to trust his suggestions when matching wine to the meal or occasion.

"Mmm, it smells delicious, Gabe. I always lose weight when I travel to London. Their food is so... so brown. Except for the Indian food. The Brits do love their Indian food."

"How have you known me this long and are still so ignorant about food? You cannot describe how something tastes using the color 'brown.' You need to use your words." He rolled his eyes.

"Selective ignorance is a talent of mine," she said, winking as she snagged a piece of fried okra. She moaned at the flavor that exploded in her mouth. "I'm dying. This is heaven and I am dead."

Eddie came in from the back of the house with a flourish and told Gabe to sit down and quit fussing with everything because Alex had a juicy story for them. He had changed and now wore what he called his evening clothes. Alex compared her comfy t-shirt and sweats to Eddie's stylish lounging suit, a dark blue trimmed with random large gold spiraling swirls. She shook her head and smiled. The dude was a fashion diva.

"Right. So, I get on the plane and guess who sits down next to me?" She paused for effect. "None other than Finley McAlister."

They both stared at her. Eddie broke the silence and asked, "The actor?"

"Yep."

"For real?"

"Yep."

The guys looked at each other for a second. Gabe drank from his wine glass, then quietly commanded, "Start talking," as he passed the cornbread.

While they ate dinner, Alex told them of her flight, how charming and polite the guy was, how normal he'd seemed, and pieces of the conversation they'd had, omitting any personal details. Once they were satisfied she had shared everything from the encounter, the guys began listing the movies Fin had starred in, and a lively debate ensued over which was the best and worst.

As they finished dinner and cleared the table, Eddie asked Alex why Finley was in Houston. She shrugged. "I don't know. I'm not sure he realized I recognized him, and I got the impression he enjoyed the anonymity, so I didn't ask too many questions. He said he was in town for a work-related event, then a vacation. You know, I felt bad for him. Even as I left the airport, people started recognizing him. It must suck to get mobbed everywhere you go."

"Price of fame, baby. Price of fame."

"I guess so," she agreed. Alex considered mentioning that Fin had asked her out, but didn't want to disappoint them when he never called. Better to omit that part than have them upset with someone they admired. "Anyway, now I have one of those 'I once met someone famous' encounters to tell my future children about."

A yawn caught her by surprise and Eddie told her, "Okay, sugar, it's time for you to get some sleep. Since you spent your ten-hour plane ride yapping your gums instead of resting, you better get off to bed."

"Yes, Mother." She smirked as she got up to leave.

"Don't you get sassy with me, young lady," Eddie replied as he shooed her toward the door. "We'll see you later. Sleep tight."

"Goodnight, Eddie Boo." She shouted back down the hall to Gabe, "Goodnight, Gabriella," and took off to her duplex.

Chapter 4

Saturday

ALEX SLEPT SURPRISINGLY WELL. She woke early and went for a run. Running was her least favorite mode of exercise, but living in The Heights made it more palatable. The neighborhood, dating back to when Houston was first founded, contained splendid historic houses and majestic oak trees too wide to put her arms around. The scenery seeped into her bones and her energy soared, making her morning jog enjoyable and invigorating. With her favorite podcast playing in her earbuds, getting in a quick workout was no problem.

This morning's podcast of choice focused on major current events. Reporters followed a particular news event from inception to the current state and gave in-depth information behind the story. After joining an international company and working with an international team, she'd observed how her foreign coworkers were incredibly knowledgeable about world events. To her chagrin, they often knew more about her nation's politics than she did. This realization prompted her to educate herself, and she found listening to this podcast helped get her up to speed on current events while multitasking.

After thirty minutes around the neighboring blocks and an education on how the Middle East came to be, she arrived back home. She jogged up the driveway to the back of the duplex and bent over with her hands on her knees. Her phone rang, and she frowned at the unknown number.

"This is Alex," she answered as she tried to control her breathing.

After a pause, he spoke. She would know his voice anywhere, she realized. It slid through the airways like butter on a hot roll. "Hello, Alexis. It's Fin." He dropped an octave as he asked, "Am I interrupting something? Ye're breathing awfully hard."

She stood so fast her head spun. Good lord, had her name ever sounded so sexy? She could feel her insides go all melty. As his words registered and his implied meaning sunk in, her face heated with more than just exertion from her run. "Um, hi. You caught me at the end of a jog, and I haven't fully caught my breath yet."

Fin chuckled in her ear as Eddie came around the corner dragging a water hose, with Dixie trotting happily behind him. Eddie scanned her face and stopped, blatantly listening to her end of the call while the dog ran to Alex for belly rubs.

"Aye, the weather's quite lovely here, isn't it?" Fin continued without waiting for a reply, "I thought I would follow up on our agreement to get together. I'm booked today, but free afterward. What works for you?"

"Um..." Alex was thrown off balance by this phone call. She'd never expected him to call. "Tuesday is volleyball night," she blurted.

"Okay. Would you like to have dinner before then? How about we do something tomorrow night?"

Eddie, the busybody, wandered closer and she shooed him away, rolling her eyes when he ignored her.

"Um…" She inhaled deeply to clear her head. "I usually stay in Sunday night, getting ready for the upcoming work week."

His silky-smooth voice flowed over the line again. "That sounds wonderful. Why don't we order something in?"

"Seriously?" Alex squeaked, her voice rising two octaves as the question escaped. She cleared her throat and asked, "You want to come hang out at my place and eat in?" She couldn't imagine this A-list movie star wanting to spend time with the common folk like her.

"Why, I'd be delighted. Thank ye for asking. When and where should I show up and what kind of food do you like?"

Oh my god, she thought, *I did not just invite him over. What is happening? How did he turn this all around on me?* She didn't normally get flustered so easily, but she honestly had not expected to hear from him again.

By now, Eddie stood right beside her with his eyes so wide she imagined them popping out of his head.

"Alex," Fin inquired, "are you still there?"

"Yes. Um, I'll text you the address. I have to go."

He chuckled again, as if he knew the effect he had on her. "Don't forget to send me the time and your food pref-erences."

She stammered, "Yeah, okay. Gotta go," as she ended the call and swung around to look at Eddie.

"What just happened?" they both exclaimed together.

After a fit of laughter at the coincidence, she answered, "Somehow, I got swindled into inviting Mr. Hot and

Dreamy over for dinner tomorrow night. What *did* just happen? And why the hell did I sound like a stammering schoolgirl when I talked to him?"

Eddie squealed like a little girl himself and shouted for Gabe to come around the side. As the big man came strolling around the corner, Eddie scooped up Dixie and looped his arm through Alex's, pulling her toward her door.

"Gabe, darling, Alex has a date with her movie star. He's coming here tomorrow night. We *must* help with this. C'mon, girl… let's go peruse your wardrobe." Before she could object, he cut her off and continued, "I know you look fabulous when dressing for work, but your casual outfits are a bit too butch. Sweats, tank tops, and t-shirts will not work for this kind of casual date. Gabe, what are you waiting for, darling? You need to put together a menu while I work on the girl. We are cooking for this man. No takeout for us!" And with that, he handed the dog off to Gabe and whisked Alex inside.

FIN HUNG up the phone and smiled. It had been a long time since he had interacted with anyone so unpredictable. No, that wasn't right. Unpredictable described the situation, not the woman. Alex was natural and true to herself, unlike the people he usually dealt with. He sighed as he noticed his assigned guide for the press junket walking towards him. He tucked away his feel-good moment and put on his professional face. Time to work.

Fin began his rounds, talking to reporters and other industry heads as he promoted the new film. Typically, he had an assigned room in the suite rented by the movie producers. The interviewers would come in and ask questions during their twenty-minute slots. That meant anywhere from fifteen to twenty quick interviews with a few strategic breaks in between, depending on how packed the schedule was.

Over the years, he and Addie had worked hard on cultivating an image with the press that screamed "stay away from my private life if you want an interview," and this image helped him navigate events like this much easier. When he'd first started drawing attention in the industry, they'd been more interested in who he dated than the work he did. These days they focused on his work, and any newbies who hadn't gotten the message didn't get invited back for future interviews. Word spread and people played by the rules. Mostly. Occasionally, he still had to give his dead-eye stare until the interviewer moved on to another question. He had perfected that stare. He'd only used it twice in this morning's torture rounds.

During the lunch break, Fin found a spot at a corner table away from the crowd. A loud clang rang out as his costar, Mac, pulled out the chair beside him, bumping the base on the leg of the table. Fin grinned. Francis "Mac" McBrewster was a veteran actor who had more movies under his belt than everyone in the room combined. Yet somehow, he stayed in the background and the press didn't hound him as much. Fin wished he knew Mac's secret.

"Finley! How's it going?" Mac asked boisterously.

Fin's grin broadened at his friend's cheeriness. "Great," he declared sarcastically. "Only eight more to go. What I want to know is how you have all this energy and how do you keep it up? I'm already exhausted halfway through."

"Ah, that's easy. I love this shit! And I'm an extrovert. I

get my energy from people. You, on the other hand, are a diehard introvert. People suck the life out of you. You need a massage or some other spa treatment tomorrow to get your groove back."

"Mm-hmm." Fin nodded in agreement, thinking it odd that his introversion had come up twice within twenty-four hours.

"So, what all are you appearing at this week?" Mac waved the brochure containing the scheduled promotional events. "I haven't yet decided which of these affairs I'm attending. I'm thinking about the one down at the Space Center."

"Aye, the NASA tour looked appealing," Fin agreed, "but I'm not planning to attend any others. I'm sticking to the required events and taking some time off before our next leg."

"Ah, a bit of 'me time.'"

"Precisely."

Mac clasped his hands behind his head and stared at the ceiling for a few seconds, then looked back at Fin. "Ya know, that sounds inviting. Maybe I'll take a minute or two to myself. Texas is a great place to get lost. It's so big, you know." He waggled his eyebrows at Fin and laughed at his own joke. "And the women here are gorgeous!" Thinking of Alex, Fin agreed with his assessment.

They spent the lunch hour discussing their various interview experiences from the morning, the state of Texas, and how Mac could wrangle up some company for his Texas adventures. Soon the junket staffers came to collect their charges and Fin left for this next round of interviews, feeling lighter after lunch with Mac.

Miranda Cole slid behind a column, hiding from the three men at the far end of the hallway. She'd managed to avoid Finley McAlister all day and didn't want to blow it as her interview time approached. When her colleague, another reporter from *Celebrity News*, had fallen ill, she'd jumped at the chance to take his place.

Finley McAlister was the one blight on her otherwise successful track record. They'd bumped heads early in her career as a Hollywood beat reporter, and he had actively blocked her access to him ever since that one ugly run-in. It frustrated her that she had identified him early as someone to watch and then been denied the opportunity to do so. Well, that hadn't stopped her. She'd followed his career from afar and watched him rise from a local stage actor to an international film star nominated for and winning multiple awards.

Everything she'd read about him said his life was ideal, but Miranda knew this business. No one was *that* perfect. She wanted the real story, the one he kept hidden. McAlister exasperated her, guarding his privacy like a hungry dog protecting a bone.

She'd had minions following him for years, but her last promotion had given her the clout to get back into his inner realm. Miranda had clawed her way into a position that commanded respect and came with the chops to demand airtime from him. And she intended to get it.

However, his success gave him clout of his own. McAlister blacklisting her meant she had to carefully plan her reinsertion into his orbit. The opportunity to represent the entertainment news company at this event was her way back. His schedule still showed her colleague's name on this afternoon's interview. She planned to use the misprint to catch McAlister off-guard and see what juicy tidbits she could get out of him. Every good reporter knew the key to getting the scoop was a surprise attack.

FIN OPENED a fresh water bottle and scowled as the reporter for his last interview session walked into the room. This woman was on his "no fly" list. In fact, she was on his "no way, not ever" list. By nature, she was ruthless. And they had a particularly ugly history. He wanted nothing more than to demand how she'd made it in the room, then show her the door. But that didn't fit the professional image he and Addie had cultivated over the years, so instead, he lingered for a minute at the refreshment station and shored up his defenses for the upcoming confrontation. *You are a professional*, he reminded himself. He would get through this, and then rip someone a new one for allowing her anywhere near him.

Fin ambled back to his chair and coolly acknowledged the woman as he sat. "Ms. Cole."

Miranda Cole smiled back at him with a smarmy look in her eye. *Great*, he thought, *she's looking pretty smug at manipulating her way onto my schedule.*

"Finley, how have you been?" she purred.

"Fine. Shall we begin?" He cut off any attempt at small talk and pushed to move the interview along. *Twenty minutes*, he reminded himself, *it's only twenty minutes*. He hoped he could get through this without losing his cool.

She began with a few customary questions about the film and how he'd approached his character development, which he fielded with his standard answers. Then she leaned forward and arranged her face into a serious, probing look. Fin wondered if she practiced the look in the mirror. Perhaps she regarded the pose as the one that would propel her to the top. *Here it comes,* he thought, *the question that makes my head explode.* He mentally braced himself while schooling his features to show no reaction.

"So, word is you got off the plane yesterday with a rather attractive blonde. Care to share with your fans exactly who she is?" she asked.

Fin was so surprised by the question he burst into laughter. "I didn't."

"Didn't what?"

"Well, let's see… technically, I guess I did. I, along with 200 other passengers, walked to the baggage claim area together to pick up our bags." He yawned and blinked at her, hoping she would take the hint and move on.

"My sources say you walked side by side with one woman the entire way through the airport," she insisted.

"Ms. Cole," Fin's voice dripped with disdain, "it's a direct path from the gate to the baggage area. Is it truly newsworthy if I walk the same route as a fellow passenger? Your access to interesting news must be limited if *that* is the story of the week. I can see the headline now: 'Finley McAlister Walks to Baggage Claim beside Random Passenger.' Titillating news in the entertainment world today."

He examined his nails as her face reddened with anger. She looked down and brushed at her skirt, then raked him with her eyes. Her icy tone scraped his nerves. "Your fans want to know about you, Finley. Why are you so selfish? Why don't you share with them? They are, after all, the ones who put you where you are today. You owe them everything. What's her name and what is she to you? Your fans want to know."

"Right." Fin stood up to leave the room. "We're finished here." As he walked away, he could hear her sputtering behind him. He released a slow breath, relieved he had kept himself composed, and held it together at her last statement.

As he opened the door, he found Mac walking by. Mac glanced at Fin's face, then peeked behind him into the room. "Oh, boy... how'd she get in there with you?"

"I don't know, but I'm on my way to find out."

Mac patted him on the shoulder and said, "I assume you need some damage control? Let me see if I can help you there." As Mac moved into the room, he bellowed, "Miranda Cole! It's been ages since we've talked. How come you haven't interviewed me? Well, no problem, we can fix that... Now, what questions do you have for me?" Mac's voice faded as the door shut behind him.

Fin approached the main room, determined to find the event coordinator and give her a piece of his mind. On his way, he ran into Buck Cabot, one of the film's producers. Buck took one look at Fin's face and pulled him off to the side.

"What's wrong, Fin?"

"Why is Miranda Cole here?" Fin asked without preamble.

"She's the lead reporter from a popular entertainment news show. Why wouldn't she be here?"

"Because she's on my fuck-all-the-way-off blacklist, explicitly given to the production company and written into my contract in large bold letters. She should never have gotten anywhere near me, much less put on my schedule. Who fucked that up?" Fin practically shouted the last bit.

Buck stepped back and held up his hands in a placating gesture. "I can see you're upset. I can't say what happened, but I will look into it and get back to you."

"Good, because I'm done. You're lucky this was the last scheduled interview. And I won't be at any of the other public events. I'm out of here."

THE ROOMY SHOWER cube in the suite's master bath came with a massaging shower head. After making the water as hot as he could stand it, Fin adjusted the massage setting to "beat the hell out of me" and let the hot water pound the stress out of him as the past came rushing back.

He'd met Fiona while attending university. They had been together for two years and engaged for one when she'd discovered she was pregnant. Fin was thrilled and wanted to marry right away, but Fiona insisted they wait until she finished her degree the following year. Little Rodney came along and was the light of their lives for the four months he had been in the world.

Fin slid down to the floor of the shower and sobbed as he remembered the fateful day when he'd gotten the phone call. He'd been on set for his first major film role, and their location was conveniently close to Glasgow, where he and Fiona lived. They had just wrapped up one of the more emotional scenes in the film when the assistant producer came rushing up, holding a phone out to him. The lack of color in her face screamed something was wrong. Fiona's mother was on the line. Fiona and Rodney had been in a serious auto accident. Fin had driven to the hospital like a madman. Frankly, he was lucky he hadn't been in an accident himself. By the time he'd arrived, they were both gone.

The investigation showed an American reporter had identified them as the family of an up-and-coming Scottish actor while they shopped. This reporter had hounded them as Fiona walked away, then had the audacity to follow them in her car as Fiona drove off. The faster Fiona drove trying to get away, the faster the woman chasing her went, until they rounded a corner and Fiona lost control of the car. Rodney had died instantly, and Fiona slipped away during surgery. The American reporter had at least called emergency services, but walked away with no repercussions. Fin had pushed for criminal charges, then pursued civil action against her, but to no avail. He had finally settled for an injunction that kept her at a distance.

Over the years, Miranda Cole's career had blossomed just as Fin's had. She was now famous in her own right and carried weight in the world of Hollywood. Fin had her on his blacklist, but judging by the interaction this morning, the studio didn't seem to care when it came to promoting its products. Hopefully, it was merely some terrible mistake. With a groan, Fin carefully wrapped up the broken bits of his heart and packed them away again, then finished scrubbing the day from his body.

He sighed and stepped out of the shower stall. The original restraining order, as they were called in the U.S., only worked in Scotland. Cole had backed off following the accident, and he'd never needed to file a similar complaint in the States. But if she was making a move to insert herself into his life again, he needed to consider it.

Fin exited the bathroom in his suite with his towel wrapped snug around his hips. Hearing his phone ringing in the other room, he walked from the bedroom to the living room and snatched it off the coffee table.

"Hey, Addie," he tiredly greeted his agent.

"What the hell happened, Fin? I got a panicked call

from Buck. He said he'd never seen you this upset, dropping f-bombs—which is highly unlike you—and giving a scathing lecture to the lady in charge of scheduling. Are you okay? I mean, this is seriously uncharacteristic of you."

Fin collapsed onto the cushy settee and exhaled loudly. "Miranda Cole was my last interview segment of the day," he responded, his voice low.

Silence greeted him as she processed his statement. He waited.

"Fuck," she said.

"Aye," he agreed.

"Okay, I'm on it. I'm sorry this happened. I'll determine who screwed up and make sure the right people know this will never happen again."

"I'm so tired, Addie."

Addie spoke quickly, "I know, *pobrecito*. But she's nothing. An annoying reporter. Let me deal with her for you. You take your vacation and get refreshed. Book a massage, go sailing... Houston's near the ocean, right? You take care of you and I'll take care of that bitch."

Fin blew out a breath, too tired to respond. Before he could say anything, Addie spoke again.

"Fin."

"Hmm?"

"Fin, don't get in your head about this. I'm on it. You. Do. Not. Worry. About. This. *¿Comprende?*"

"Aye, Addie, I understand. Goodnight."

"Bye, Fin-Fin. I love you."

"I know." His standard response to her declaration of love fell flat without the usual smugness he interjected.

He lay there, spent. The quiet humming of the air conditioner unit in the background soothed his senses. Fin's eyes fluttered closed, then popped open again as his phone dinged with a text message. He smiled as he read Alex's brief note about handling the food. He closed his eyes again and slipped into the sleep of the emotionally exhausted.

Chapter 5

Sunday

Alex spent Sunday morning cleaning the house and doing laundry. For lunch, she reheated leftovers from Friday night's supper with Eddie and Gabe, then ate while she made her grocery list for the week.

When Alex had first moved into her own place, she had tried to manage her kitchen the way her mother ran the ranch house back home. Mom kept a fully stocked kitchen with certain staples always on hand, ready to whip up a meal for ranch hands and visitors at a moment's notice.

She learned quickly this approach didn't work for her, when her frequent business trips resulted in wasted food. She now planned meals week to week and had an arrangement with Gabe where he could make use of all perishable items in her kitchen when she was out of town.

After cleaning up her lunch dishes, she checked in to see if Gabe needed anything for tonight's dinner with Fin. She received an amused no and headed to the carport.

Yesterday, the boys had taken over planning for the meal tonight and she'd happily let them, still reeling that she had a date with a movie star. She'd worried about having a strange man over to her house, and asked the guys to chaperone. Of course, they'd been delighted to be included, but she hadn't updated Fin on the additional company. She hoped he wouldn't be upset about the change of plans. Alex shrugged as she unlocked her Nissan Juke. Better to ask forgiveness, than permission.

She slipped behind the wheel of the little black and red car. The Jukester, as she affectionately called it, was the NISMO edition, modeled after the Nissan Motorsport racing car division. The cute compact car came with a manual transmission, and its peppy engine made it super fun to drive. Nissan no longer made the Juke, so she constantly received offers to buy hers, which she politely declined each time.

She made a quick run to the store and got everything she needed, plus a few things she didn't. Who could resist cookie dough ice cream on sale? Back at home, Alex unloaded the groceries. As she put away the last bag, she glanced at the clock. She still had a few hours to fill before Fin arrived, so she sat down at her laptop and worked on her project plan for the new PMO department.

Just after five, Eddie walked in after giving a single knock. Upon seeing her at her desk, he stopped short and bellowed, "What in the Sam Hill are you still doing in your gym clothes? You only have an hour and a half until he arrives!"

"Geez, Eddie, it only takes me thirty minutes to get ready. Calm your tits," she replied patiently as she saved her work. "Did you need something?"

"I came to check on you and bring over this hair clip my sister left the last time she visited. I thought it would go perfectly with the outfit you chose. And don't tell me to calm my tits. I hate when you say that," Eddie sulked.

"Well, I wouldn't say it if your tits didn't need the occasional calming." She laughed at Eddie's mock outrage. "Oh, that's pretty," she exclaimed as she crossed the room and reached for the clip.

He handed it over and pushed her gently towards her bedroom. "There ya go. Now go get ready. We'll see you in a bit."

"Thanks, Eddie." Alex headed off to shower and dress for her date.

AN HOUR LATER, Alex left Eddie's side of the duplex through the back door after checking with the guys that everything was on schedule. Her stomach twinged and she pressed a hand against her abdomen, hoping to calm her nerves. She rarely invited strangers to her house and, despite knowing *who* he was, she still didn't know him. She hoped he wasn't too upset that she'd included her friends.

As she walked the short distance to her back door, a black sedan pulled into the driveway. She tracked the vehicle as it drove around to the lot behind their house. Fin emerged from the backseat and waved the driver on. She watched as he glanced around and took in the compound. Wow. His casual attire of jeans and a blue long-sleeve t-shirt showed off his physique and played up his striking blue eyes. His damp hair hinted at a recent shower.

His eyes swept over the flower bushes, landing on her. Fin moved toward Alex, smiling. "Hello," he greeted her cheerfully.

"Hello, yourself," she answered as she led him to her side of the duplex. "This is my side of the house. Come on in and I'll show you around."

Fin followed her through the door, where Felix welcomed him with a loud meow from the top of the clothes washer in the tiny utility room to the right. "Hello there, cat." He reached over to scratch behind Felix's ears.

Alex grinned and introduced the two males. "Felix likes to inspect all new arrivals. He's open to bribes of rubbing and petting. Sorry for bringing you in the back way, but we're not very formal around here. You are now officially a backdoor guest."

"Nice. Who's 'we?' Just you and Felix?" he asked as gave the cat a final rub and followed Alex to the heart of the house.

"Mmm, yes, only Felix and I live here, but I was actually referring to me and my neighbors. We're all connected via the parking lot in the back and treat each other like a bunch of grown siblings. In fact, we are dining with my landlord and his partner tonight. They live next door," she explained as she pointed to the southern wall of her living room.

She noticed the frown that appeared on Fin's face. "Don't worry, they're harmless. And Gabe is a premier chef at one of the hoity-toity restaurants in town so the food will be fantastic." She assumed he was worried about being exposed, especially at the mention of her gay friends. One of Fin's critically acclaimed films was about a homosexual couple trying to adopt a child. The film had catapulted him to the top of the gay community's favorite stars list. The frown cleared from his face, followed by a slight shrug, then he shifted to look around her home.

She wondered what he saw and stopped to consider the room through a stranger's eyes. The ceiling had exposed wooden beams with a matching mantle over the stone fireplace. The warm tones of her decor complemented those elements as well as reminded her of the ranch house she'd grown up in. Splashes of color in the form of pillows, vases, and paintings spread throughout the living room, reminiscent of palettes often found in the southwest. Those warm tones extended from the living area into the kitchen, separated only by a large sit-down bar, the cabinets having the same rich wood hues as the living area.

"This is charming," he told her. "It's very homey. Cozy, without being too small." Alex thanked him for the compliment, then explained the setup of Eddie's "compound" and how it suited her perfectly, especially with them willing to look after Felix when she traveled.

She checked her watch. "Okay, Gabe said to come on over when you got here because appetizers would be available. You ready to go over?"

He hesitated a moment, then told her, "Thanks for letting me invite myself over, Alex. I realized later that I might have been pushy about it. I appreciate you letting me step outside my world for a bit and just be a regular guy."

"Sure, big-shot Hollywood dude." Her face sobered as she added, "I imagine you don't get to do that often. I'm delighted to be of service." She turned to leave.

"Wait." He caught her arm before she moved. "You… you know who I am?" Fin looked stunned. "When did ye know?"

"When you sat down on the airplane, silly."

Fin gaped at her. "And you said nothing the entire time?" he asked, his voice raising an octave at the end.

She gave him a sad little smile as she answered. "You looked like you wanted to be," she added air quotes with her fingers, "'just a regular guy' so I treated you like one. You ready to meet Eddie and Gabe? They know who you are, but they'll be cool." She waited for his stiff nod before leading him next door.

Fᴉɴ ʀᴜʙʙᴇᴅ the back of his neck as he followed Alex, unsure what to expect now. He was astonished to learn she had known who he was from the beginning. She had acted so normal, far different from his usual experience with people in general and women in particular. He absorbed this as he walked behind her. It appeared he was in for an intriguing evening.

She led him around to the front and knocked on the door to the other side of the duplex. The door swung open to reveal a giant beast of a man. "Lexi Bear," he crooned in a deep base that brought images of Barry White to Fin's mind. "Come on in."

They stepped into the hall and Fin shook his hand as Alex introduced Gabe. *Ah,* Fin thought, *the chef,* not *a bodyguard as one might think.* The three of them moved into the living room, where a slender man rushed in to greet them. He wore a suit wild with colors, dark blue palm tree leaves scattered across a light blue backdrop, with a touch of red and gold accents. The trousers matched the jacket, which might have been overwhelming but for the solid white dress shirt underneath. That blast of color wasn't something Fin would wear, but it worked on the man he presumed was Eddie.

"Hello, Finley. Welcome to our home." Eddie smiled as he swept his arm out, indicating the interior of the house. "Please make yourself comfortable. Would you like something to drink? We have everything."

Alex laughed and told him Eddie wasn't exaggerating.

They kept a well-stocked bar. She asked Eddie for a glass of wine and Fin followed her lead, ordering the same. As Eddie sauntered off to the kitchen area, Gabe brought over a tray of mixed crackers and cheeses for them to snack on and sat down. Eddie returned with the drinks and sat beside Gabe.

"Okay, to eliminate any awkwardness, we are aware of your celebrity status and we don't care as long as you don't mess around with our girl," Eddie proclaimed as Alex sipped her wine.

Alex choked and sputtered, "Jesus, Eddie, don't do that when I'm taking a drink. I almost spewed all over every-thing!" She laughed as she seized a napkin and wiped her face, then mouthed, *I'm sorry* to Fin.

Eddie shrugged and looked pointedly at Fin. "So, you guys met on the airplane. That's neat."

Fin took the comment as his cue and replied, "Aye, I'm in town for a thing. We hit it off. Here I am."

He noted the grin that appeared on Gabe's face, but Eddie continued to stare at him. Fin stared back.

"Okay, enough of the inquisition," Eddie declared with a flap of his hands. "So, did you get a chance to venture out yesterday and see the sights? Or is that later on your agenda?"

Apparently, the big-brother interview segment of the evening was concluded. Fin relaxed and answered, "No, yesterday was a workday for me. I had a round of interviews promoting the new film. But I am working on my schedule for the week. Tuesday I'm playing some volleyball."

Alex swung toward him with a question in her eyes. He threw a smug grin her way. *Yes*, he thought, *I'm coming with you just as I promised.*

"Well, we have some phenomenal places to eat around

here. What part of town are you staying in?" Eddie continued without waiting for an answer, "We can recommend restaurants all over town that won't be too crowded. You might actually be able to dine without being noticed at a few of them."

"That's right. Alex told me there was a chef in the house. What type of food do you specialize in, Gabe?" Fin asked, diverting the focus from himself.

The four of them discussed local foods and favorite spots with the best cuisine. Gabe moved them to the dining room, where the topic migrated to entertainment and everyone's favorite bands. Even as the topic dipped into movies and awards, it never focused on Fin or his works. They asked his opinion on other films as if he were one of the gang and didn't have an inside track on what happened behind the scenes.

The food was delicious, the conversation engaging, and the company exquisite. Fin couldn't remember having a more comfortable meal with someone outside the industry. Discounting his family, of course, with whom he would always feel comfortable.

As they cleared the table, Fin pushed up his sleeves to help with the dishes. Gabe noticed his actions and said, "Oh, no, you don't. You are the guest."

"But I should help clean up," Fin protested as he appealed to Alex for support.

Alex snorted. "Guest or not, Gabe doesn't let anyone into his kitchen. You won't do it right." She squealed and moved sideways as Gabe popped a kitchen towel at her.

"She's absolutely right, and you know it," Eddie chimed in.

Gabe grinned sheepishly and shrugged. "Busted," he admitted.

Eddie asked if they wanted coffee, but Alex declined and told them she thought they would wander over to her place and watch some TV. Fin perked up at the idea of having her to himself. While he had enjoyed the company, he was here because of Alex. He had accepted earlier in the evening they were doing a double date, but now found himself eager to be alone with the woman who had intrigued him since their shared flight.

Fin shook hands with both men and thanked them for the wonderful evening. As he and Alex walked outside, he looked back at the two men deep in conversation, Eddie talking nonstop and Gabe smiling at whatever he said. They seemed happy together.

THE SKY HAD GROWN dark during their meal, and Alex realized she'd forgotten to leave her porch light on. She took Fin's hand to guide him along the path, and thought how perfectly hers fit in his. They walked quietly, listening to the neighborhood sounds.

"That was lovely. Your friends are wonderful," he said out of nowhere.

"Yeah, they are. I'm glad you enjoyed them. I didn't think you would mind, and they aren't ones to fawn over you like other fanboys might."

He chuckled. "I still can't believe you knew who I was this whole time. I thought I had gotten away with being plain old Fin."

Alex let go of his hand and pulled open her door. "Maybe *I* should be an actor." She laughed. "I don't know if you genuinely want to watch TV, but I thought the timing was good for us to escape before they started feeling a little too comfortable with you." She caught his slight nod and knew he understood he had just been rescued.

Fin followed her in. "Whatever you want to do. By the way, I both appreciate and approve of your exit strategy." He smiled at her.

Alex pointed at her couch and offered him a drink. "I've got soda, iced tea, and wine. Or water. The non-fizzy type."

"Whatever you're having, thanks." He sank into the massive sofa while Alex collected two glasses and a bottle of wine, which she set on the coffee table in front of Fin.

She then plopped down beside him and promptly rolled towards him, sinking into the soft cushions. "Whoops!" she cried. "It's been a while since I shared my couch, and I forgot how it sucks you in." She could feel her face turning bright red as she disentangled herself from him. She put her hand on his chest and pushed away. He placed one hand on her shoulder to hold her steady and the other hand hovered around his lap.

As she got herself more stable on the couch, she looked from his lower hand to his face. "Did you just protect your manly bits from me?" She burst into laughter.

He smirked. "Sorry. Instinct."

She covered her mouth and tried not to giggle. "That reminds me of the time on the ranch when my friend decided he wanted to ride one of our bulls. He was wearing gym shorts, which have absolutely no protection for manly bits." She told him the story of her high school friend attempting—and failing miserably—to ride one of their younger animals, and how he needed an ice pack afterwards.

Fin laughed and shared a few stories of him and his mates' misadventures in that department.

As they talked, Alex poured two glasses of wine. They

slipped right back into the easy camaraderie they had shared on the plane.

Except this was different. They were in her home... her space. And yeah, the chemistry between them sizzled. On the plane she had written it off to the excitement of meeting someone famous, but here in her comfort zone, she couldn't explain away the heightened awareness of his every movement. While they talked, an occasional brush of fingers or an innocuous touch while one of them changed positions caused undeniable heat to zip along her spine. They weren't even sitting particularly close. They both sat sideways on the couch, facing each other with at least a foot separating them. Even with the space between them, Alex was acutely aware of everything about him.

While laughing at Fin's rendition of a scene gone wrong in one of his movies, Alex was abruptly struck by a yawn. "Oh, gosh. Sorry." She yawned again. "I guess I'm still recovering from jet lag."

"And you have to wake up early tomorrow for work. Unlike this guy," Fin pointed to himself, "who is now officially on vacation. I better go."

He stood up and pulled her along with him. "I can't tell you how wonderful this has been. I had the crappiest day yesterday, and today it's all behind me."

Alex raised her eyebrows in question.

"No, not tonight. Let's not ruin it," he answered her unspoken question. He typed something on his phone. "Since I didn't know how long the evening would go, I told Blake to stay close, so it shouldn't take him long to arrive."

"Blake?" Alex asked.

"My driver."

"Oh." Reality crashed back in. He had a driver. He was a movie star. He operated in a different world.

"Listen, Alex..." Fin interrupted her thoughts. His gaze sharpened and she stared up at him until he cleared his throat. "What time and where is volleyball on Tuesday?"

Alex snapped out of it and switched into planning mode. "Where are you staying?" Ignoring his raised eyebrow, she continued, "It might be easier for me to pick you up depending on what part of town your hotel is located."

"Oh, I see. I'm at the Hotel Granduca... ehm, in the... Gallery Area?"

"Galleria," she corrected. "That's perfect, as I have a meeting Tuesday afternoon at our Post Oak office. I'll be right up the street from you and can swing by and get you. Say around five-ish? That gives us time to get there and eat something before my first match."

Fin hesitated and Alex asked, "Problem?"

He rubbed the back of his neck. "There are some security issues I need to consider. I'm happy to ride with you, but I'd like to get the address to give to my driver in case I need to make a quick getaway."

"Oh, I never thought of that. I'll have to look it up, but I can text it over before Tuesday. Does that work?"

"Sounds perfect. Also, I'll likely have to sneak out a side door at the hotel, but can text you ahead of time where to pick me up."

"Awesome."

He laughed, and she asked, "What?"

"'Awesome,'" he repeated. "It's definitely an American word. You guys use it extensively."

"You mean like how the British use 'lovely?'" she teased him back.

"Precisely."

His phone dinged, signaling his driver was outside.

He wrapped his arms around Alex and gave her a brief hug, then kissed her cheek. "Thank you again for tonight. I look forward to Tuesday."

She trailed him out the door and watched him walk to the car. Alex answered his wave goodbye as he got into the backseat, then followed the car with her gaze as it drove away. Her heart was still pounding from the chest to chest contact and the feel of his arms around her. *I wonder if he knows he's sending me to bed with butterflies in my stomach,* she thought.

Chapter 6

Monday

Monday morning, Alex sat at the conference table in her office surrounded by the three other individuals who comprised her global financial systems team, or the GFS, as they referred to themselves. Both Grace and Sam had previously worked as accountants, then system experts with deep experience in supporting accounting teams. Natalie was the newest member and was still learning how to fulfill her role as a systems admin support person. Without guidance, she tended to get lost in the weeds and forget that the end users were her first priority.

Alex loved her team. She considered herself lucky to have such consummate professionals who were as dedicated to their team's mission as she was. Alex considered her role to be one of troubleshooting and clearing the path for these guys to do their job.

Normally, they met once a month, but she wanted updates on a few hot-button items that Grace and Sam had handled while she was out last week, and to share the news on the PMO approval.

Natalie had derailed the conversation again, talking about her weekend activities and was trying to pry information from Alex about her personal life. As she expertly dodged the inquiries, Alex realized she needed to have a formal discussion with her employee about boundaries, something she'd never needed to do with either Grace or Sam. They seemed to understand inherently that Alex never discussed her personal life at work. She'd learned that lesson long ago when a hostile colleague had tried to undermine her achievements by bringing up her personal life. And she'd vowed never to find herself in that position again. Anything outside of work was nobody's business.

Recognizing an opening to change the topic, Alex asked, "Okay, any other updates?" When they all shook their heads no, she gathered up the papers in front of her and put them aside.

Sam pushed back from the table, but Alex stopped him before he rose. "I've got one more topic to discuss."

He settled back in and Alex waited until everyone focused on her. "Frank gave us the go-ahead on the PMO proposal."

The room exploded with their responses.

"What?"

"That's fantastic!"

"I can't believe it."

Alex made a pushing motion with her hands. "It's not official. They haven't approved it yet. But, if we can pull together a decent proposal quickly, and they approve it, we may move on it as early as next fiscal year. Frank wants the new department in the budget for next year."

Grace's eyes widened. "Next year. As in two-and-a-half months from now?"

Sam scoffed. He waved his hand dismissively and said, "We already missed the deadline."

"The deadline for the *first* pass," Alex corrected. "Frank said if we can pull this together, he was sure we could get it added before the final pass."

"Can we do it?" Grace asked. Alex could always count on Grace to keep them grounded.

"I think we've got an enormous jump on it from our preliminary analysis. We need to refine what we have and verify our numbers are solid. Where I'm concerned is that our original projections assumed we would start with existing projects our team is working on and the four of us would form the foundation for the PMO. We used our GFS salary projections as a basis."

The team nodded and Natalie asked, "But?"

"But our assumption was we'd do this in the middle of a year and slowly transfer existing budget resources as needed from other departments to the new PMO department. If we are raising it from scratch at the beginning of the year, shouldn't we plan for more people? Doing so means those numbers would change."

Sam nodded. "Yeah, I get you. This is an opportunity to do it right rather than piecemeal it together. I think we need to present two options, the first based on the number of upcoming projects with a fully fleshed-out team, and the second option being to transfer team members in phases."

Grace cleared her throat. "The other item we need to talk about is that our primary function is support for the financial department. With our previous plan, we would have time to plan and develop the support structure. If the PMO launches at the first of the year, how do we make that transition? If we're all focusing on projects, how will we support the existing applications and our users? Going live with the PMO in January means we don't get the transition time we need. I mean, it's already October. And the holidays are coming up, which means even less time."

There it was. That something that had niggled at the back of her head, but never evolved into a full-blown thought. Trust Grace to nail it down so succinctly.

Alex blew out a breath and leaned back. "You're right, Grace. As usual, you're able to spot the weak spots we need to focus on. At the end of the day, the PMO will be a separate department working with our GFS team. We're a unique group already, so we need to decide where this team will land in the grand scheme of things."

They kicked around other changes and concerns to consider with the accelerated timeline while Alex made notes. She sensed both anticipation and trepidation from her team, similar to her own emotions. The issues Grace and Sam raised suggested some reluctance on their part that she needed to get to the bottom of. And for the first time, Alex and Natalie seemed to be on the same page. They were both excited at the prospect of getting this in place earlier than expected.

As the discussion wound down, she stood and gathered her things. "Okay, I'm meeting with Frank tomorrow at ten to go over these points, so if you have any other thoughts before then, shoot them over in an email. Sam, with me focusing on the PMO, I'll need you to take over leading the planning system project. Does that work for you?"

"Yeah, we're at the point where I'd be more involved anyway. I'd have balked if you hadn't already done the schmoozing the big guys part." He chuckled.

"What, you don't like sweet-talking the bosses and

convincing them to part with their budget money?" Alex grinned at him before dismissing the group. "Thanks, guys."

As the group dispersed, Alex captured her thoughts on her laptop on what to discuss with Frank before she forgot. First among those was what happened to her current team if the new department was pushed forward now.

Chapter 7

Tuesday

MAN, *what a start to this week,* Alex thought while typing her notes Tuesday afternoon. Yesterday had been a typical Monday, with issues creeping up all over the place. She hadn't gotten home until late last night. This morning, she'd come to work thinking today would be lighter, but that concept flew out the window early. One of their reporting systems went down and her team spent all day in crisis mode working with IT to get it back up. Thankfully, this last meeting had adjourned with no actions for her, leaving a smile on her face as she shut down her laptop.

With today's trials behind her, Alex was ready to hit the courts and spike some balls. She was packing up her things when her phone pinged, notifying her she had a message from Fin.

Alex smirked when she saw the image of a cloak-and-dagger cartoon character looking sneaky, followed by Fin's cryptic message. *"Location: Side door, north side, towards the back. What time should I be there?"*

She typed in *"30 minutes"* and hit send. In reality, his hotel was only five minutes away, but based on prior experience, Alex rarely left the building without someone stopping her. People always seemed to come up with "a quick question before you go" right as she was leaving. She looked forward to the evening with Fin, which led her to tell everyone to email her or call her tomorrow when she typically would have stopped and chatted.

When Alex finally pulled her car around the corner of the hotel, twenty-nine minutes had passed since her last text. She eased the Juke forward, looking for the side door when a resounding thump reverberated through her car. Startled, she braked and looked around. She almost didn't recognize him, which she supposed was the point. He wore black jeans and a long-sleeved denim shirt, unbuttoned down the front, exposing a crisp white t-shirt underneath. A black fedora reminiscent of Dave Navarro covered his ebony curls, and dark sunglasses hid the top half of his face. He carried a gym bag slung over his shoulder.

Alex unlocked her car, and he slipped in, throwing his bag in the backseat. "How are ye?" he asked as he closed the door and buckled in. She grinned and told him again how much she loved his Scottish accent.

He checked out her car as she put it into gear and drove forward. "Cool car," he told her. "You don't see many manual gearboxes here in America. I'm impressed you drive one."

"Well... farm girl here, so it shouldn't be a surprise, but yeah, The Jukester is a wonderful car and lots of fun to drive. She's peppy. Nice hat, by the way."

"You don't like it?"

"I do like it. It works well on you. Not something I would expect to see on any of my colleagues or teammates, so it's unusual."

"I was trying to blend in and not draw attention. Sounds like I only stood out more."

Alex smiled and asked, "Did anyone recognize you?"

"No."

"Then it worked. No problem." She laughed, and he flashed a grin at her before asking where they were going.

"It's a place in the northwest part of Houston called Rally Up Sports," she told him as she maneuvered around an irritated driver. "Any other time, I would take the freeway. But rush hour would add at least half an hour if we went that way. So, we're taking the back way." Alex shrugged. "It's a much more pleasant drive, anyway."

"Nice. Most of my trips with Blake are more in the downtown area, so I haven't been out this way yet."

"Blake is your driver, right?" At his nod, she continued, "So what have you guys been doing?"

Alex wove through the neighborhoods, avoiding any major streets and congestion, while Fin told her of his explorations of the city of Houston. He was quite the storyteller and had her giggling at his observations.

As they drove, Alex pointed out interesting houses or sights and he commented on the varying architectural styles of the houses they passed. Eventually, they came to a major street that merged onto one of the major freeways.

"Okay, hold on. We have to travel on 290 for a while, but we're almost there," Alex told him as she shifted gears and punched the gas.

"Whoa!" he exclaimed, and grasped the handle above the door. He held on as she jockeyed for position among the other vehicles on the freeway. "Watch out for—never mind," he trailed off as she sped up and moved into the left lane, dodging a pickup truck whose driver veered into their lane without bothering to see if anyone was there.

"Only another ten minutes, then we're away from these crazies," she informed him. She noticed his tight grip on the handle. "We call that the 'oh, shit' handle."

Fin emitted a nervous laugh. "I understand why."

She snickered and made her way toward the upcoming exit, where she eased over to the right lane, waving at the guy who made room for her to change lanes.

After a few more turns, she pulled into a parking lot adjacent to what looked like a large tin barn and a fenced-in field containing large sandboxes. Alex parked the car and shut off the engine, but didn't move.

"Are you ready?" she asked Fin. "Because I'm a bit nervous."

His eyebrows rose in surprise. "Why? Because of me?"

"Yes. Two reasons. First, I've never brought anyone with me, so I would get loads of ribbing and speculation about this, anyway. Second—and this is the primary reason —you're famous. So that makes this whole scenario even more weird. Why would you want to hang out with a bunch of average Joes, anyway?"

He peered at her for a moment before responding, "I am sorry if I put you on the spot. I didnae think of it from your point of view." He looked away and rubbed the side of his face. "I guess I wanted to escape from my life for a bit and be that average Joe, as you say. Should I call Blake to come get me?"

"What? Oh, no... I'm just telling you to be prepared for a shit-ton of crap. They will not be cool like Eddie and Gabe." She paused. "I mean, they might be cool like that, but there will probably be someone who is *so* not cool." With that, she laughed and exited the car.

HERE WE GO, Fin thought. He grabbed his gym bag from the backseat and followed Alex into the building, looking around to see if anyone recognized him. He was taking a risk by going out in public, but Sunday's dinner with Alex and her friends had emboldened him. Hopefully, this group of friends would be as low-key as Eddie and Gabe.

Alex showed him to the men's locker room where he could change, and left to do the same. While he put on his workout gear, he considered what she'd told him about being the first man she's brought to meet her friends here. Fin wasn't sure if he felt humbled that she'd let him in her inner circle or concerned that he'd bullied her into something she didn't want to do. He shoved his street clothes into his bag and wandered out into the main eating area. When he didn't see Alex anywhere, he sat at a table nearby and looked around.

The concrete floor flowed throughout the metal building. A large wooden bar worthy of an old western saloon ran along the wall closest to the parking lot. Stools lined the bar where you could sit comfortably and peruse the enormous collection of bottles filled with various alcohols on the shelves behind it. Numerous neon signs decorated the walls, and tables of all sizes spread throughout the interior. To the far side of the room was a billiard table and an area set up for throwing darts. And the last wall across from the bar had several industrial-sized garage doors that were open. These doors led to a covered wooden deck and beyond that, Fin could see the volleyball courts.

"What do you think?" Alex startled him.

"Nice. Not very crowded."

"Yeah, that changes with the weather. October's a fairly mild month for us, weather-wise. Right now, everyone's probably outside on the deck. Shall we join them?" she asked.

"After you, m'lady." He bowed and waved his arm forward.

Alex snickered and walked out the closest garage door while Fin followed. She was wearing athletic shorts and a tank top with a sports bra underneath, which gave him an excellent view of her toned arms and well-defined legs.

Once outside, Alex aimed for a loud group of people who were scattered across two long picnic tables and laughing at the story one guy was telling. The group was a diverse mix of men and women whose ages ranged from early twenties to mid-forties. And the style of clothing varied from bikini swimsuits to t-shirts and leggings. It appeared to be quite an eclectic group of people.

As Alex drew near, the curly-headed man finished his story and shouted her name, then ran over and swooped her up in a hug. The group followed with a variety of greetings and a few more hugs.

"When did you get back? Your team's been sucking without you," the curly-haired dude said as he popped a French fry into his mouth.

"Hey, asshole!" exclaimed a male voice on the other side of the table.

Alex laughed and replied, "Got home late Friday, Andy, and I doubt the boys have sucked without me, thank you very much. Also, guys, this is Fin. He's hanging out with us tonight."

A chorus of "Hey, Fin" rang out while someone found a couple of chairs and made room for them at a table. As he was sitting, Fin noticed the curly-haired man—Andy—was staring at him, and braced himself for what was coming.

"Dude, you look just like that actor dude, what's-his-face."

Alex replied before he could, "Hey, Andy, pass me a fry, will ya? And, yes, he is that actor dude. I met him coming home from London. He's got some time on his hands, so I told him how cool my peeps are and here we are. Where's Daisy? I'm starving. Fin, are you hungry?"

Everyone at the table stopped talking and stared at him.

"Holy shit," someone said.

"Dang, Alex," another chimed in.

"Cool!"

"Well, all right-y then."

Fin looked at Alex who was waiting for his reply and said, "Aye, I could eat a bite."

The entire group roared with laughter, and that ended the introductions. A few more whispers went around the table, but in general, people went back to what they were doing. The waitress came over and took their order while the conversation returned to who was leading the tournament and updates on injuries.

Fin relaxed when no one probed further, but still felt on edge at the occasional click of a camera shutter or the quick motion of someone putting their phone back on the table. While it seemed like Alex's friends were nonchalant about having a celebrity in their midst, his shoulders itched with wariness that their easygoing nature was a facade.

Their food came and, before Alex had taken more than a couple of bites, a brown-headed man across the way yelled over at her, "Alex, we're up."

"Oh, crap. Gotta run, Fin." She pointed to a middle court as she nabbed a few more fries. "We're on court four. You should be able to watch from here. See ya in a few." She ran off, shoving fries in her mouth.

Fin watched as the two teams stretched and got ready to play. He sensed a presence beside him and looked up. The waitress held her pen and pad close, as if shielding it from him.

"Um, Mr. McAlister? Can I get your autograph?" she asked.

"Aye, what's your name?" he asked as he reached for the pen. He hid his disappointment behind his Hollywood smile. Perhaps his goal to escape unnoticed had been too lofty.

"I'm Daisy. Please don't tell Alex I bothered you. She'd kill me."

"No worries, Daisy. There you go now." He handed everything back to her.

"Thanks. Next drink's on me." She blushed and scurried away.

Fin turned his attention back to Alex's court, where she and two men played against a team with two men and two women. Fin leaned over and asked the red-headed bloke next to him why Alex's team only had three players.

"They've never been able to find another girl who they mesh with," he responded.

The ginger turned and offered his hand. "Hi, I'm Scott. Alex and my girlfriend, Melissa, are tight."

"Lovely to meet you," Fin responded as he shook Scott's hand. "What do you mean by 'mesh?'"

"Oh, you know, they couldn't find a steady rhythm with anyone else, so they just play with the three of them."

"Doesn't that make them handicapped?" Fin asked.

"You'd think so, but not really. They play well together so they don't need a fourth. In fact, I think they actually won the league last time. Or maybe it was the time before. Anyway, they hold their own."

Fin watched as Alex dove across the sand to keep the ball in play. He gasped, hoping she wasn't hurt, but she bounced up and kept playing. In the next volley, her blond teammate set up the ball and Alex spiked it, earning a point for her team.

"Wow," he exclaimed.

"Yeah, she's good. You should see her with her women's team—also my girlfriend's team. You know, the net out here is higher. Only a few of the girls can spike on it. She's a beast on a women's net." Scott's voice filled with admiration as he watched the match.

"Scottie!" Andy hollered from across the deck. "We're up. Court two."

Scott stood up. "Gotta go. Hey man, they've got some foreign beers here if you're not a fan of 'weak Yankee beer.'" He laughed. "Probably not what you're used to, but you might find something you like. Just tell Daisy to put it on Alex's tab. We settle up at the end of the night. See you after the match."

"Thanks, mate," Fin replied and turned back to the match. When Daisy came around again, Fin inquired about the foreign beers and ordered a Heineken.

A few minutes later, Alex plopped in the chair beside him. "Man, I'm still hungry!" she exclaimed. Daisy dropped off Fin's beer and she ordered another appetizer for them.

One of Alex's team members came by and held out a hand to Fin. "Hey, I'm Rick," he said as Fin shook it. He spoke to Alex. "Jules is coming later so we can play with four. Good with you?"

"Sure, dude. We played well with her last time. If we sync again tonight, we might have our fourth, yeah?"

"Yep. Sounds good. Nice to meet ya," he directed at Fin as he walked away.

Alex grinned at Fin and asked, "So, how are you holding up? Feeling out of place?"

"No, actually. I am having a lovely time. There's plenty to watch with all the different matches being played. And your friends are cordial. They talk to me as if I'm one of them." He smiled at her skeptical look. "Truly, I'm having fun."

They sat with the group eating, drinking, and laughing until her next match. This time, her team had four players and appeared to do just as well. Fin understood what Scott had been saying about meshing, and the new girl seemed to fit in well with the team.

Alex settled into her seat afterwards and told Fin she was finished with her scheduled games for the evening. They could stay and hang out or leave whenever he got ready. Before he could answer, Alex's ginger friend called his name from the courts.

"Fin, you up for a match? We're down a player."

"Eh, sure..." Fin looked at Alex and whispered, "Scott, right?"

"Yes," Alex confirmed.

"Sure, Scott," he responded as he rose from the table. "Although I must tell you I haven't played in a while."

"Just like riding a bike, man," Andy shouted from the sidelines where he sat nursing a twisted ankle.

Fin stretched a bit while Scott filled him in on the rules, emphasizing that a girl must touch the ball at least once during each play.

As they played, Fin relaxed and enjoyed himself. He caught Alex's eyes a few times during the match and smiled her way. They lost the match, but everyone was happy, and he received several thumps on the back as he made his way to their table.

Alex looked up at him as he sat down and told him, "You were great. You're very athletic and graceful." She blushed as she said it, and he wondered if her discomfort came from watching his athletic assets, as it were. He hoped so. He'd hate to think the attraction was only one-way.

They drank more beer and played together in a few pick-up games on the free courts. During one of these, he and Alex both moved toward the ball, colliding during the play. They wound up tangled up on the ground together. He felt a spike of attraction as their bodies brushed against each other. He disentangled himself from her and offered her a hand up, laughing at how much fun he was having. She took his hand and pulled herself up.

"My bad... I should have communicated better," she chuckled.

"I thoroughly enjoyed your miscommunication," he quipped with a leer, and moved back to his position. She stood for a second gaping at him as her cheeks turned bright red, then shook her head and got into position for the next play.

After their third pickup game, Alex declared she needed to head home, as she had to work tomorrow. Several boos and hisses went up around their table along with calls of "party pooper," but she waved them off and reminded them all they were doing this all again in two days.

As Alex and Fin collected their things, someone asked, "Fin, will you be back again?"

He glanced at Alex who seemed interested in his answer as well and responded, "Not sure what my agenda is, but I've had a great time so if I can, I will." Shouts of approval rose around the table and he added, "I wanted to thank everyone here for making me feel so welcome and let you know I had a great time tonight. Cheers!"

The group raised their glasses and said their goodbyes.

"Don't we need to settle our tab?" he asked Alex as they walked toward the building.

"Nah, I closed out earlier when I went to the ladies' room," she assured him as she led him around to the outdoor showers, where they washed the sand off their feet. "Some people only get their feet sandy, but I get it everywhere." She rolled her eyes at the last statement.

"Well, after the spill we took, I probably have sand everywhere as well." He grinned.

Once they were back in the car, Fin touched her hand before she put it in gear. Alex looked over at him and waited. "I had a fantastic time tonight. It's been so long since I've spent an evening doing nothing but killing time and having fun. Thank you for that." He gave her hand a squeeze and let go.

"You're welcome. Everyone deserves an occasional night of responsibility-free fun," she responded.

After a much quicker ride home due to less traffic, Alex pulled the car up to the side door at the hotel. As she put the car in neutral and applied the parking brake, Alex said, "I had a good time, too, Fin."

He leaned over and brushed his lips against hers. "Let's do it again. I'll call you tomorrow and we'll go somewhere classy for dinner. Yes?"

"Okay," she whispered, absently touching her lips.

He squeezed her shoulder before getting out of the vehicle. "Good night, Alexis," he said before closing the door and walking away. "Keep walking, Finley," he told himself aloud. "Just keep walking."

ALEX WALKED out of her bathroom, rubbing her wet hair with her towel. The long, hot shower had helped soothe her muscles and remove any remaining sand from her body. She picked up her workout clothes scattered about the room and threw them in the hamper, then hung her towel on the bathroom rack to dry. She slid into bed with a sigh.

When she picked up her phone to check her alarm, she noticed the voicemail indicator and hit play. Fin's voice greeted her. "Hey, Alexis. I wanted to call and tell you again how much I enjoyed tonight. And... And to, um, apologize for the kiss. I wasn't expecting that to happen, it just did. It felt so natural to kiss you goodbye and it didn't occur to me until afterward I might have been out of line. Anyway, I'll call you tomorrow and see about plans for dinner. I hope you're still interested. Goodnight."

Alex played the message three times before setting her phone aside. That kiss! It had taken her completely by surprise. It had been a fleeting touch, nothing but a gentle caress of lips. But that brief touch of his lips had zipped electricity through her body right down to her toes. From the beginning she'd been aware of the attraction between them, but she kept telling herself it was his celebrity status that fascinated her. The man had been voted this year's "Hottest Man Ever," for Pete's sake! Who wouldn't feel attracted to him? But tonight, after that kiss, she acknowledged that the chemistry between them was more than some starstruck reaction.

She considered their interactions the last few days. Alex had noticed right away Fin was a toucher. He used his hands to communicate, and part of that included touching people. He held her elbow to guide her through people at the airport, he touched her back, guiding her through a door, he touched her shoulder when pushing in her seat for her... all respectable and chivalrous ways to show consideration for someone. And Alex had noticed every single one of those touches because she was *not* a toucher. Ever. She could tolerate hugs from friends, but a business-like handshake was as close as she came to touching anyone outside of her inner circle. Funny how she hadn't minded those touches from Fin at all.

She groaned and rolled over, trying to put thoughts of Fin's touch out of her mind. Eventually she drifted off to sleep, dreaming of soft kisses and baritone voices with sexy Scottish accents.

Chapter 8

Wednesday

ALEX'S MORNING had been busy. She'd completed several documents on one team project, then reviewed and approved a revised draft from Grace on another. Man, she loved working with competent people. Afterward, she emailed the final documents to the stakeholders for approval with instructions on how to submit e-signatures.

She and Sam were in the IT department finishing up a meeting with the infrastructure guys about the availability of virtual servers for yet a third project. As they wrapped up the meeting and exited the conference room, Alex's phone pinged. She glanced at the text message from her friend Melissa stating, *"What the heck did I miss?!?"* She smiled and stopped to say hello to a systems analyst who had helped her on a previous project.

Lunch came and went before Alex made it back to her desk. She was deep into updating the PMO proposal when her office phone rang.

"This is Alex."

"What happened at Rally Up last night? Are you actually dating a celebrity? Why wouldn't you tell me this?" her friend Melissa fired off at her. Surprised at hearing her friend's voice on her office phone, Alex glanced the phone's display and found she had answered her cell phone via Bluetooth connection on the desk phone. She laughed, realizing she had been so imbedded in her work she'd failed to screen her calls as she normally did.

"No, I'm not dating a celebrity. How did you know about him, anyway? Scott told you?" She saved her work and stretched her back, grateful for the break.

"Yes. Plus it's all over their website."

"What?" Alex yelped. "Hang on, let me go look." Alex pulled up her search engine and found the Rally Up Sports page. Sure enough, the site contained multiple pictures of Fin and herself plastered on their home page. "Ugh, I've never been on their page before and now I'm splattered all over it! Who took these anyway?"

"Looks like Daisy or possibly that new bartender took most of them, but anyone who tagged Rally Up last night got posted as well."

"Ugh. I hope no one from work sees these. I've spent years cultivating my professional reputation, working to get my coworkers to see me as an authoritative figure and not some barbie doll pretending to be one."

Alex clicked through the images until she came to one with her and Fin sitting together. She was laughing at someone to the left, and Fin's gaze focused on her. The longing in his eyes was almost palpable. "Oh, man..." she murmured.

Melissa chuckled and said, "Sounds like you found the one that caught my attention. Scott told me you guys bumped into each other on the flight home and you offered him a reporter-free evening. Which seemed totally plausible until I came upon that picture and how he looked at you. Now I want the real story. Drinks later?"

"Um, I can't tonight," Alex stammered, her eyes never leaving the photo on her screen. "I have a dinner date."

"With him?" Melissa's tone sharpened, and Alex pictured her friend sitting up straighter.

"Yes. He's in town for a week. Or was it two? Anyway, we hit it off, and he's having fun acting like a regular guy. I genuinely like him. He's not what I expected at all," she ended quietly.

Melissa paused and then said, "It's kind of surreal, yeah?"

"Yeah, definitely. But temporary. Might as well enjoy it while I can, right?"

"Yes, enjoy it as much and as often as you can," Melissa laughed. "Every chance you get before he leaves."

"It's not like that!" Alex opened her mouth to defend herself but stopped when Sam stuck his head in her office. "Melissa, I've gotta run, but I'll call you tomorrow and give you all the details, okay?"

They said their goodbyes and Alex closed her browser before following Sam to his office to address the latest process issue.

AROUND FOUR O'CLOCK, Alex's cell phone pinged with a message from Fin asking if she had time to talk. Silently thanking the stars she wasn't in a meeting, she answered in the affirmative. Her phone rang shortly afterwards.

"Hey, you." She smiled into the phone. "You sore at all?"

"How did ye know?" He groaned before continuing, "I

thought I was fairly fit considering the workout regime I've been following for the film, but I am sore in places I never knew existed."

Alex laughed and responded, "Apparently being a superhero uses different muscles than being a volleyball player. Do you have any bruises from the ball? When I took up playing again, my arms were covered in them."

She could hear him shifting around on the other end.

"No, no bruises here. You really got bruises?"

"Yeah. I hadn't played for five years and I was banged up pretty good those first two weeks. The bruises were bad enough that one lady at my office quietly came up to me and told me places existed where I could get help. And I didn't have to put up with that sort of treatment. It took me a minute to understand she believed someone was abusing me."

"How did you respond?" Fin asked.

"I thanked her for her concern and told her it wasn't what she thought. I explained the situation, but I don't think she believed me. She didn't say anything further, but looked at me like I was covering up for someone," Alex said.

"Wow."

"Yeah. At first I laughed, but then... her assumptions were unsettling. Anyway," Alex dismissed the somber topic, "I'm okay with a few bruises in the name of fun."

Fin burst out laughing and Alex groaned as her cheeks grew warm and her ears burned. "I mean... Oh, geez... never mind. Insert foot in mouth now."

He chuckled some more, then asked what time she wanted to do dinner. "I've made reservations for six, seven, and eight o'clock because I wasn't sure what your normal eating time was."

She laughed. "Good lord, talk about being prepared.

Were you a Boy Scout? Do they even have Boy Scouts in Scotland?" Before he could answer, she continued on, "I'm an early eater. How about you?"

"Honestly, I have no set schedule and eat when time's available. Which works better for you, six or seven? This is me asking what 'early' means to you."

"I'm okay with either. If I need to change clothes, then seven o'clock is better. Traffic, you know. But if I can come straight from work in my suit, then six is okay," she informed him.

"Let's dress up. I'll pick you up at your place at six-thirty. I believe that will give us plenty of time to make our seven o'clock reservation."

"Sounds good, Fin," she concluded. "I'll see you at my duplex at six-thirty."

Fin laughed. "Do you always repeat and confirm?"

"Oh. I never thought about it. I'm so used to making sure everyone is on the same page and we have no misunderstandings, so I guess I do. Um, oops," she giggled.

"Love it. See you then," he responded, and disconnected.

Alex glanced at the time and figured she could get a few more things done on the PMO project before she needed to leave. After finally catching up to her boss with questions, she'd put together the draft budget proposal, but it still needed some polish and formatting. She wanted to finalize the numbers so Frank could review it before presenting to the management team. Knowing how she tended to lose track of time when focused, she reached over and set an alarm on her phone so she wouldn't be late for dinner with Fin.

～

Alex checked her appearance in the mirror one last time. Why was she so nervous?

The dress was one of those "little black dress" things made from a stretchy material that gathered in all the right places, and ended between mid-thigh and the top of her knees. She liked the way the dress clung to her body, giving her the suggestion of curves. The black material stopped beneath her collarbone, blending into a delicate lace pattern that extended up into a rounded neckline and out into long, lacy sleeves that came down past her wrists. Lace wasn't something she was normally drawn to, but this dress made her feel soft and feminine.

Her hair fell in smooth waves and she wore a soft pink shade of lipstick, something she only did on special occasions. The sleek silver hoops she wore in her ears matched the bracelet on her right wrist.

For the final touch, she slipped on her black suede ankle strap heels. They put her height just shy of six feet tall, so she rarely donned them for a date. Given that Fin still had several inches on her even with the heels, she felt almost giddy at being able to wear them tonight.

The doorbell rang. Alex jolted, then ran her hands over the dress one more time, smoothing down imaginary wrinkles. She opened the door and swallowed. Fin stood on her porch wearing dark blue jeans and a black long-sleeve button-down shirt under a silvery gray vest. His rolled-up sleeves showed off his muscular forearms. Sexy couldn't even begin to describe him.

"You look lovely." He pecked her cheeks in greeting, similar to how her European colleagues did. "Are you ready? I think we have plenty of time, but my experience with traffic is on the unsure side."

"Thanks. And yes, I'm ready," she responded as she

gathered her black clutch purse and a light wrap. He waited while she locked up, then walked her to the car with his hand lightly resting on her lower back.

Fin introduced her to Blake, who got them settled in the backseat, then drove them confidently towards the freeway. As they rode, Fin told her about his day exploring the city. Apparently, Blake had lived here his entire life and knew the coolest places to see. She laughed several times throughout his observations and appreciated seeing the city through the eyes of a newcomer.

Twenty minutes later, the car slowed, and Blake dropped them off at the front door of an elegant restaurant situated on Buffalo Bayou. Alex recognized the upscale steakhouse and looked forward to an enjoyable experience. The hostess led them outside to a secluded corner on the patio, away from the main crowd, and a young man in a crisp uniform took their drink order.

Fin finished filling her in on his explorations of the city, ending with a funny story about getting Blake lost with one of his sight-seeing requests. Alex wiped the tears from her eyes when their waiter swept in with perfect timing to deliver their wine and take their meal orders.

Finally, they were alone. Fin raised his wineglass and made a toast. "Here's to good company."

"Cheers," Alex agreed as she clinked her glass against his and tasted the wine. "This is awfully swanky, Mr. McAlister. Much different from me taking you out to roll in the sand."

His lips curved up in response. "May I say you look comfortable in either setting, Ms. Tanner?" His gaze took in the area around their table. "When I made the reservation, I requested a secluded table where we would be less visible to other patrons. This is lovely."

They talked about the beautiful setting of the restaurant on the bayou. Alex told Fin about the terrible flooding that had occurred during Hurricane Harvey and how the people of Houston had come through like troopers helping one another.

When their meal came, they discussed foods they liked and didn't like. He talked about his experiences in his travels and they compared favorite foreign cuisines. They laughed at the more notorious things they had eaten, like the dish in Singapore Alex swore looked like fried spiders.

About midway through their meal, Fin turned to Alex with a serious face and hesitated. "Alexis, I can't tell you how refreshing it has been to spend time with you. It's just the break I needed."

Alex set her glass down. "After dinner at Eddie's, you mentioned you had a crappy day at work on Saturday. We've never slowed down enough to talk about it. Was that related to you needing a break?"

Fin raised an eyebrow at her. "You are a perceptive one." He took another drink of wine and stared into his glass. "I know this sounds like an oxymoron, but I hate being in the public eye. I lost someone long ago as a direct result of a reporter chasing a story."

Alex held her breath, not sure what to say.

He pursed his lips and continued, "Saturday was a press junket for the new film. We do a series of interviews throughout the day. This same reporter snuck in. The moment was stressful, to say the least."

Alex reached over and covered his hand with hers. "That sounds terrible. I don't know much about it, but I can sympathize. Can't you block them somehow?"

"Aye, she's on my 'no fly' list, but somehow got in despite that fact. Anyway, that was the bad day I referred to on Sunday. But then my week got better." He grinned that sexy grin women everywhere swooned over.

"Yeah, well, I'm not sure how you'll feel when I tell you that your photo is all over Rally Up's social media pages. Apparently, they took pictures Tuesday night. A friend called me to let me know."

Fin shifted toward her, his brow furrowed in concern. "How do you feel about it?"

Before Alex could answer, their server came to refill their glasses and ask if they needed anything. She considered the question while waiting for him to finish. She hadn't had a moment to think about it, but her initial reaction was shock at seeing her picture everywhere. Alex had seen photos on the Rally Up site before, but if she was in any of them, she'd been in the background or on the courts, never in one of the featured images. She was private about her personal life and utterly content to be in the background.

"It's uncomfortable. I'm not one to chase the spotlight and I keep my private life private. When I was younger and living in a small town, I was in the local newspaper's sports section every week. Strangers would come up and talk to me as if I knew them. I don't remember it bothering me then. Other than feeling surprised and awkward. But as an adult, and as a female in particular, I'm more cautious and don't share my personal life. Even my closest work colleagues don't know much about me outside of work. I guess I feel... wary." She shrugged and took another bite.

Fin grimaced. "I've been doing this a long time, and the fame starts to wear on you. It's crossed my mind to drop out of sight and attempt a normal life, but I couldn't imagine doing anything else. I love the work. I do. But the lack of privacy... and not knowing if the people around you are sincere about you or if they are there because of who you are... that gets to me sometimes."

"Yeah, I get that," Alex said. "Does she like me because I'm the 'Hottest Man Ever?' Or maybe because I have mad style skills? Or is it because I'm super smart and funny?"

He laughed, and she was glad he took the joke as she meant it.

"In all seriousness, though," she continued, "I know what you're saying. How do you know if someone is in your world because of you or because of what they think you can do for them? How do you find anyone to trust?"

Fin set his fork on the plate and pushed it away. He wiped his mouth with his napkin, then covered his plate with it and sat back. "Well, in my case, you have a select few in your inner circle, and you hold everyone else at arm's length."

"That sounds hard. And a little lonely. But I get it. Even in my not-a-movie-star life, I have many acquaintances and lots of 'fun to hang with' type friends, but very few who really know the whole me. I'm good at compartmentalizing the pieces of my life. I think that just makes me weird, but sounds like it's a survival tactic in your world."

"I never thought of it that way," he said. "But hey, let's not talk about depressing things. Do you want dessert?"

Before she could answer, a loud crash clanged close by and a bright flash struck her eyes. Fin muttered, "Damn it" as he captured her arm and guided her up out of her chair. He picked up her purse and handed it to her as he led her away from the table. She looked over her shoulder, her eyes widening at the crowd of people sporting cameras and climbing over the rail onto the patio.

Everything seemed to slow down. She watched Fin texting on his phone as he guided her along. He wrapped his arm around her waist and moved toward the hostess station, pulling a wad of cash from his coat pocket and shoving it at the woman. Alex assumed he was paying for their meal and apologizing for the abruptness of their departure. He whisked her outside, where a crowd mobbed them with microphones and more flashing lights.

She felt a tug on her arm and heard fabric ripping as someone yelled at her, "Over here, miss." Yanking her arm away, she walked briskly as Fin continued to move her down the walkway toward the waiting car. Another voice shouted, "Finley, who's the girl?" And yet another called "Is she your new lover?"

Blake held the car door open and blocked the crowd as she and Fin rushed into the backseat. The door thudded shut, muting the noise from outside. A brief cacophony of shouting assaulted her ears when Blake got into the driver's seat before silence descended once again.

When her heart finally slowed down, Alex noticed Fin held her tight. She moved and he let her go at once.

"Are you okay, Alex?"

She looked at her sleeve where the lace was ripped beyond repair. Her wonderfully exquisite dress that made her feel so feminine was now ruined. Her fists clenched and she seethed in anger. Tears threatened, the loss of control infuriating her.

"WHAT THE HELL WAS THAT?" she shouted.

Fin winced. "Alex... I'm so sorry." He tenderly touched the ruined sleeve. "That," Fin raised his arm in a wide arc, "was a taste of my life." His eyes looked so haunted.

Chapter 9

Still Wednesday

ALEX CLOSED the door to her duplex and headed to the bedroom. Felix greeted her, and she bent down and rubbed his head. "Hey, boy. How's your evening been? I bet not nearly as confusing as mine."

She pulled off her shoes and stripped off the dress, flinging it on the chair in the corner of her room as she moved into the bathroom. It wasn't exactly how she had imagined the dress coming off this evening. She doubted the delicate lace sleeve could be fixed. She sighed as she turned on the hot water in the shower.

Fin hadn't wanted to let the evening end on a sour note, asking her quietly to come to his suite so they could talk about what happened. When she'd balked, he'd suggested coming here where she felt comfortable. But she held firm. She needed time to process. Alone. Without his pheromones or her hormones getting in the way. They had parted with Alex saying she'd talk to him tomorrow.

She absentmindedly washed her face, then rotated around to let the soothing spray of hot water melt the tension in her shoulders and neck. What had gotten into her this week? She had determined long ago that relationships and her ambition didn't mix. Her confidence, intelligence, and independence drew men to her. And those same characteristics that attracted them in the beginning later became the sticking points. She had been accused of loving her job more than him (maybe true), not needing him (definitely true), and cheating on him rather than working late (absolutely false). At some point, she had decided she didn't have time for the drama. From that moment on, her interactions with men had been strictly casual, and the minute she sensed any sign of it getting serious, she bailed.

Of course, this approach meant the men she dated either had similar philosophies or they weren't the caliber of man she would ever consider long-term. Unfortunately, casual often meant shallow, which resulted in Alex not dating much. A lack of social life made it easier to focus on work. And she had good friends in her life if she wanted a deeper connection.

When the hot water ran out, she finished up and dried off. As she got ready for bed, she thought about her mom. Debra James had been a beautiful, carefree, aspiring artist working on her fine arts degree when she'd met and fallen in love with Tom Tanner, a country boy from West Texas focused on animal science and agriculture. He'd been a senior and her, a freshman. When he'd graduated, she'd dropped out of school and followed him home to the ranch.

Mom still painted when the mood took her, but she spent the bulk of her time managing the household and assisting Dad with chores on the ranch. While Alex knew they were happy, she'd never understood why her mom had given up her life's dream to follow someone else's. Alex had decided at an early age she would *not* be like her mother and sacrifice everything for some boy.

Her thoughts drifted back to the present as she slipped into bed. Fin was a complete surprise. She genuinely liked him as a person. He was intelligent, kind, considerate of others, and not at all arrogant as you might expect of someone who seemed to have it all. Honestly, except for the fame complication, he ticked all the boxes of the man she *might* be interested in at some point in the far future. A point in time that wasn't anywhere on her radar right now. She had too much to accomplish before she started to think of settling down. Or rather settling, as she thought of it.

And the fame part of it... Tonight was like a scene from a movie. It didn't even feel real. What a nightmare. How could Fin live like that? He had said a few things over the last several days hinting that he struggled with it, but good lord, what if his life was like that all the time? She would not want to be a part of that world.

Alex pushed those thoughts away, determined to focus on tomorrow's schedule, which she should have been paying more attention to anyway. She drifted off to sleep with thoughts of deadlines and task lists floating in her head.

FIN SAT in despair in the car's backseat. He replayed the evening over in his head, wondering how the press had found them so quickly.

"Mr. McAlister?" Blake interrupted his thoughts. "We've arrived at your hotel."

Fin sighed and pulled himself together. "Thank you, Blake. Nice rescue back there. I appreciate your search and rescue capabilities more than you know."

"No worries, sir. I hope Miss Tanner is okay."

"Aye, I hope so too. Thanks again, mate."

Fin closed the car door and made his way toward the hotel entrance. He'd like to have a drink before bed, but didn't think he could manage a quiet moment alone in the hotel bar. He made his way to the elevator, ignoring the flutter of activity his presence caused in the lobby.

Once alone in his suite, he poured himself a whisky and thought about Blake's last words. What was going through Alex's head right now? They'd been so relaxed with each other. In fact, it had felt as if they were the only ones in the world. Things had been going well until the end, when they had been attacked. Attacked! Alex had literally had her dress ripped. Fin clenched his fists, thinking of someone putting hands on her.

"Feckin' hackit dobbers," he cursed. What the hell was he supposed to do about the press? He thought he'd recognized the photographer who had grabbed Alex. If he was correct, the man had worked for Miranda Cole before. Was this her doing? The photos Alex had mentioned on the Rally Up social media site had likely caught Cole's eye. If so, it was easy to draw the conclusion that she'd put out feelers to all her bottom-feeding lackeys to be on the lookout for Finley McAlister in Houston. Anyone from the restaurant could have posted a photo on the Internet for the paparazzi to find and put them on the hunt.

He pulled out his phone and sent a text to Addie. *"Bombarded by paparazzi on a dinner date. Suspect Cole's minions. Lady friend's dress ripped. Look into legal options? Talk tomorrow. Too tired tonight."*

He sipped his whisky and leaned his head back, picturing Alexis in that dress. When she'd first opened the door, his visceral physical reaction had taken him by surprise. The dress hugged her in all the right places, emphasizing her feminine shape and showing off those long, gorgeous legs of hers. The high heels she wore gave him a bit of a thrill as well. Her feet were rather delicate looking, with her toenails painted a surprising bright red. Alex didn't exude a particularly feminine mystique, but these hints kept popping up and taking him by surprise. Like the lace on her dress. Who knew lace on a self-proclaimed tomboy would be so tantalizing?

His phone pinged, and he read Addie's reply. *"Fuckers. Will talk tomorrow."*

He appreciated Addie's unceasing loyalty. Fin finished his whisky and tucked away all thoughts of Alex and the evening. He reached for his tablet and the new script, intending to lose himself in the story that had captivated his attention from the beginning.

Chapter 10

Thursday

ALEX GLANCED at her watch and noted she had thirty minutes before her first meeting of the day. She had arrived early to complete the PMO proposal for Frank's approval. She never knew what kind of feedback to expect from her boss when sending items for review. His responses were either "Looks good" with no changes, or a total rewrite of multiple sections. *We shall see what Mr. Lambert thinks of this one,* she thought as she attached the document and clicked send.

Her phone vibrated, and she grew concerned when her mother's picture popped up on the screen. "Hey, Mom," she answered, "is everything okay? You don't usually call during the day."

"I saw you on TV! Are you dating that movie star, Finley McAlister?" her mom asked.

"What? Oh god." Alex rarely watched TV. All her news came from printed sources, websites, or the radio. And she never watched those silly entertainment news shows. Office gossip had made her life miserable early in her career, so she refused to contribute to the problem by taking part. In her mind, watching those entertainment shows was another version of participating, and she wouldn't support them with her patronage.

"So, it's true?" her mom persisted. "You won't date normal men, but movie stars are okay? What is going on?"

"Mom," Alex said, "we're not dating. I sat beside him on the airplane coming home from London. He asked me to dinner. I thought dinner with him would be entertaining. I was wrong. The end."

When her mom launched into a list of movies Fin had starred in, Alex closed her eyes and pinched her nose, attempting to stave off the headache developing behind her right eye. The older woman began adding her personal critiques, and Alex realized she had to stop her.

"Mom, I've got to go. I have a meeting. We'll talk later, okay?"

"Alex, I'm worried about you. Do not brush me off on this. I mean it," she threatened.

Alex hung up and leaned back in her chair, staring at the ceiling. She loved her mom and had wonderful memories from growing up on the ranch, but their worlds were so far apart that they had little in common as adult women. She made a mental note to call her back as soon as she got a quiet moment.

She still had twenty minutes available before the meeting, so she searched the Internet for Finley McAlister. The pictures of them fleeing the restaurant came up right away. Fin's jaw was clenched and his gaze locked forward, his right arm wrapped protectively around her while his left stretched out to block unwanted advances. Alex's own face was pale and drawn, and her eyes appeared glazed over in shock.

She found other photos as well. The two of them sitting

at the dinner table together, laughing, touching each other. Those images screamed cozy and romantic. The photographer must have been hiding in the bushes left of the balcony. Alex groaned and closed her browser, mentally shoving the images aside, then gathered her things for her meeting.

A few minutes later in the conference room she'd reserved, she projected the meeting agenda on the screen and opened the conference call as the first attendees walked into the room. She greeted the callers on the line and turned back to her laptop as one of the IT admins who frequently worked with her team sauntered over to where she was sitting.

"So, Alex... Anything you want to tell us?" He stuck his hands in his front pockets and looked up at the ceiling, then cut his eyes back to her.

"Yes, I'm proud of you for arriving on time for once to a project meeting. Good job," she said with a smile, returning her attention to her laptop.

"Well, I wanted to show up early and get the gossip on Mr. 'Hottest Man Ever.'"

Alex stopped typing and met his gaze. Beyond him, the other attendees stood still, staring at her and awaiting her response. A beep on the conference phone announcing a new arrival saved Alex from answering. She addressed the room and told them they were waiting a few minutes for everyone to arrive and would begin soon.

To give herself time to recover from the jarring question, Alex got up to shut the door to the conference room. *Good lord,* she thought as she walked to the door, *do people actually follow celebrities this closely? Seriously?*

Alex kept the meeting on track, finished early, and left

the room before anyone else could ask about her personal life.

She'd worked hard her entire career to keep her personal life separate from her work. When you were the only woman among a sea of male managers, it became second nature to tuck away anything that reminded them you were different. This strategy had worked well for many years. Suddenly having her private life exposed for everyone to disseminate unnerved her. She feared losing the traction she'd made in her career over a stupid dinner date with some temporary guy.

Her stomach growled and Alex checked her phone. A lunch break would give her time to collect herself and she had enough time in her schedule to venture off premises.

Normally, Alex liked to use her lunch hour to leave work behind. She usually went out with friends or colleagues, where they avoided talking about any current job-related issues they were working on. The human interaction was good for her soul and the break from work helped her revitalize for the afternoon. Today, however, she wanted some quiet time alone. She collected her purse and let Grace know she was going offsite for lunch should anyone come looking for her.

Her phone rang as she crossed the block-sized park outside her office building and headed to a nearby deli-catessen. She glanced at the caller and grimaced when Fin's name popped up. *Nope,* she thought, *not ready for* that *conversation.* She put her phone away and walked inside the deli.

She paid for her muffuletta sandwich and found a narrow table outside in a spot that faced the park. She loved how much green space Houston had within the city, even in the downtown area. From her seat, she could see both the park and the inside of the deli. The view allowed her to enjoy nature while watching for colleagues who had the same idea. She did not want company right now.

Alex forced herself to relax and enjoy the fall weather. She watched two birds fight over a piece of bread while she ate. A flash of color caught her eye on the television inside the deli. She focused on the image and gasped, nearly choking on the bite she had in her mouth. The image showed Fin, stunningly handsome in a red-carpet tux, with the headline, "Hottest Man No Longer Available?" Her mouth went dry, and she had to force herself to swallow the now unappealing sandwich bite. When her stomach gurgled, she waited to see if the nausea would pass. *At least if I threw up, the pigeons would have more to fight over.* Alex cringed and acknowledged she was finished with lunch. She wrapped up the leftovers, cleaned off the table, and headed back to the office, hoping her stomach would settle down before the next meeting.

Fin had risen early that morning, gotten in a full workout and swim, and had eaten a hardy breakfast. As he showered, his mind drifted to the manuscript and where he'd left off the night before. He was eager to get back to it.

Fin's phone pinged as he buttoned his shirt. His mother loved this shirt. According to her, the navy color brought out the deep blue in his eyes. He liked it because the soft poplin button-down with the tapered cut made him feel stylishly comfortable.

He tucked the shirt into his tan chinos and read the text from Addie. "*Got something for you.*"

She picked up as soon as he dialed.

"I saw the pictures. You look great, by the way, and so does your lady friend," Addie said without preamble. "Needless to say, we do have some recourse. Do you have her dress? We can use it for evidence."

"Er, no, I'll have to fetch it from her," Fin answered. "What's the deal?"

"First, tell me what happened. I can take a guess but want to hear it in your words."

Fin filled her in on the evening. He paced back and forth as he talked, rubbing the back of his neck in agitation.

"Okay, so you were right about that jackass being one of Cole's minions. She may even keep him on retainer if my source is right. I can't believe he touched your date, much less ripped her dress. Did you know the douchebag posted a picture that shows the sleeve hanging loose? What an *el estúpido*. That's probably enough evidence alone, but I'd like to have the dress for backup. What's the lady's name, by the way? I'm not sure you've told me yet."

"Her name is Alexis Tanner. She goes by Alex. She's a project manager based here in Houston. Did I tell you she knew who I was the whole time? From the moment I sat down beside her on the airplane. And yet, she didn't fawn all over me or act like I was some big shot. She treated me like I was a fellow passenger." Fin paused, remembering the shocked look on her face last night after the attack. "I hate that she was accosted like that because of me."

Addie growled. "No, Finley, it's not your fault. That onus belongs to the Miranda Coles of the world. Don't ever take that on. You feel me?"

Fin puffed out his cheeks and blew out a breath. "I understand. I don't know why it's bothering me so much after all this time."

Addie's voice gentled over the phone, "Well... the other

women you've dated have all been in the business. They're used to the spotlight, and—let's be honest—some showbiz types encourage that kind of attention. Alex doesn't come from that world." Addie took a deep breath on the other end of the line before continuing, "And Finley, I'm sure the physical aspect of the incident brought back some strong feelings for you."

Fin sat down hard as he absorbed what Addie said. "Right." He scrubbed his face with his free hand, then scraped it through his hair. "So. What do we do about it?"

"I've already been in touch with my attorney. He's looking into getting an injunction against Cole and anyone associated with her here in the States like you have in Scotland. He's not sure there's enough to warrant it, but since it's a recurring theme with her, we have a chance. We'll know something later this week. Having the dress will help. If nothing else, we can file an assault charge, but we need to act quickly if you want to go that route."

"She left me alone for so long—writing from a distance, but not coming near me physically—that I thought she was done with me. Anyway, I'm seeing Alex tonight, so I'll ask about the dress. Thanks for staying on top of it for me."

"Tell me about Alex. What's going on there? Are you falling in love?" Addie prompted.

"What are we, school children?" Fin exclaimed. "Look, she and her friends act like I'm ordinary. Like I'm just some dude hanging out with friends having a regular day. I haven't been treated that way in so long I've forgotten what it's like to be me." He ran his hand through his hair again. "I wanted to use this break in the schedule to remember what that's like. If only I could get the rest of the world to cooperate."

"All right, I get it. Go have fun. Enjoy your vacation. I'll see if I can keep the wolves off your back."

"Thanks, love," Fin replied.

"Yep. Later," Addie said as she hung up.

Alex finally got a break around mid-afternoon and shut the door to her office. Throughout the day she had been receiving strange looks and hearing whispers. She'd side-stepped and avoided any direct questions in the same manner she had dealt with the tech guy earlier in the day, but doing so wore on her last nerve. In addition to all that, she'd received a text from Fin earlier asking if she was okay and wanting to talk when she had a chance. Never one to be rude, she'd acknowledged the text with the okay emoji, but nothing else.

Now was a good time for a follow-up. She cleared off her desk, picked up her phone, and dialed Fin.

"Hey, you," he answered, the silkiness of his voice sending shivers down her spine. "How are you today? I've worried about you since last night."

"I'm okay. I slept better than expected and have been busy most of the day so haven't had time to dwell on what happened. Although I can tell from the looks I've been receiving that more of my colleagues follow the gossip shows than I ever would have imagined."

"Funny how that works," Fin responded drily. "Listen, my agent asked if we could have your dress for evidence."

"What? Why?"

"We're looking into filing charges. The man who grabbed you works for the reporter I told you about. Addie thinks she can get an injunction against her and the dress might help with the case."

"Wow. I don't know what to say. I didn't realize we could do anything about it."

"Well, don't expect too much," he warned. "It rarely happens due to the freedom of the press banner they constantly wave, but we can still try. Tearing your dress like that could go down as assault and gives us a better case."

"Okay. The dress doesn't look repairable, so it might as well go to a good cause. Um, I wasn't planning to go home before volleyball this evening, so I'll have to give it to you later. You're still coming tonight, right?"

"Aye, I'll be there." The warmth in his voice sent a shiver down her spine.

"Cool. I gotta run. See you then."

"Bye, Alexis," he murmured before hanging up.

Alex froze with the phone still at her ear. Her body got all tingly and melty when Fin spoke her full name. Did he know he had that kind of power over her? She shook her head, put down her phone, and focused her attention on the next item on her agenda.

ALEX DUMPED her stuff at their gang's usual table and headed to the second court, where her teammates passed the ball back and forth. Julie, or Jules as Rick called her, stood next to him, so it looked like they would have a fourth again tonight. Alex waved as she began her stretching routine.

"Hey, Alex." Julie came over and stretched next to her. "You okay with me playing again?"

"Sure. We all seem to play well together. Are you joining the team permanently?"

"I'd like to, but wasn't sure how you felt about it," Julie faltered. "You know, because I'm Rick's girlfriend." She made air quotes with her fingers on the last part.

"Does that matter?" Alex asked curiously. "We've tried for two years to find another girl who works well with our rhythm and haven't found anyone. You fit right in as if you've been here from the beginning. I assumed you weren't a permanent fixture because of an outside factor."

Alex stopped stretching and looked at Julie. "Seriously, were you worried what I would think? And why?"

Julie hesitated while Alex waited. "I guess because you're kind of intimidating. And, well, I'm not sure I'm good enough for league ball."

Alex waved in a dismissive motion. "Nonsense. Of course you are. And anyway, we play for fun. Sure, we like the t-shirts we get for winning, but it's the camaraderie that keeps us coming back. And the beer." She leaned over and bumped shoulders with Julie. "Honestly, it's Rick's team. He can choose whomever he wants, and I wouldn't complain." Alex scrunched up her nose. "I take that back. I would totally complain if they sucked like Poser Dude."

"Whoa, now... no need to be vulgar." Julie laughed at the shared memory from last year when a new guy off the street had come to play and was so bad, he wound up getting people hurt. The evening had been so memorable, the poor fellow earned a permanent moniker that was now used to describe someone having a particularly bad game.

They finished their warm-up and got settled into position as the opposition lined up on the other side of the net. The team got off to a slow start, but eventually hit their stride, winning the match with two out of three games.

Alex picked up her water bottle and turned to find Rick walking toward her.

"Good match," she called before taking a drink.

"You too." He lowered his voice to add, "Hey, Alex, thanks for what you said to Jules. I don't understand why she was nervous. I told her you were cool."

"Sure. I meant it," Alex said. "I don't know why everyone thinks I'm intimidating. I get that at work too. I think I'm charming." She batted her eyelashes at him, then laughed at herself.

Rick narrowed his eyes and pressed his lips together. "I think it's because of your self-confidence. Most people aren't as secure about themselves as you are."

Alex blinked at the honest appraisal, then flipped the focus back on him. "I've never noticed you having any self-doubts."

"Yeah, well, I'm an arrogant ass," he said with a smirk. "Where's your man?"

Alex stiffened but forced herself to relax. "We didn't ride together tonight. I believe he planned to come, but not sure when."

"Cool. He seems okay." When Alex didn't respond, Rick continued, "Our next match is at seven on court five."

"Okay, thanks." Alex waved him on and took her time walking to the table. That was the most Rick had ever said to her about her personal life. Their past interactions always focused on their team. His feedback both surprised and pleased her. From as early as high school, she'd been told she was intimidating, but had never had a clue why people thought of her that way.

Rick's observations intrigued her. *Do I really give off an aura of self-confidence?* Alex wondered. Maybe that impression resulted from her never seeking approval from those around her. That attitude had caused issues early in her career until she had established herself. Coworkers had accused her of being aggressive, but her managers had never complained. The bosses were always happy with her results, so she never worried about what the nay-sayers said behind her back.

Alex shrugged off her musings as she reached the group's table on the deck. She caught Daisy's attention and ordered a burger with fries, then joined the current argument over the upcoming rule changes for outdoor volleyball.

As TIME for her next match approached, Alex finished her burger and cleaned up the table. She dumped her trash in the nearby garbage can and turned, stumbling right into Fin. He gripped her shoulders to steady her.

"Whoa, there," he said, "I didn't mean to startle you."

Alex reached up to his forearms and squeezed. "Hey, you made it." She smiled at him and before she could move away, he pulled her into a quick hug. After a brief squeeze, he let her go.

"I intended to be here sooner but was delayed by some fans. At least there were no reporters around." He grimaced, then made a silly face.

"No worries. We're up so I've gotta run, but I'll catch you after the match, yeah?" Alex tilted her head in question.

"Aye. Do you want me to order you some food?"

"Nah, I've already eaten. You go ahead. Back soon." She waved him off and ran to the court. She smiled to herself, happy he was here.

They lost the match. Alex and her teammates made their way back to the deck where Fin was telling a story.

As she approached, he pulled out the chair next to him for her to sit without breaking stride in his narrative. The story centered around some mishap that occurred on the set of one of his movies. Her friends laughed when he concluded.

Fin leaned over and said, "I wasn't able to follow close-ly." He nodded his head towards the people sitting around their group of tables. "Did you win?"

"No, but it's okay. We rarely beat that team. They've got three A-level players." She shrugged. Seeing his confused expression, she explained, "League play is divided into distinct competitive levels... that particular team has three people who play at a higher level than we do. But we still have fun. And honestly, I enjoy challenging myself against better opponents."

"It helps," Fin agreed. "When training for a new role, I often have a workout partner because they push me to keep going and reach whatever goal we've set for the day, keeping me accountable."

"Exactly. Plus, it motivates you to do better."

Alex tensed as arms slipped around her from behind. She recognized Melissa coming in for a hug and relaxed.

"Hey, lady. Long time no see," Melissa said as she kissed the top of Alex's head.

Alex turned around in her seat and squeezed Melissa's arm, then introduced Fin. Scott, Melissa's boyfriend, pulled up another chair as Melissa took the one next to Alex.

"Melissa is one of my closest friends. She ranks up there with Eddie and Gabe," Alex told Fin.

"Hello, tall, dark, and movie star. How's it hanging?" Melissa looked at Fin with eyes of innocence.

Alex snorted and Scott looked down, trying to suppress a laugh. Fin looked back and forth between Alex and

Melissa before commenting, "Hanging well, thank ye for asking."

Alex and Melissa burst into laughter, and Scott thumped Fin on the back a couple of times.

"Nice to meet you, Fin. And a little weird, but kind of cool. How do you like Houston?" Melissa asked.

Fin gave Alex a long speculative look and answered, "I'm liking it."

Daisy came to take orders and Melissa answered greetings from those seated at the table. She and Scott got caught up in a debate about the proposed zoning laws for the city and how those changes would affect several of their favorite haunts around town.

"She's a bold one. Are all Texas ladies so confident?" Fin murmured as he leaned closer to Alex.

"Melissa's originally from California. I think she's used to movie stars, so she's not as awestruck by your celebrity as the rest of us mere mortals," she teased. "So, did you do more sight-seeing with Blake today?"

"No, but I got a good workout in at the gym he introduced me to earlier this week. It's set up to do boxing, Krav Maga, and other martial arts as well as plain old-fashioned weightlifting. I've gone every day since he first took me."

"I didn't know you did all that martial arts stuff. Did you get into it because of your films?"

"Aye. I had to do some training for an action film early in my career and I loved the workout and how it made me feel, so I incorporated it into my regular workout routine."

Fin's phone buzzed and his brow furrowed as he read the text.

"Something wrong?" Alex asked.

"Eh, apparently fans have swarmed my hotel, and getting back undetected by the media will be a challenge.

With the press junket last weekend, it's no secret we were in town, but things had died down. Apparently, all this focus on you and me has stirred up more interest."

Fin rubbed the back of his head, making his hair stand up in places. Alex squeezed his hand, then reached up and smoothed the unruly curls back into place. Fin blinked at her, making Alex realize the gesture had been an intimate one.

"I'm sorry. I was feeling your pain and... you messed up your hair... um..." She trailed off.

Fin smiled and took her hand in his. "You can run your fingers through my hair any time you want, Alexis."

She blushed and he beamed at her. Damn the man! He knew full well the effect he was having on her. That knowing smile gave it away.

He broke the gaze and looked off into the distance. "I suppose I'll have to move hotels now."

"Is that common?" She frowned at the idea of having to adjust your life because of over-exuberant fans.

"Not usually, but it happens. Although moving doesn't address what I need to do tonight. I dismissed Blake for the night when he dropped me off, assuming you'd give me a lift back, but I don't want to drag you into the spotlight again. Those vultures—the media, I mean... not the fans—have a way of finding you. They once harassed the guy where I dropped off my dry cleaning. They have no shame. And don't care if people get hurt." He frowned at the memory.

"I'm done for the night, but we could stay and hang out longer. Maybe they'll get bored and disappear," Alex suggested.

"That hasn't been my experience in the past," he replied tiredly. "If it were just me, I wouldn't worry, but they can be vicious as you've seen and your safety is important."

"My safety?" Alex asked, wondering at the tension appearing in his eyes.

Fin set his jaw and stated, "I'll find another place to stay for the night and make arrangements to move tomorrow."

"Why don't you come home with me?" Alex blurted out. She froze, unable to believe she'd suggested it.

Fin's gaze snapped to her eyes. "What?"

FIN STARED at Alex waiting for her to confirm he heard her correctly.

"I mean, you could ride home with me and we could figure out what to do from there. The apartment above Eddie's garage is empty and sometimes friends spend the night when they've had too much to drink. We can ask Eddie if you can stay there tonight. Would that help?"

"Aye, that would help, but..." Fin narrowed his eyes at her. Memories flashed through his head of the funeral, the full-size casket and the smaller one next to it. He gasped and lowered his head to stave off the panic creeping up his spine.

"But what? Are you okay? What are you thinking?" Alex asked.

"A lot of things are going through my head. I'm worried about dragging you into the spotlight. I'm concerned about keeping you safe. And I don't want to be invasive."

"Invasive?" Alex snorted. "I think that ship has sailed." She pulled out her phone and scrolled through her contacts.

"Alex." Fin reached out and covered her hand with his.

"What?" She looked up at him, eyebrows raised.

"Are you okay with me staying somewhere that close to you?" Fin's first reaction was he shouldn't because he would endanger her. But the vultures knew about her already, and they'd find her eventually. Perhaps if he was closer to her, he could protect her.

"Yeah, sure. Just let me text Eddie real quick and make sure no one's using it before I commit to something I can't deliver." Alex patted his hand and sent the message to Eddie.

"Yo, guys... HELLOOOOOOO... anyone there?" Andy called from down the table.

Fin looked up to see all eyes on them and Alex responded, "Pardon me?"

"We were asking if you two wanted to play. There's a court open."

Alex's phone dinged and she showed him Eddie's response. The apartment was empty, and Eddie was thrilled to have him stay there. One night wouldn't hurt, would it?

Fin spoke up before Alex could answer, "Actually, something's come up and we have to leave. Rain check?" Now that he'd made the decision, he wanted to get away from the crowd. He raised his eyebrows at Alex, silently asking if she was ready to go.

"Yeah, sure, man. Everything okay?" Andy asked.

Alex nodded her agreement.

"Yes, nae bother." Fin stood and picked up his things. "Thanks again for letting me hang out with you lot."

Alex collected her stuff and preceded Fin to the car.

Chapter 11

Thursday Night

THE DRIVE HOME WAS QUIET. Not an uncomfortable silence, but an anticipatory one. They discussed how much more visible the stars were on a clear night like tonight and how you couldn't see as many as you could back home. For her that was West Texas, and for Fin, Scotland. It gave them a safe topic to discuss while their minds pondered deeper matters.

Before Alex knew it, and perhaps before she was ready, they arrived at her duplex. The lights were on in the garage apartment and Eddie walked toward them from the stairs at the end of the carport.

"Hello, Finley! Let me show you to the guest house," Eddie greeted them as they pulled their gym bags from her car.

Fin looked at Alex. When she shrugged and followed Eddie, he fell into step beside her, trailing Eddie around the side and up the stairs.

Alex had seen the garage apartment before, but Eddie had redecorated several times since she'd last peeked inside. The entrance led into an open living/kitchen combo area.

The cabinetry was white with seafoam green-colored walls as a backdrop. The furniture was all casual chic with airy greens and blues, giving it a beach cottage feel. Alex spotted a few accessories with an oceanic theme and congratulated herself on getting better at identifying a specific style. Eddie had been trying to educate her for years in the aesthetics of design. Her habit of picking things she liked regardless of how they blended with a color scheme horrified him.

"The unit is an efficiency apartment. Living area, kitchen, utility closet." Eddie pointed around as he talked. "The door on the right is the bathroom and through here is the bedroom."

The beach house motif continued into the bedroom, which contained a dresser, a nightstand, and a queen-size bed. On the right were two doors, an open door leading into the bathroom and another door beyond it, which Alex presumed led to a closet.

Eddie continued the tour. "As you can see, the bathroom is accessible from the bedroom as well as the front room. That way when you have guests over, you don't have to give them access to your boudoir if they need to use the facilities."

Fin held up his hand, and Eddie stopped talking.

"The apartment is lovely, Eddie, but I only need one night."

Eddie cleared his throat. "Well, from Alex's text, I assumed you needed new accommodations for the rest of your stay here in Houston."

Fin's eyebrows rose and he glanced at Alex. "Oh," she said. "I didn't think beyond tonight. *Would* you want to stay here for the rest of your vacation?"

Fin hesitated. "I need to check with Addie and make sure I don't have any legal obligations. The hotel room is tied to the press junket so..." He trailed off and raised his hands.

Eddie bustled about. "Sure, sure... check with your people and let me know. The apartment is yours for the night, and it's available if you need it through the end of the month. Honestly, it's available for the remainder of the year. We haven't put the place up for rent since the last tenant left, and it's become more of a 'just in case' spot for friends who drink too much. Here are the keys... drop them off tomorrow if you're not staying." Eddie smiled and made his way toward the door. "Ta ta for now."

And just like that, they were alone. Alex looked back at Fin, who was still holding his gym bag and inspecting the bedroom. He dropped the bag on the bed and faced her.

"Well, that was unexpected," she said.

"Aye. My head is spinning."

"I have an idea." She pointed at him. "You get showered and changed—I'm assuming you have something to wear in your bag—then come to my place and we'll have a glass of wine or something stronger and relax a bit. We can put together a plan."

Fin smiled and agreed.

"Give me at least twenty minutes. I have more hair to wash than you do," she called as she left.

FIN PULLED what he needed from his gym bag and headed to the bathroom. The open shelving was fully stocked with both male and female grooming products, proving again what an excellent host Eddie was. He jumped in the shower and washed the day from his body. Seeing the shaving supplies in the cupboard, he considered the stubble on his face, but decided he was too eager to hang out with Alex to mess with it.

Happy that he always carried spare clothes in his gym bag, Fin pulled on the extra track bottoms and a t-shirt. This would work for tonight, but if he ditched the hotel, he needed to retrieve the rest of his things soon.

Fin found his phone and dialed Addie.

"Hello, darling, how are you?"

"Hey, Addie, I'm good. Listen, according to Blake, a mob has swamped the hotel, and I may need a new locale for the rest of my stay here."

"Well, fuck. So much for relaxation, eh? Let me see what I can find... same area?" Fin could hear her shuffling papers in the background.

"No, I might have a place lined up already, but needed to run it by you."

"Oh?"

He grinned at the question. Funny how Addie could say a million things with a simple two-letter word. "Yes, ehm, Alex's friend has a garage apartment available if I want to use it. I'm just wondering if I need to do anything at the hotel... if I have any obligations tied to the press junket, producers, or movie?"

"Okay, number one, screw them. They didn't protect you from that Cole bitch, and that *was* in your contract. So no, you do not owe them anything. And truth be told, you weren't obligated to stay there, anyway. We booked that hotel for the convenience. Now about this apartment... nothing shady there, right? Do I need to look into this 'friend?'"

A comforting warmth spread through him at the protectiveness Addie displayed. He must be overly stressed to have his emotions so close to the surface like this. Addie was always protective and fierce. Nothing new here.

"Nothing shady. In fact, I think he's a matchmaker type," Fin said, thinking of the sly looks Eddie gave him and Alex earlier. "Addie, have I told you lately that I love you? You are my best friend and you look after me like family. I'm closer to you than my own sister."

"Well, my god, Fin, you don't have to get all maudlin on me, for fuck's sake." Addie sniffed on the other end of the line, and he could picture her tearing up. "Listen, you can do what you want as far as where you stay. You want me to have them collect your things? I can check you out remotely and arrange it so all you have to do is swing by and pick everything up. Or better yet, have Blake do it."

"Let me double-check with Alex before we commit to anything," Fin told her, "but I like the idea of having everything ready to go so I can send someone for my stuff. I'll text you later to confirm. Possibly later tonight, but tomorrow for sure."

"Okay, sounds good. I'm sorry you're having to deal with this, Finley. I hoped you would get your break from the limelight. You're too popular right now." Addie snorted. "I never thought I'd complain about a client being too popular. Who knew?"

"Your client sounds like a pain. Night, Addie."

"*Such* a pain, but he's worth it. Sleep tight, Fin. Later."

Fin pocketed his phone, grabbed the keys to the apartment, and locked the door behind him. The porch light at Alex's back door was on, so he headed that direction instead of around front.

FIN KNOCKED on the back door. A muffled response came from somewhere inside the duplex. He opened the door and stepped inside.

"Alex?"

"In the kitchen," she called.

He slipped off his sandals and left them by the door. The cool tile soothed his feet as he made his way down the short hallway. Alex stood at the kitchen counter. She wore loose cotton pants and a large, oversized t-shirt. Her damp hair was pulled up with a bright orange band of material and her feet were bare. Music played softly in the background and she moved in time with the beat, her ponytail swishing back and forth.

"What are you doing?"

She turned and grinned at him. "I know we ate at Rally Up, but I'm starving. I'm putting together some cheese and crackers for us. Or would you rather have fruit?"

"Cheese and crackers are fine. What can I do to help?" Fin asked.

"Pour our drinks? I'll have a glass of the Riesling in the fridge. I have soda, more wine, water—again, no sparkling water—and iced tea. Oh, and if you want something stronger, I have liquor up there." She nodded towards an upper cabinet on the left.

Fin pulled out the wine and poured her drink then moved to inspect the contents of her liquor cabinet. "Ah, you have a superb Scottish whisky up here. I approve."

Alex grinned. "I'll let Gabe know. I'm more of a spiced rum girl myself, but I keep that here for him."

"Nice," Fin replied as he found a glass and poured himself a drink. He watched her making the snacks and examined the cheese tray. "What is the white cheese with the red and green in it?"

"That, my friend, is jalapeño Havarti. It's delicious."

"Jalapeño?" He raised his eyebrow. "In cheese?"

"Oh, yeah. Texans put them in everything. You should try jalapeño cornbread. It's to die for. Here, try some," she coaxed as she held a piece of cheese up to his lips. Fin opened his mouth and took the bite. The spicy flavor of the pepper blended surprisingly well with the buttery sweetness of the Havarti cheese.

"That's scrumptious," he commented as he licked his lips. His gaze caught hers and held it. Alex blushed and rubbed her lips together as if she could also taste the cheese. He found himself leaning closer.

She cleared her throat and said, "Let's go sit down."

"Right. Shall I carry the drinks?" *Cue the sexual tension,* he thought with a grin.

She picked up the tray while he held their drinks and followed her to the living room where they made themselves comfortable on the couch.

ALEX WATCHED as Fin situated himself. The t-shirt he wore stretched tightly across his chest. His hair was still damp from the shower and she wanted to run her fingers through it. Instead, she raised her glass and waited for him to raise his.

"Tonight, we are celebrating. Last week in London, I was invited to submit a project initiation request for something I've been pitching for a while, and today I officially submitted it."

Fin clinked his glass to hers and raised his glass. "Congratulations. What did you propose?"

Alex sipped her wine and explained, "I want to set up a

single department to manage all administrative and IT projects within the company, rather than having them managed by whomever proposed the idea. This would standardize and streamline so many things for us. And leading this team means my position would move up a level from manager to director."

"Wow, that sounds like a significant opportunity."

"Yeah, that's why I'm so excited. I'm looking forward to the challenge, but at the same time, it's a bit daunting. If they approve it, I have a shit-ton of work to accomplish in the next two months. Lots of overtime."

She assembled a cracker and cheese sandwich and shoved it in her mouth, pausing as she took in his grin. "What?" she asked, her mouth full.

"Your sayings amuse me. 'Shit-ton?'" He paused for a drink and continued, "Sounds ambitious."

She swallowed her bite. "It is. Anyway, I wanted to get that out of the way before we talked about your current living situation."

Fin cocked his head as a new song came on. "What *are* we listening to?"

Alex laughed and asked, "What, you don't like Theory of a Deadman? This channel plays hard rock, which essentially means alternative, hard rock, and metal. I can find something else if you like."

She reached for the system remote, but Fin stopped her. "No, it's fine. I just didn't have you pegged as a headbanger. After hearing about your cowgirl life on the trip over, I assumed you would listen to western music. You are an intriguing woman, Alexis Tanner."

Alex felt the heat creep up her face. When do you outgrow blushing like a schoolgirl? "No, I generally avoid country and western music. Too much of it growing up, I suppose. I enjoy dancing to it, though. And I do a mean Texas two-step. Do you like to dance?"

"I have been known to step out on occasion."

"Hmm... maybe we need to go dancing and I'll teach you how to two-step. That's assuming you don't already know how, of course."

"I don't believe I do." He smiled and finished his whisky. "So, about Eddie's apartment..."

"Right, back to business. It's rather nice. He's redone the place since I was last in it. Did you like it?"

"Aye, it reminds me of a cottage I stayed in once on the East Coast. I checked with Addie and she confirmed there's no issue with me moving from the hotel. But I have a few questions about staying here."

While Fin had been talking, his hand had moved along the back of the couch and his fingers slowly drew circles on Alex's arm where it rested. The tingling sensation running from where his fingers touched down to her spine made it difficult for her to concentrate on the topic at hand.

"Um... wh-what are your questions?" she asked. She leisurely turned her hand palm up and raised her fingers to brush the underside of his arm as he continued to draw circles on hers.

"First, how much should I pay Eddie? I'm unsure what the going rate is for a rental."

"I don't think he expects payment. He never charges his friends anything." She shrugged. "But if you're concerned, you should ask him. He'll be straight with you." Alex shivered as Fin's circles made their way from her elbow to her palm.

"Okay, then the most important question..." He paused and leaned forward to tug gently on her ponytail.

"Yes?" she asked as she subtly shifted closer and ran her fingers up his arm to wander through his hair.

Fin smiled. "You're distracting me."

"Am I?"

"Most definitely," he answered as he took her glass and set it on the coffee table along with his. "Now, where were we?" Fin reached out and pulled her closer. Alex was practically sitting in his lap at this point.

"You were asking me the most important question," she whispered as his hand circled around her back and up into her hair. She felt the band holding her ponytail slide out and her hair fall around her shoulders.

Fin groaned and captured her mouth with his. The kiss began as a gentle exploration, but molten desire exploded through Alex's body and she curled her fingers in his hair, pulling him closer. She leaned backward, bringing him with her, falling back so he stretched out on top of her. Alex adjusted her legs, cradling his body between them. She broke off the kiss and gasped for air.

Fin moved from her mouth to her ear, trailing wet, searing kisses along her jawline. Alex raised her hips up in an attempt to move closer. The evidence of his arousal pressed against her, causing shivers of anticipation along her spine. She gasped as one of his hands explored under her t-shirt, moving her bra aside and finding her breast. She felt the sudden dampness between her legs and uttered, "Jesus."

Fin's hands stopped moving and he went still. Alex wasn't aware they had been grinding against each other until he stopped. *Don't apologize*, she thought, *please don't apologize.*

He didn't. But he slowed down. He whispered something unintelligible in her ear. Maybe a foreign language? He peppered light kisses back along her jawline to her mouth. Not as passionate as a minute ago, but definitely smoldering and hot.

Fin raised up on his elbows and focused on Alex. His hair was a mess of curls and she imagined she looked just as disheveled. He twirled a lock of her hair in his fingers before speaking. "I knew we had chemistry, but that fire roared fairly fast. You okay?"

She smiled shyly up at him. "I wasn't expecting it either. Wow! I think I might have attacked you or something."

His smile turned sultry and he tugged on her hair. "I could handle being attacked like that. You caught me by surprise, and I responded on a visceral level." His gaze moved down their bodies. "Am I crushing you?"

Alex instinctively wrapped her legs around him before he could move off of her, unintentionally moving them into a more intimate position. Fin cocked his head and raised an eyebrow at her.

She found herself breathless at the feeling of him resting snugly between her legs. "Um, I... I didn't want you to move." She gulped. "Wh-what was your last question? Before we got... distracted."

His face sobered and he asked, "How do you feel about me being so close to you?"

Alex stared at him for half a second and then burst out laughing. "Seriously? You ask that right now? While we're lying here stuck together like glue?"

Fin grinned. "Okay, I admit the timing is awkward."

Alex moved her hands to either side of his face and pulled him toward her. She kissed him lightly on his forehead, then his nose, and then his mouth. "I don't care," she said against his lips before plunging her tongue into his mouth and squeezing him tight with her legs.

Chapter 12

Friday Ups and Downs

FIN WOKE to the sound of water running. He opened his eyes and looked around. He was in Alex's bedroom. The closed bathroom door muffled the running water of the shower.

She'd surprised him last night by taking the lead. His intention in coming over had been to make sure she was okay with him staying so close to her for the rest of his trip, not wind up in her bedroom. When she had reached for his pants, he'd halted her. He hadn't been prepared for this and didn't have any protection. No worries, she had told him, and had proceeded to withdraw a box of condoms from her nightstand drawer. She had informed him that she never relied on someone else to look out for her well-being.

Fin stretched, then tucked his hands behind his head as he remembered their activities last night. Alex had been a delightful combination of shyness and adventure. He could tell when they wandered into areas new to her by the way she grew timid and let him lead. Then she would join in with enthusiasm and had even taken control a few times. The night had been a mix of slow, sensual lovemaking and fast, furious sex with languid bouts of quiet talk between. They had made a sizable dent in her condom stash. He made a mental note to buy some more.

Recounting the memories from last night stirred thoughts of joining her in the shower. He moved to do so when the clock on her nightstand caught his attention. Why was she up at such a deplorable hour? It occurred to him then that she was getting ready for work. And had an important meeting this morning, which she had mentioned during one of their quieter periods last night. A distraction this morning might not be appreciated.

He sighed and decided it was time to find coffee. He located his sweatpants discarded on the floor, pulled them on, and headed to the kitchen.

Fin had finally managed to pour himself a cup of coffee when Alex walked into the room. She was dressed to kill in an ebony pencil skirt and matching jacket. The blouse underneath the jacket was a shock of purplish-blue color, reminding him of the Scots bluebells from back home.

"Your coffee machine is fantastic, but your selection is abysmal," he said by way of greeting.

She laughed. "Yeah, that machine mostly sees hot chocolate. Any coffee you found was left over from a family visit." She walked up to him, sliding her hands up his bare chest and around his neck. "Good morning, handsome." She kissed him lightly, and when it threatened to turn into something deeper, pushed away. "My god, you're addictive. How can a simple good morning kiss make me want to throw you down and have my way with you?"

Fin's body was already reacting to the kiss, but the suggestion of her ravishing him had everything standing to attention. She noticed and gave him a wry look. He told her, "Aye, you're not the only one with thoughts along that line."

He grinned sheepishly and placed the second coffee cup he'd retrieved earlier back into the cabinet. "The only reason you didn't wind up with company in the shower was because I remembered your morning meeting."

Her eyes widened and he thought for a minute he had said something wrong before she responded quietly, "That's incredibly thoughtful of you, Fin. You're not what I expected a celebrity to be. At all."

He leaned against the counter and sipped his drink, watching as she moved into the living room and surveyed the damage from last night. Her face went pink as she picked up the trail of clothing they had left in their wake.

"I've got to run. You okay to show yourself out?" she asked.

"Aye, I can do that."

"Okay, there's a spare key hanging on the rack in the laundry room. If you don't mind, lock the deadbolt behind you and I'll get the key back from you later." She gathered her computer bag and purse but stopped as her gaze landed on the abandoned snack tray from last night.

As she moved toward the tray, he told her, "Leave it, Alex. I'll clean up before I go."

She stopped and looked at him. "So, you're good in bed, thoughtful in the morning, *and* you clean up? Am I in one of those Hollywood movies where everything is perfect?" She laughed as she tossed his shirt to him. "I'm so sorry I have to run off. Next time, let's do breakfast," she said, before turning bright red. "Um, I mean... boy, that was presumptuous of me."

Fin walked to her and kissed her forehead. "Not presumptuous. I am definitely up for breakfast next time. Now go, before you're late."

As soon as she left, Fin picked up the room and put

their dishes in the dishwasher. He finished his coffee, then moved into the bedroom and straightened up in there as well. He wandered into Alex's bathroom and looked around. It still smelled like her, fresh from the shower. He spotted her makeup bag and was surprised at how much she possessed. He hadn't thought she wore enough makeup to have a bag that full. And... now he felt nosy.

He switched off the bathroom light and turned to go. As he was leaving the bedroom, he spotted the black dress from Wednesday night crumpled up in the corner chair. Fin retrieved it and headed in search of the utility room. A plaintive meow caught his attention, and he spotted Felix looking mournfully at his empty food dish.

"Did we forget about you, buddy?" Fin picked up the cat, scratching his ears as he checked the cupboard for cat food. "I appreciate the assist you gave me last night by being discreet and staying hidden. Ye're a good wingman."

Fin found the food, read the directions for serving size, and filled the cat's dish. He located a pen and paper, then left a message on the counter letting Alex know he'd fed her cat and had her dress. He found the keys, locked up, and headed back to his new temporary home.

"ALEX." Alex looked up at the mention of her name. Her boss stood in the doorway with some papers in his hand.

"Hey, Frank. What's up?"

"I reviewed your project proposal last night and forwarded it to Jeff. He wants to meet with us this morning to review it."

"Holy crap, that was fast." Alex blinked up at him.

When Frank raised his eyebrows at her, she asked, "He wants to meet right now?"

"Yes. He wants to discuss a few points, and he's aware of the tight deadline to add it to the budget, so are you available? Because he won't be if we don't get up there now... he's got a meeting in thirty minutes and is booked the rest of today."

"Okay. I need to have Grace reschedule something." She paused. "What do I need to bring? Never mind... I'll bring my laptop so I'll have everything."

Alex unplugged her laptop from the docking station and followed Frank down the hall. They stopped at Grace's office, where Alex asked her to push back the mid-morning meeting they had scheduled for one of their other projects.

As they walked to the executive suite, she breathed deeply through her nose, trying to quell the nervousness in her stomach. She'd hoped to have her project approved, but this seemed to be moving too fast. Her heart raced, and she realized the adrenaline coursing through her system would have her bouncing off the walls if she didn't calm down.

They reached the CEO's office, where Frank knocked twice on the door before walking in. Jeff greeted them and pointed to the round conference table to the right while he finished a phone call. Alex followed Frank's lead and sat down, opening her laptop on the table.

Jeff Davis was a former engineer who had risen through the ranks to the top spot at the company. He was down-to-earth and easygoing most of the time, but a stickler for perfection and known to call out anyone who tried to bullshit him. His mercurial moods could change him from a pleasant guy to a ruthless shark in a flash if he thought you weren't being level with him. While Alex admired his vision and work ethic, she was intimidated by him as well. She hated not knowing which Jeff would appear each day.

"Alex, Frank." He nodded at them both. "Thanks for coming so quickly. I'm excited about this new department and the idea of standardizing our approach. It's been a pet peeve of mine for a while how all our project proposals come up through various channels and in different formats. I didn't realize how much it annoyed me until someone proposed something different."

They all chuckled and, after grabbing a pile of papers from his desk and pulling on a pair of reading glasses, he continued, "So far, everything I've seen looks good. Am I reading the plan right? You would need to hire additional project managers?" He looked at Alex.

Alex cleared her throat and answered, "Yes. Originally, we thought the department would grow organically over time, but with the push to establish it by January, we worked it up as a fully functioning department from the beginning. We expect growing pains as the stand-up period is rather short, but with more project managers on staff up front, we can mitigate several of those issues by having a more knowledgeable team and a deeper bench."

"Makes sense. Planning to hire from within?"

"If we can. I'd prefer to build the team from within the company—you can't beat tribal knowledge—but doing so depends on several factors. How politically correct I have to be about 'stealing' people from other departments, what the salary level is for those folks, and if we want to relocate anyone or not. Those are just a few considerations that will influence what we do. Once we have the green light to talk to people, we can narrow down our requirements, which will allow us to firm up these numbers."

Picking up her point on the salary levels, Frank added,

"Some of our folks have been with us long enough to have achieved a high salary via annual increases, so the numbers may change if we find someone who fits our needs but comes with a price tag."

Jeff rubbed his chin as he considered this. "Gotcha. I know several engineers who have been here as long as I have and make a pretty penny. Although I can't see any of them in this role."

He took off his reading glasses and focused on Alex. Everything in his body language told her his next statement was critical. She waited.

"Who will run the department?"

"Me," she replied without hesitation. "I'm a certified project manager and have been studying the PMO structure since I realized we needed one. I've researched what others have done and read several case studies on starting up a project management office in an existing corporation."

"It's an ambitious plan to have this in place by January. Will you have time with all the extracurricular activities and celebrity acquaintances you have going on right now?" Without waiting for an answer, he looked at Frank and added, "Might think about putting Steve in charge of this," effectively dismissing Alex.

Alex blanched as she gawked at him. *What the fuck? Did he just refer to my dating life? And threaten to take away my idea because of it?* she thought. A low thrumming started in her ears as she felt the blood rush back into her face. She was sure her cheeks were bright red.

"*Excuse me?*" she asked.

Jeff swung his attention back to her. "Alex, you're great at what you do. I don't want to overburden you with this. You have a great deal going on—"

"Are you married, Jeff?" she interrupted him.

"Uh… yes."

"Do you have kids, Jeff?"

"Yes, but what does that have to do with anything?"

"Not a *damn* thing," she told him. "In fact, I didn't know until this minute your marital status or that you had kids, but not knowing about your personal life didn't change the way I thought about you professionally. At all. Funny how I expected the same consideration from you."

Frank sat up and spoke, "Alex—"

Alex closed her laptop with a snap. "Until this moment, I admired you. I have watched you steer this company toward continuous improvement and have been thrilled to be a part of that effort. I never expected you to think of me as anything other than a competent employee helping you reach your vision." She straightened her back and lowered her voice. "My personal life outside this office has never and will never affect my work. My relationship status is none of your damn business. And furthermore, you would *never* have brought it up if I were a man." She pushed back from the table, preparing to stand.

"Alex, wait."

Alex froze where she was. Her hands shook, and she clenched her fists to hide it. She didn't know which was worse… his treatment of her or that she had told him off. She was mad enough to quit on the spot. Or would Jeff Davis fire her for insubordination and save her the effort? She stared him in the eye as she waited.

Jeff's gaze slid from her to Frank, then out the window. He stared outside a minute before focusing again on her. "Alex, I apologize. You're right, I was out of line. I should never have brought your personal life into the conversation." The corner of his mouth raised in a half-smile. "And you called me out on that bullshit too. I knew you were tough." His smile slid away. "I'm sorry for both questioning your ability and for making a remark about your private life."

"A sexist remark," Alex said before she could help herself.

"Alex—" Frank began.

"No, she's right, Frank. My comments were sexist and inappropriate." Jeff again peered at something beyond the window before turning to Alex. "I'm ashamed of what just happened and hope you will forgive me. I have nothing but high regard for your work. And," he hesitated, "in my defense, I think I slipped into overprotective dad mode rather than boss mode, which is where I should have stayed. You remind me of my daughter and I have watched your success here with pride as I do hers. Please forgive me for overstepping."

Jeff and Frank watched her, waiting for a response. She was still shaking, although she couldn't tell at this point if it was from anger, shock, or disappointment. Neither of these men had ever been less than professional with her in the past. She didn't trust herself to speak.

"Honestly, I need to go cool off. If you will excuse me?" she asked.

Jeff nodded and Alex snatched her laptop off the table then fled the room. Frank called her before she got two steps down the hall. She turned and waited for him.

"Alex, take off the rest of the day. I know that hit hard, and if it's any consolation, he's never expressed any doubt to me privately about your abilities. And I believe his remark about slipping into dad mode. I'm not sure if you knew, but you're the same age as his daughter." Before Alex could protest, Frank raised a hand and continued, "At any rate, take a break. Your team can handle things for you. It's

Friday. Take the weekend and let's talk first thing Monday. Okay?"

She nodded once and turned to go. Frank didn't follow, but went back into Jeff's office, shutting the door. Lord only knew what that exchange would be like.

On her way back to her office, she pulled her phone from her pocket and called Fin. When he answered, she asked, "Hey, Fin... you remember that gym you told me about? Can we go there? I need to hit things."

Chapter 13

Friday Aftermath

FIN HELD the punching bag as Alex attacked it. Her call had first surprised, then delighted him. Earlier in the week, Blake had introduced him to Pete, the owner of Pete's Gym, and Fin had come here for his daily workout ever since. He had mentioned it in passing to Alex, but had never thought to invite her along. Now they were here sweating together while she worked out her frustration from the meeting with her bosses. She had said little about what happened, but it must have been bad because she had thrown punches for ten minutes straight with a fury he never wanted to see unleashed on himself.

"You know," Alex finally spoke, "I expect to run into the chauvinistic bullshit from the guys in the manufacturing plant and the sales dudes in the field. They're rough. They're used to talking shit and being the big man or greasing the wheels through the good old boy system. But he completely blindsided me this morning. I never expected to hear that shit from the highest-ranking person in the company. And my boss just sat quietly beside me, saying nothing. I had to fucking defend myself!"

"What happened?" Fin asked, thinking she was ready to talk.

"You happened." Alex punched again with force. "He approves of my project and certainly seems excited about it, but wasn't sure if little ol' me could handle all that pressure, especially since I'm so busy dating a Hollywood movie star." She bent her head forward and punched again.

Fin winced. "Truly? He brought up your love life?" The last thing he wanted was to cause problems for Alex.

"Right? If I were a man, my personal life would never have come up. But women are judged harshly in that area. We can't promote you because you might have babies and leave us. We can't pay you the same because you will spend too much of your time focused on your family rather than the job. Or worse, we can't pay you the same or promote you because your work isn't as good as a man's. Utter. Bullshit." She gave the bag a double punch.

"You know," she continued, "I've paid my dues. I've dealt with harassment, both subversive and blatant. Do you know that I once had my work double-checked by some guy in IT because he didn't think I knew what I was talking about?" The question was obviously rhetorical because she continued before he could respond. "Do you know what a subject matter expert is?"

Fin shook his head no.

"A subject matter expert is someone who—as the name suggests—is an *expert* on the topic. The finance department chose me to represent them—the entire global community of our finance organization—on the project. Aside from that tidbit, I was a fucking controller at my last job. I mean, the company was smaller, but I *was* the top accountant. I signed the tax returns and bank papers, dealt with auditors and attorneys..."

She trailed off before scowling and added, "And yet some snot-nosed, holier-than-thou network guy ran my work by a *male* accountant to make sure I was right."

Fin held the bag steady as her punching grew furious again.

"I've put up with comments about my legs, about how I dress, about how I *don't* dress, and about how I won't date anyone in the office. I've had men whom I outranked in seniority ask me to make the coffee!" She gave another hard double punch to the bag. "I finally reached the point where I thought I had earned my seat at the table... where I would no longer be subjected to crap like that."

Alex paused, breathing heavily for a minute before she glared at him. "Do you know how I knew they finally accepted me as 'one of the boys?' I was at a pub with some sales managers on a business trip when one of them talked about a vacation he'd taken with his mistress. They suddenly realized I was a woman and swore me to secrecy because they didn't want *his wife* to discover his cheating ways. That disgusting moment was when I knew I had been accepted." Alex hung her head, collecting herself before continuing. "But it seems I was wrong. Apparently, I'm still fighting that battle."

She closed her eyes and took another calming breath. "He said something weird. Jeff, the CEO." When she opened them again, she looked directly at Fin. "He said he was thinking like a dad when he made the comment. Like he was acting protective of me. What does that mean? Does he think he's protecting me by *not* giving me challenging work? By *not* advancing my career? *Humph.*"

Her eyes filled with tears and one slipped down her cheek. Fin let go of the bag and gathered her up in his arms.

"Damn it! I hate it when I cry," she said into his chest.

"Men are arseholes," he replied as he kissed the top of her head.

She laughed and agreed, "Yeah, they are."

Alex moved away, and Fin let her go. She wiped her cheeks and smoothed her hair, as if those actions would erase the distress she felt. "I'm starving. You hungry?"

Fin raised an eyebrow. "Are you finished hitting things?"

"Yes. I'm still mad enough to spit, but we've taken the edge off so now I can think clearly." She rolled her eyes. "In fact, I just now realized I didn't even ask you if you were available. I hope I didn't interrupt anything?"

"Nothing I couldn't rearrange. Blake has been showing me some of the historical landmarks around the area and educating me on Texas history. Let's go get cleaned up and grab a bite to eat. Sound good?"

"Yeah."

An hour later, they sat in the back of a Mexican food restaurant, eating fajita nachos and drinking margaritas. Alex had given him the details of what happened with her bosses. She shared additional stories from her career, highlighting the blatant sexism and misogyny rampant in corporate America. Fin was rather shocked at the things men had said to her over the years. When he'd read of sexual harassment cases, he'd always assumed the guy was a total creep. Alex was talking about ordinary men walking through an ordinary day on the job. He had no idea the problem was as prevalent as this.

When he told her this, she snorted. "It's everywhere, Fin. Of course, it's worse in male-dominated industries or for women in professions normally held by men, but it's everywhere. Society has conditioned us to think it's normal behavior."

"Well, I for one will pay more attention and make sure it's not happening where I work," Fin stated. He made a mental note to follow up with Addie, his sister, and other women in his life on this topic.

Alex tilted her head as she considered him. "You are, aren't you?"

Confused, he asked, "I am what?"

"You're that guy... the one who takes action when discovering some injustice."

Fin warmed at the admiration she conveyed and shoved a nacho in his mouth to cover his awkwardness.

"Do you realize we've only known each other a week?" she asked. "How did you become such a huge focus in my life in one freaking week?"

Fin took in Alex's furrowed brow and decided to lighten the mood. "I don't know, but I suggest we continue because I'm enjoying your company immensely. In fact, in celebration of our anniversary," Fin continued despite Alex's raised eyebrow, "I suggest we do something special this weekend. Your boss did tell you to get away and not think about anything."

"And what do you suggest?" Alex leaned back and sipped her margarita, eyeing Fin with wariness.

"I haven't thought that far ahead."

They burst out laughing, and Alex raised her drink. Fin clinked her glass with his and they sipped their margaritas while smiling at each other.

A camera flashed in the background, and Fin groaned. "Och, not again." He searched the room and found that the camera wielder wasn't a reporter, but a fan. He glanced at

Alex for her response, and she shrugged at him. Fin smiled at the teenager who timidly stepped closer. He waved her over, and she rushed forward with a wide grin.

"Mr. McAlister, I'm such a fan. Can you sign this for me?" She held out a pen and ticket stub from his latest film.

"Aye, what's your name, lass?" Fin asked as he took the pen from her.

"Bethany," she answered.

Fin penned a note on the ticket and handed everything back to the girl.

She read it aloud, "'Bethany, lovely to meet you. Finley McAlister.' Oh, my gosh! My friends are going to *scream*. Thank you so much!" She squealed and ran back to her table.

"That was gracious of you," Alex commented.

"Aye, but we should leave soon, or everyone else will come by. They often leave you alone until one brave soul breaks the bubble, then they all come. I don't mind sharing myself with the fans, but there's only so much to go around." He winced, then signaled the waitress for the check.

Alex sucked down the rest of her margarita, and they made their way to the car before any other fans stopped them.

ON THE WAY HOME, Alex glanced sideways at Fin. "You serious about getting away for the weekend?" she asked.

"I'm free and available. What do you have in mind?"

"Let's go to Galveston. You mentioned an interest in local history, and Galveston is one of the oldest cities in the vicinity, with a rich history, including pirates. It's only an hour-and-a-half drive. We can rent a beach house, go to Moody Gardens, or hang out downtown. It's nothing fancy, just a fun little side trip that gets us out of our heads. What do you think?"

Fin smiled and declared, "Road trip!"

"Awesome." Alex pushed the Bluetooth button on her steering wheel. At the beep, she said, "Call Gary Jones."

They arrived home as Alex finished the call with her friend Gary. He owned a couple of properties down in Galveston that he rented out when his family wasn't using them, and he had a cute little two-bedroom cottage on the west end of the island available this weekend. The call ended with him promising to email Alex the instructions for getting to and in the house.

Alex parked the car and turned to Fin. "If we get on the road now, we can get there in time for dinner out, or we can pick up groceries along the way and make our own at the beach house. Which do you prefer?" she asked. "And before you answer, understand that I am a terrible cook so don't expect anything fancy."

"Well, I am an excellent cook, so we have options and won't starve," he joked back. "Let's stop for groceries. We've had a full day, and that way we can settle in and avoid the outside world. I'll pack a bag and meet you at your place?"

"Sounds good. I need to check in with Eddie and Gabe to make sure they can watch Felix. See you in a bit." She closed her car door and headed straight to Eddie's side of the duplex while Fin walked toward the garage apartment.

By the time they arrived at Gary's beach house, the sun had set. Stopping at the grocery store had been both enlightening and surreal. Alex's method of grocery shopping was to grab what you needed and get out. Fin, however, liked to browse the selection for inspiration on what to cook. She assumed that was the difference between someone who rarely cooked and someone who enjoyed doing so. She'd blushed when Fin boldly strolled down the birth control aisle and picked up a large box of condoms. At the checkout counter, they'd briefly argued over who would pay, but Fin insisted that since she had arranged the accommodations, he would handle meals.

Her navigation system led them to a bright blue and white cottage, where Alex pulled into the driveway and shut off the car. The cottage, like all houses in this section, was up on stilts and had storm shutters over the windows and doors.

She found the key where Gary told her it would be, then helped Fin unload the car and carry everything upstairs. Alex took their overnight bags to the master bedroom while Fin unpacked the groceries.

"You ought to feel right at home here with this beach motif," she observed as she took in the combination living and kitchen area.

"Ha. You're a funny woman. I could hear the ocean when we got out of the car. It sounds close."

"Yeah, from what Gary sent me, the beach is a short walk from here. I packed a flashlight if you want to check it out after we eat." After unpacking their groceries, he started on their meal and she set the table. After the late afternoon nachos, they had agreed to a light supper of Caesar salad with pre-cooked chicken, since they weren't sure about the grilling situation at the cottage.

As they sat down to eat, Alex told Fin what she knew about Galveston's history. "There's a museum downtown we can check out tomorrow. In 1900, a massive hurricane came through and wiped out the entire island. The storm destroyed almost everything, and thousands died. They rebuilt and added the seawall to protect the island from future storms. The museum has tons of information on it."

"Have you been through a hurricane?"

"Oh, sure... Downtown Houston is about fifty miles from the coast and we get storms every year. Some small, some large. Mostly we see the edge of a storm that has landed somewhere else along the Gulf Coast. But sometimes we suffer a direct hit. You constantly hear stories about the bad ones. Tropical Storm Allison in 2001 caused a crazy amount of flooding around town. Hurricane Ike in 2008 was only a category-two storm, but it spun off tornados around Houston causing a great deal of damage. And I was here for Hurricane Harvey in 2017. That was a nightmare."

She had been lucky and hadn't flooded, but two of her friends had gone through hell, losing their houses and rendered homeless for a while. Eddie and Gabe had come through for a few of their mutual acquaintances by setting up temporary campers around their yard and the parking area behind the duplexes. Alex had volunteered at the shelters, handing out water and supplies.

"Why continue to live here with that kind of danger?" he asked.

Alex shrugged and took a swig of her drink. "Tornados in the Midwest, wildfires in California, earthquakes along the West Coast... I mean, it can be dangerous anywhere you live. Why not live somewhere you love and deal with nature the best you can?"

"Fair enough," he said.

They finished eating and cleaned up. With a flashlight in hand, they headed down to the beach where they walked hand-in-hand, spotting crabs and talking about other beaches they had visited. After Alex yawned for the third time, Fin insisted on returning to the beach house.

The cottage had two bathrooms, so they each took one to shower off and get ready for bed. Alex fidgeted with her hair and adjusted the straps on her tank top for the fifth time. *Stop being nervous*, she told herself. *He's seen you naked before.* She closed her eyes and slowly inhaled, then exhaled. She repeated this mantra two times before she annoyed herself, switched off the light, and walked into the bedroom.

Fin sat in the chair by the window, looking at a book on seashells. Alex stopped in her tracks and inhaled sharply. He wore thin cotton pants and no shirt. She always joked with her friends that she "was a chest man herself," but the reality was, she wasn't kidding. Fin's chest made her want to rub her hands all over him. His body was well-defined from his regular work-outs, with a thin sprinkling of hair to cover his muscles. She watched those muscles ripple as he turned the pages.

He looked up at her and grinned. "Some of these shells are stunning. Look at this one." He held the book up and showed her the picture of a large conch shell with iridescent coloring on the inside. His damp hair curling around the back of his neck combined with his enthusiasm reminded Alex of an excited little boy. She sat on the bed and watched him pour excitedly over the pictures.

"Which side of the bed do you want?" she asked.

Fin put the book aside and moved toward her. "It doesn't matter to me. I don't have a side."

She yawned again and pulled back the covers. "Me neither. I wind up sleeping around Felix and typically end up in the middle." Alex slid under the covers and sighed. The bed was surprisingly comfortable.

Fin turned off the light and climbed in next to her. He pulled her close to him and wrapped his body around her, tucking her in tight. "Sweet dreams, lass," he whispered.

Alex wanted to stay awake. She wanted to make love to this beautiful man, but exhaustion from the day's events pulled her into a weightless, drifting place. The warmth of the man behind her induced such a feeling of safety and security that she sank into slumber without another thought.

Fin listened as Alex's breathing deepened, amazed at how fast she'd fallen asleep. She must have been exhausted. He winced, thinking the walk on the beach might have been too much. He should have realized the emotional toll of the day would wear on her.

He had been intrigued when she'd called that morning, wanting to punch things. Alex was already fit and had taken to boxing naturally. He'd enjoyed sparring with her. Initially, he'd been impressed at how physically strong she was. Even now, he wasn't sure how much of the strength came from her anger and how much was natural. And she had been howling angry. He didn't blame her. He regretted that her interaction with him had caused the conflict with her boss.

Fin sighed and pushed the thought aside. The day had been perfect, exactly what he'd imagined a break from the showbiz world would be, and the woman beside him was a part of that. The more time he spent with Alex, the more he realized how complex she was. She often masked her keen intelligence with light-hearted banter. Her friends from volleyball seemed to paint her as emotionally distant, but she'd been uninhibited with him. From everything he'd learned about her this past week, she seemed conservative in her personal relationships, but she hadn't hesitated to get physical with him or take the lead when the chemistry between them had ignited. He tightened his arms around her and kissed the back of her head. And he liked this woman. He rarely let people in, but she had quickly found a spot in his inner circle. He expected them to remain friends and keep in touch even after he left Houston.

Fin's thoughts became sluggish, and he drifted off to sleep in a state of contentment.

Fin slowly awoke from the most incredible dream. He'd dreamt a gorgeous woman was making slow, sweet love to him. As he came more fully awake, he discovered the source of his subconscious' motivation as Alex's hands wandered leisurely over his chest and arms.

The night was still dark, but enough moonlight filtered in through the windows that he could see her face. Her eyes locked on his and she moved her hands upward, tracing along his jawline and finally up into his hair.

"You are so beautiful," she whispered. She pulled on him, and he complied, moving close enough so their bodies pressed against each other. "I'm bedazzled by muscular chests, and yours is spectacular."

Fin groaned and covered her mouth with his. He took his time exploring her body, tenderly removing her night clothes and tracing his tongue over her skin as the fabric disappeared. He had discovered her shyness the first time he'd moved his mouth to her more intimate parts, but her reaction once she relaxed told him she enjoyed it. Fin worked his way down her body, intent on giving her the same pleasure again. She moaned and gripped his hair in her fists.

"Oh, god, Fin. Please..." Her breath hitched, then her body tightened. "Oh!" she exclaimed as she went over that cliff. Her body relaxed, and he crawled back up toward her face, planting kisses along the way.

"You're awfully good at that," she whispered.

He smiled and kissed her. He pressed his erection against her and deepened the kiss. The soft whimpering noises she made maddened him as he explored her mouth with his tongue. She tugged at his bottoms and he rose up to help her push them off. As he settled back on top of her, she wrapped her legs around him.

"I need you. Now," she commanded. "Now, please." She strained toward him, trying to take control.

"Patience, love," he whispered. Fin reached over and plucked a condom from the box on the nightstand. He had strategically placed them there before bed so as not to break the mood should the need arise. He tore open the wrapper with his teeth and swiftly donned the protection before turning his attention back to Alex.

He flipped over, pulling her up so she sat on top of him. She gasped at the unexpected movement, but quickly maneuvered him into position and slid down on him. Fin sucked in his breath at how complete he felt in that moment, buried deep inside her and looking up into her eyes. Then Alex moved, and he lost all coherent thought.

Chapter 14

Saturday at the Beach

ALEX AWOKE to the smell of bacon. The empty spot beside her told her Fin was the source of the smell. She stretched and took stock of her body. She grinned to herself at the strange combination of soreness from using unfamiliar muscles and complete satisfaction from feeling sore in those places. While she hadn't had many lovers, she had enough experience to recognize that Fin knew what he was doing. He knew exactly how to fine-tune her body and make it sing. Her mirth grew at the musical comparison, and she threw back the covers to go find the subject of her thoughts.

She wandered into the kitchen and burst out laughing when she encountered him frying bacon wearing nothing but an apron. "Are you making a fashion statement?"

Fin turned to her and beamed. "Must protect the manly bits."

She walked up behind him and slapped his naked butt cheek before palming it as she peeked at the stovetop.

"Good morning," he said as he pecked her cheek. "You looked so sweet in your sleep. I didnae want to disturb you."

Alex pinched his butt and moved to the refrigerator. "I

am not sweet." She poured herself a glass of orange juice, then held the jug up to Fin in question. He shook his head no, nodding to the coffee cup sitting on the counter. "I've noticed your Scottish brogue seems to come and go."

"Aye. I get more formal under stress. Almost the opposite of you. I've noticed your Texas drawl shows up more when you're excited."

Alex cocked her head sideways. "Huh. I've never thought about it, but you're probably right. The more wound up I am, the more I sling those words out."

"Or chop them off." At her raised eyebrow, he added, "You seem to lose the letter 'g' at the end of your words sometimes."

"Are you tryin' to tell me somethin', Mr. McAlister?" She playfully batted her eyelashes at him.

"Aye, you're thoroughly delightful with your Southern charm. Now pass me the eggs, will ye?"

Alex handed Fin the eggs and made toast for them. They sat down to breakfast and planned their day while they ate. After cleaning up, Fin hurried them into the bedroom to get dressed.

"Take a look at my new disguise," Fin said as he donned a baseball cap embroidered with the Houston Astros logo. "I noticed my fedora stood out more than blended in."

"Go Astros!" Alex cheered. "That'll work." She took in the rest of his outfit. He wore dark blue jeans, a blue t-shirt with buttons at the neck, and a lightweight suede jacket. "You look nice."

"Thanks. You too," he responded as he looked her up and down. She also had on jeans, although hers were white-washed and barely blue anymore. She wore a navy and white striped t-shirt with a faded jean jacket. Her feet were encased in white sandals, but she planned to stash her socks and ankle boots in the car in case the temperature dropped later.

They spent the morning exploring downtown Galveston. The historical town was reminiscent of New Orleans and had an old-world vibe to it, in contrast to the shiny, modern skyscrapers of downtown Houston. They wandered in and out of the shops, looking at the different wares targeting tourists. Occasionally, there would be a stir of recognition from the surrounding crowd. Fin deftly maneuvered them back to the street when it happened.

They visited the museum and read about the destruction from the massive hurricane that had come close to obliterating the landmark town at the turn of the twentieth century. The images were awe-inspiring reminders of both the forces of nature and human resilience.

After a pleasant lunch on the boardwalk, they drove over to Moody Gardens. They strolled through the aquarium and the rainforest, making a game out of dodging any would-be autograph seekers. Alex noticed throughout the day that the more people around, the more likely Fin would be recognized. As the afternoon wore on and they finished their tour of the rain forest, they found themselves surrounded by a pack of women who had been trailing them throughout the exhibit. Fin graciously signed their autograph books, papers, and pictures and the women left happy.

"That wasn't nearly as frightening as last time," Alex commented.

"Aye. When it's the fans alone, it's generally a pleasant experience. Most of them are polite and aware they are interrupting my personal time. It's when the media gets involved that things get unruly. Are you getting hungry?"

"Starving. I know it's early, but I'm ready to eat. Must

be the salty sea air," she exaggerated her drawl and fanned herself, mimicking a proper Southern lady.

"Aye. Or perhaps all the physical activity." He waggled his eyebrows at her, making her laugh. "I found us a highly rated seafood restaurant to dine at when you were in the toilet earlier."

She wrinkled her nose at his phrasing. "I know it's what the British call restrooms, but saying 'the toilet' just sounds weird to me. Because the toilet is what you use *in* the restroom."

"And yet you also call it a 'bathroom' when there's no bath in the room," he replied. "Don't get me started on your strange language habits."

They volleyed shots back and forth all the way to the car, laughing at each other's attempt to outdo the other. The restaurant Fin found was close, so their banter didn't last long.

THE CUISINE WAS EXCELLENT. They coordinated their orders so they could sample and share each other's food. Alex was a huge fan of crab and Fin ordered the steak.

After settling into their meal, Alex asked the question she had been wondering all week. "Fin, if you hate the publicity, why do you do it? Isn't fame part of the package?"

"Fame is part of the package if you become famous. I read a study once claiming several hundred thousand actors exist around the world, along with a million more aspiring actors. How many of them are famous?" He took a drink of his water. "I do it because I love the craft."

"What does that mean? What is it about the craft that you love?"

"Look, acting is more than merely pretending to be someone else. It's storytelling at its finest. And for me personally, it's the opportunity to see things in a completely different light... to experience the world through the perceptions and emotions of someone new. It allows me to see this world in ways I've never seen it and perceive things I've never noticed before. And that's just talking about the character. We haven't even gotten into the story the character is walking in."

"You can actually adjust your thinking and see things differently?"

"Yes. I suppose that's why people like me. They believe me because I become that character."

Alex nodded. She had seen several of his films and he seemed like a different person in each one. "I think I understand what you mean. Some actors are completely unique in each film they star in, like yourself." She nodded to him. "And then you have those who are always the same person, no matter what the story is. Don't get me wrong." She held up her hands and continued, "I'm not knocking them because I can't imagine portraying someone other than myself."

She slowly sipped her wine. "You must have great empathy to transform yourself like that."

Fin shrugged. "Perhaps. I've never labeled it. I just love doing it."

Before he could say more, Alex's eyes widened at the man who walked up and clapped a hand on Fin's shoulder.

"Yo, Scotsman! What the hell are you doing down here?" Mac McBrewster wore a cowboy hat, a large belt buckle, and cowboy boots.

"Mac!" Fin stood up and shook his hand, throwing one arm around his shoulders in a half-hug. "Hey, it's good to see you. I thought you'd be in Los Angeles already."

"No, I followed your lead and did the tourist thing. I wound up down here. I have a couple of lady friends meeting me here soon, but got here early enough to check out the bar." Mac tipped his hat at Alex. "Ma'am."

"Let me introduce you to Alex. Alex, this is Mac McBrewster, one of my costars on my latest film and someone I consider a friend. He helped me navigate the press junket last week."

"Nice to meet you, Mac. Would you like to join us while you wait for your friends?" Alex asked. She smiled as Fin's brows rose in question.

"Are you sure? I don't want to intrude." He hesitated.

"Of course. No problem. We were talking about acting or 'the craft' as Fin called it, so your timing is fortuitous." Her grin grew as Fin cleared his throat and ducked his head at her reference. *Interesting*, she thought, and made a mental note to ask him why it embarrassed him to discuss his trade.

Mac made himself comfortable as Fin signaled the server to take Mac's drink order. Once he was settled, the discussion moved back to acting. Alex asked him questions about his career, and Fin even asked a few himself. Mac entertained them with stories of mishaps and misadventures until he spotted one of his companions arriving for their dinner date.

"Before you go," Fin said as Mac stood up to leave, "how long will you be in Houston?"

Mac admired the leggy blonde walking toward them from the front of the restaurant and replied, "Undetermined. At least until Tuesday, but maybe longer if things go well tonight." He looked back at Alex and gave an exaggerated wink. "Why?"

"I'd like to meet with you and talk further about your production ideas. I've also been considering doing something on my own, and I think the two of us should discuss a partnership. From what I can tell, we think alike on the important stuff and would complement each other on the outliers."

Mac narrowed his eyes at Fin while he considered this and replied, "Sounds intriguing. Call me."

"You got it," Fin said as he shook Mac's hand.

Mac turned to Alex. "It was a pleasure to meet you, Miss Alex. I hope to see you again."

"Thank you, Mac. Good luck tonight." She winked at Mac and nodded at the lady approaching their table.

Mac gave Alex a thumbs up and his attention shifted to his date. "Darling! You look magnificent."

Alex giggled as the couple walked away, and Fin grinned at her.

"I like him," she said. "I've seen a ton of his movies. He's one of those actors we talked about who completely sells you on his character, regardless of the role."

"Aye, he's won multiple awards. But you wouldn't know it to be around him. He and I became friendly during this last project, and he's quickly becoming part of my inner circle."

"Did you just propose a business deal with him?" Alex asked before sipping her wine.

"Aye, Addie and I have discussed starting our own production company so we can have more control over the projects I work on. At one point during filming, Mac had mentioned a similar desire, and I think we would work well together. In fact, if you don't mind, I'll set a reminder right now to call him on Monday." Fin pulled out his phone after she waved him on and keyed in a reminder.

They spent the balance of the meal discussing the business side of Hollywood and how things worked. Alex was fascinated with the similarities and differences in Fin's industry compared to others she had worked in or studied. She asked questions, several of which prompted Fin to make some notes on his phone. Alex enjoyed the speculative nature of the discussion and asked "What if...?" and "How...?" type questions. From the answers Fin gave, she could tell he had given this topic considerable thought.

When they finished eating, Fin and Alex drove back to the cottage, looking forward to another walk on the beach.

Chapter 15

Sunday Headed Home

Sunday afternoon found Fin sitting in the living room marking up the manuscript with some closing notes. Last night had been another wonderful night of exploring each other's bodies. Their activities ranged from slow, tantalizing lovemaking to frenzied, hardcore sex. He'd finally gotten her naked in the shower, where they'd narrowly avoided a mishap from the slippery tiles.

Earlier today, they'd eaten breakfast, watched a movie, and packed a lunch to eat at the beach. They played in the ocean some, but this late in the year, the water was getting chilly. After showering together, they moved to the bed, where Alex promptly fell asleep following their activities. Fin left her there undisturbed and decided working on the new project was a great way to spend the afternoon while she slept.

His phone buzzed, and Addie's face popped up on the caller screen.

"Afternoon, love," he greeted her warmly.

"Finley! I've got news. I started the process for filing the injunction against that Cole witch. We can't do much about her, but we can target her man, the one who assaulted Alex. We're filing a restraining order. We can file one of these without having to go to court. If he violates that, then we have reason to take him to court and get an injunction. Additionally, if it goes that far and we wind up in court, we may be able to tie everything back to Miranda Cole. At least, that's my understanding. We should hear something back this week from my guy in Texas."

"That's something, I suppose. Thanks for following up on it. Listen, I wanted to talk to you about our production company. I think we're closer."

"You found the unicorn?"

Fin laughed at her reference. The first time they'd talked about forming their own production company, it had been in jest. But through the years, the idea kept finding its way into their conversations to the point where they had decided if they found the right project, they would stop talking about it and actually do it. All they needed was that one magical unicorn to launch their company.

"Aye. I believe I have. A manuscript fell into my hands before I left London and I've been marking it up and making notes. I expect to finish today and will send it to you this evening so you can review it. It's got all the elements we're looking for... characters you care about, a plot that keeps you invested, a story that runs the emotional gamut, yet leaves you satisfied at the end."

"Fin, this is exciting. It seems like everything we've looked at lately is focused on big, action-packed super hero stories. How'd you get it again?"

"An unexpected source. One of the production assistants slipped it to me one day. A friend of hers had written the script based on a book. I'd read the book a while back and remembered the story, so I told her I'd give it a look. I'm happy I did."

Fin rattled off the name of the book and the author so Addie could look it up later.

"I look forward to reading it," she said.

"I think you'll love it. And there's one more thing. You remember meeting Mac McBrewster a few years ago?"

"Your current costar? Yes, I remember."

"Right. Well, while shooting this last film, he and I talked at length about what it takes to run a production company. He's got experience in this area as he's partnered with others before on previous projects. And he shares our same values and work ethics. I think the three of us would be brilliant together. I'm talking with him on Monday to pick his brain some more about the process. If you're open to it, I want to invite him to join us."

When she didn't respond, Fin added, "I know it's a change to what we planned, but it feels right. Just think about it and get back to me, okay? We can set up preliminary meetings to make sure he meshes for you like he does for me." Fin held his breath, waiting for her to say something.

"Okay. I will. Send me the unicorn." Addie cleared her throat, signaling a change of topic. "So, I haven't seen you in the news lately. How have you managed that?"

Fin relaxed. "I took the weekend off. Alex and I have been hiding out down on the coast. It's been brilliant."

"You're spending lots of time with her then?"

"Aye, this weekend was what I imagine life is like for normal people... hanging around at the beach, driving to town for groceries or dinner, making... ehm, lunch together.

You know, normal stuff like that." Fin pressed his hand to his forehead as heat crept into his cheeks. He'd almost said *making love*. Addie would never have let him live that down.

Addie was quiet, and Fin asked if she was still there.

"You're falling for her," she whispered.

"Pardon?" Fin's mouth gaped open and he stiffened at her declaration. But as he thought back over the last week, he slouched back against the couch. "Ooft, I'm a numpty, Addie." Fin dragged his hand through his hair and looked toward the bedroom door. "You're right. I think I'm falling for her. What terrible timing."

"No, Fin, it's perfect timing. Don't you see? I've been so worried about you. You've been showing classic symptoms of burnout. You've been bored, fatigued, and rarely excited about anything new. But this week, you've started making moves to take control of your life again. I thought maybe you had finally had enough of Miranda Cole and that was the catalyst, but now I'm thinking it's because of your Alex. She might be the spark you needed. It's exactly the right time."

Fin still felt flabbergasted. "Addie, I have to go. I need to think about this. I'll call you back tomorrow after I talk to Mac, okay?"

"Absolutely. Hey," she said before he could hang up.

"Aye?"

"I love you, Fin. I'm here for you. Don't overthink it. She's come into your life at exactly the right time. Don't let her get away without telling her. That's it. Later."

She disconnected before he could respond. Fin tossed the phone on the coffee table and stood up. His skin crawled with the need to do something. Anything. He left a note for Alex, letting her know he was going for a run, donned his trainers, pocketed his phone, and headed to the beach.

When Alex found Fin's note, she grinned and began preparing to leave by tidying up the beach house. She removed the bed sheets and put them in the laundry bin with the bath towels. Gary employed a service to do the heavy cleaning, but he requested his guests do some minimal picking up to help, and she happily did her part.

She was almost finished emptying the refrigerator when Fin returned from his run. She handed him a bottle of water and watched him drink it. He wore only his running shorts, and sweat gleamed on his body. His hair was windblown, the soft curls unruly. Her insides turned gooey all over, and she thought they'd never leave if she got distracted every time he looked good to her.

He drained the water and crushed the bottle before throwing it in the recycle bin. "Did you have a good nap?"

"Yes, I did. I rarely sleep during the day so that was refreshing. How was your run?"

"Hot. I can't believe it's still this warm in October. But running along the beach was lovely." He looked around at the kitchen and into the bedroom. "You are packing up to leave?"

"Yeah, I'd like to be back in Houston earlier rather than later, so I have time to get ready for tomorrow. Is that okay with you?"

"Aye. Let me shower and I'll help. Back in a sec," he called as he headed to the bedroom.

They were on the road and on the way back to Houston an hour later. They drove in companionable silence, but

Alex got the impression Fin had something on his mind. His body language and tone of voice had been more contemplative than what she typically witnessed in him.

"Something bothering you? You've been awfully quiet since your run," she commented.

He gazed at her, his eyes probing. Startled at the intense look, she focused her attention on the road again. "I talked to Addie before my run. Addie is more than my business partner, she's my best friend. She's helped me manage things when I had no clue what I was doing and has been a sounding board for any personal issues."

He paused long enough that Alex wasn't sure if he would continue. "Okay?" she prompted.

"She observed something I hadn't even realized myself, and I'm still processing it. I'm going through a change right now. In my life. And..." He paused a beat before continuing. "I think you're part of it."

"What do you mean?" Alex asked.

"I mean, you've reminded me what it's like to be Fin and not Finley McAlister, movie star. I've been feeling lost for a while, unsure which direction I wanted to go, but unsatisfied with where I was. Meeting you, hanging out with you this week... I've remembered what it feels like to just be me. I feel motivated again. I feel energized and capable of taking on those projects that have been moping around in my head, collecting dust."

He stopped talking and stared off into the distance for a minute before turning back to her.

"I'm not sure I'm saying this right, but I would like us to talk about the future. This past week has been wonderful, but we've been living very much in the present. I like you. I feel like we will be friends going forward regardless, but I want more than that. I believe we have something between us we should explore and allow to grow."

Alex kept her eyes on the road and let his words wash over her.

"I'm having a hard time getting a read on you, Alex. What are you thinking?"

When she finally spoke, her voice croaked. She cleared her throat and tried again. "Just to be clear, you are saying you would like to start dating? As in, we would be a couple?" She looked over at him for confirmation.

"Aye, that's what I'm saying."

She swallowed and looked forward again. "Okay. Don't be alarmed, but I have to step back and reframe things. I assumed all along I was a side trip for you, a temporary distraction while you were in town." She smiled over at him to soften her words. "And I'm totally okay with that. The chemistry between us is off the charts. And, yes, I like you too. You're smart, funny, and caring."

"But?" he asked, sitting completely still.

She nodded her head, acknowledging a "but" coming. "*But* I honestly hadn't considered anything beyond these two weeks. And it certainly never crossed my mind that a relationship might be something you wanted to pursue."

"That *I* wanted to pursue?" Fin's brow furrowed. "What about you, Alexis? How do *you* feel?"

"I have no idea how I feel!" she exclaimed. "You've completely caught me off-guard, and I don't know how to process this. I mean, how would it work anyway? You're leaving to go back to your Hollywood life, and... we don't even live in the same country."

"Ah, lassie, those are merely details. What I'm more concerned about is if you feel the same way." Fin adjusted himself in his seat. "All right, you're a logical thinker, let's approach this in a way that works for you."

Fin held up a finger. "We know the sex is phenomenal, so we can tick that one off." He gave her a wolfish leer before raising a second finger. "I'm assuming you also like me because you've spent a good deal of your week with me, and I don't see you as someone who would waste her time." He raised an eyebrow, waiting for an answer.

"Maybe I'm just using you for sex," she blurted.

"Always a possibility," he calmly replied. "But we talk about deep, meaningful topics of substance, and I don't think you'd do that with someone whom you were just using for sex."

Alex made a show of looking over her shoulder and changing lanes. She was fine in the lane she was in, but the action gave her more time to consider the situation she found herself in.

"Yeah, okay, I like you too. We talk about deep things. You have a beautiful mind."

He grinned at her flippant response and raised a third finger as his face sobered. "All right. Now a serious question. Is my fame a problem?"

Alex exhaled harshly. "I'll be honest, it's a tad overwhelming. Not just the dealing with the public, but the idea of actually dating the guy who's in the movie I'm watching and is known as the 'Hottest Man Ever.' It's a bit surreal." She paused as she considered the past week. "But this week, there's been less... interaction than I expected. So, I think the jury is still out on that one." Alex couldn't believe she was having this conversation, much less genuinely considering a relationship with Finley McAlister.

"Fair enough. And I'll be honest with you. The intrusion comes and goes. This week has been fairly light, given the promotion we were in town for. I've experienced both more and less disruption." He shrugged.

Fin sat quietly for a moment while Alex navigated among the cars on the freeway. Sunday was a light day for traffic in Houston and she was glad for it. Discussing this topic during rush hour likely would have resulted in a fender bender.

"Now the hard question," he spoke again. "Take away everything else... my career, your career... do you think we could be more than just 'friends with benefits?'" Fin made air quotes with his fingers as he spoke the last words.

She looked over at him then. The look in his eye told her he wanted her to say yes, but was already bracing himself for a no. Alex looked back at the road. How had she come to care about his feelings so quickly?

"Fin, I'm not saying no, but I'm in a state of shock right now," she began. "Most of the men I have dated have attracted me with their brain or their body, never both. Based on that, I'd say there's potential for something."

From the corner of her eye, she could see him sitting motionless, waiting for her to continue. "The sticking point is this: you sound like you're in a place in your life where you're ready for that type of commitment. I'm not." She raised one hand in a half-shrug. "It's not even on my radar at this time, which is why I'm reacting like this. I love my life right now as it is. A serious relationship was always an ambiguous concept that might or might not happen some-time in the far future."

Alex thought about Fin's stipulation to put her career aside for the moment and continued, "As for ignoring my career, I can't. My job... my career... it defines me. Every-thing in my personal life revolves around what I do for a living, and I can't *omit* that piece when thinking about the future. I mean, I'm fixin' to launch a career-making project that will consume every bit of my time in the next year at least. It's a terrible time to enter a relationship. I'm just..." Alex stopped and breathed for a moment. She could feel herself getting emotional. "I'm a little overwhelmed right now. And, frankly, I'm feeling a bit trapped having this conversation in my car."

Alex wiped her eye at the tear that threatened to escape. *Damn it*, she thought, *don't fucking cry!*

Fin reached over and squeezed her leg. "You're right, I'm a *dunder heid* and my timing is terrible. I shouldn't have brought it up where you wouldn't feel comfortable."

Alex snorted, "I'm pretty sure *I* brought it up when I asked why you were so quiet."

They rode in silence for a few moments before he spoke. "What exactly are you fixing?"

A laugh erupted from her. "Right. I meant I'm about to launch my project." She inhaled deeply through her nose. "Look, my perception of 'us' just got knocked off its axis. Can you give me some time to absorb what you've said? Just give me a day or two to realign and let's talk about it then. Okay? I'm not putting you off, I just... need a moment."

"Nae bother... I mean, no worries," he corrected himself. He gave her leg another squeeze and faced forward in his seat again. "I'm meeting with Mac tomorrow and will be busy with Addie afterward. Why don't we reconvene on Tuesday?"

Alex giggled. "You sound like a businessman setting up a sales meeting."

Fin beamed at her. "You must be wearing off on me."

"Tuesday is volleyball night. You want to set a date for dinner on Wednesday?"

"Oh, right. Okay, Tuesday we play ball and Wednesday, dinner at my place. I'll cook."

"Sounds delicious." Alex smiled in relief. "We'll talk before then and you can let me know what I should bring."

"What is this shite we're listening to?" Fin asked as he turned up the volume on the radio.

They spent the last hour of the ride home debating what constituted good music and what did not.

Chapter 16

———————

Margaritas and Girl Talk

FIN UNLOADED his bags from the car and set them on the pavement, then helped Alex unpack her things. Once she'd locked the car, he pulled her in for a slow, sweet kiss.

"I'll see you on Tuesday at volleyball. Call me if you want to ride together; otherwise, I'll just meet you there," he whispered against her lips.

"Okay," she answered. "Fin. Thank you for giving me time and not getting butt-hurt when I freaked out a little." She kissed him again.

"I don't know this phrase 'butt-hurt,' but I ken its meaning." She felt his grin against her lips and saw the laughter in his eyes.

He gave her a final kiss, then gently pushed her away from him, as if physically setting her aside was the only way to stop kissing her. "Bye, lass. Sleep well tonight," he said as he picked up his bag.

"Bye, Fin. Talk soon," she answered and turned toward her duplex.

Alex dropped her suitcase on her bed and texted Eddie to let him know she was home. Her head was spinning with everything she and Fin talked about in the car. She needed to talk to someone, but Eddie wasn't the right person. She tapped the "Favorites" icon on her phone and dialed Melissa.

"Hey," Alex said when Melissa answered.

"Hey, yourself. You okay?"

"Yeah. It's just... I need to talk to someone. You busy?" Alex inquired.

"Not at all," Melissa said. "What's going on?"

"I need to talk about Fin," Alex said.

"Okay. Is this an over-the-phone convo? Or is it one of those 'we need margaritas' situations?"

"God, we might need margaritas," Alex groaned.

"Awesome! I'm coming over. I have the margarita mix. Do you have snacks or do I need to pick something up?"

"I have snacks and tequila. I'll make queso."

"I'll be there in twenty minutes," Melissa said before she hung up.

Alex unpacked her bag and changed into a long-sleeved cotton t-shirt and her pajama bottoms. She got the cheese warming up in a saucepan on the stove, then set a can of spicy Ro-Tel on the counter to be added later. By the time Melissa pulled into her driveway, the queso was almost done and the tequila and chips were ready and waiting.

Melissa walked in carrying a canvas bag and Alex's cat, Felix. "Look who I picked up on the way in!"

Alex took Felix from her and buried her nose in his fur. "Hey, little man. How was your weekend with the boys?" She refocused on Melissa as she set Felix down. "You ran into Eddie?"

"Yeah, he was bringing Felix over, but when he saw me loaded with margarita mix," she motioned to the bag on her shoulder where the bottle protruded from the top, "I think he assumed I was here for girls' night and skedaddled."

"That sounds like Eddie." Alex pulled two bowls from the cabinet and filled them with the queso as Melissa made their drinks. Their hands filled with plates and glasses, they headed to the living area to get comfortable.

"Right," Melissa said as she got settled on the couch. "So? Tell me about it."

"So. I met a guy." Alex slouched forward and slumped her shoulders. They burst out laughing.

"Understatement of the year," Melissa teased her.

"Right? Okay, so set the whole Hollywood complication aside and there's already a problem. He's not the type of guy I usually date. I'm *not* looking for a permanent relationship. There's no time in my life for that crap. I'm busy, I've got things to do."

"And...?" Melissa prompted as she stuffed a chip into her mouth.

"He's not the type of guy I date," Alex repeated. "He's smart... funny. And he's caring. I feel completely at ease with this man and I've only known him for a week. And yet, I feel like we've become close friends. I know way more about him than I should in such a short time frame, and vice versa."

Melissa spoke around the chip. "Definitely not your usual type if you actually *know* something about him."

Alex snorted. "Yeah, so you see my problem. Geez, I just pitched my dream job to the management team this week, and I think I'll get the go ahead. If the approval comes through, I'll be working so much overtime in the next few months, probably well into the next year. And likely traveling more than I am now. This is the worst possible time to be considering an actual *relationship*."

Melissa perked up, tilting her head to the side. "Are you considering a relationship?"

"Well, I wasn't. But apparently, he is. I mean, what the hell?" She inhaled deeply and exhaled in a slow release, then sipped her margarita.

"Seriously?" Melissa yelped.

"Yes. Driving back from Galveston this weekend—"

"Wait, you spent the weekend with him? At the beach?" Melissa interrupted.

"Er, yes... did I fail to mention that?"

"Spill," she commanded.

"We rented one of Gary's cottages and spent the weekend together in Galveston. Two days of awesomeness."

"Sex?" Melissa asked.

"Mind-blowing," Alex answered.

"Ha! I knew it. Anyway. On the way back...?"

"On the way back, he hits me with wanting to see more of me beyond this week... wanting to date and be a couple. Those are my words, not his. From the things we've talked about, he seems to be at a point in his life where he wants more than what he's getting from his career. Apparently, this past week has brought that into focus for him. And that brings us to problem number two. The Hollywood matter. I have no idea how to deal with that aspect."

"But don't you think he does? I mean, you could take your cues from him," Melissa said.

Alex sipped her drink, collecting her thoughts. She turned back to Melissa, who sat quietly, waiting for her to continue.

"I suppose. It's a complete unknown for me right now." Alex paused to grab another chip. "The third major concern, and probably the most important, is I'm not at that point in my life. I'm still exploring and having fun. I'm not ready to settle down. I mean, am I just supposed to give up everything I've worked for just to follow some big-shot celebrity around? I don't think so."

Melissa scooped up a hefty dollop of queso with a chip, shoved it in her mouth, and held up a finger while she chewed. She followed up with a long sip of her margarita and faced Alex.

"Alex," she began, "I've known you a few years and feel confident saying this... you've got relationship issues. You think your mom sacrificed her career for a man and you've sworn never to do that. I think this perspective short-changes you. Yes, you are busy. But you make time for your friends and doing the things you like to do. Why couldn't you make time for a relationship with a guy? The Holly-wood matter is intimidating and somewhat surreal, if we're being honest. But if Finley McAlister ticks all the boxes for you, then why not give it a chance?"

Alex opened her mouth to argue, but Melissa continued before she could speak, "You know, there's a bonus here you haven't considered. In every one of your previous dalliances, you held all the power."

"What do you mean?"

"You made more money, you had a bigger title, you trav-eled all over the world... You set *all* the rules of engagement. Every single one. If you really think about it, those were problems for you. You felt like the only grown up in those relationships. Dating a world-wide movie star would elimi-nate every one of those issues."

Alex slumped back against the couch, staring at Melissa. "Huh. I've never thought about it that way. But you're right, I've always been the one calling the shots. And Fin and I would be equals. Hell, probably not even equals. *He* would have the power."

"I doubt it," Melissa said. "I've never known you *not* to have the power, also known as control." She laughed, and Alex grinned at her.

"This is true," Alex said, and raised her glass in a toast.

"Okay, so tell me what all y'all did this weekend. Go anywhere good?"

Alex filled Melissa in on her weekend activities, slowly relaxing as their conversation shifted to her friend and other noteworthy happenings in their lives.

After Melissa left, Alex cleaned the kitchen then slipped in to bed, reviewing everything her too-wise-for-her-years friend had brought up. Melissa was right. Alex's past relationships had contained an inequity to them. Alex had always been in charge. She'd decided to engage, and she'd inevitably broken it off when the arrangement no longer suited her. Arrangement. That was the right word. They weren't relationships; they were *arrangements* she had with guys who also wanted the company without the commitment.

Fin had asked for more than that. And Melissa was right about the balance of power, too. Fin was a strong, commanding person who could handle her independence. Her career ambitions wouldn't be off-putting for him, given what he'd accomplished in his.

Two external downsides she could see were the interference from outside and coordinating schedules. One she didn't know enough about, and the other was what she did for a living. The big unknown was how dating a celebrity would affect her career and how people at work would treat her. This one made her the most nervous.

She decided she would play it by ear and see what this coming week brought. As if guided by fate, her phone rang with Fin's face on the screen. The image wasn't one from the Internet, but a photo she had taken while they lazed around in bed Sunday morning. His tousled hair framed his face and the laughter in his eyes spoke more about his mood than the smile on his face.

"Hey," she answered softly. They talked more about his ideas for his production company, shared stories about their families, and never strayed into the dangerous territory of relationships. Two hours later, her yawns signaled the need for sleep and they said their goodbyes. She drifted off into a world filled with soft Scottish brogues and soft, sleepy kisses.

Chapter 17

Monday Full Throttle

ALEX FINISHED her early morning conference call, then walked to the office kitchen to refill her drink. She felt light and airy this morning, like nothing could bring her down.

"You're awfully cheery this morning." Grace fell into step beside her as they headed back to their wing.

"I had a rejuvenating weekend at the beach. Just what I needed. How about you?"

"Oh, I did some gardening and puttering around the house. Very boring." Grace waved her hand as if pushing the topic aside. "I came to tell you Frank came around earlier looking for you. You might want to follow up with him. He had a strange look on his face. Is everything okay?"

Alex realized she hadn't debriefed her team on what had gone down last Friday.

"Should be. I need to update you guys on what we discussed on Friday, but let me check in with him first. Then I'll tell y'all what we talked about and how they pissed me off." Alex smirked at Grace before turning and heading towards Frank's office.

"We'll be waiting!" Grace called after her.

Alex found Frank in his office making a call. When he noticed her, he hung up the phone. "Good, you're here. I was just calling you."

"Grace said you were looking for me. What's up?"

"Jeff wanted to follow up with you this morning. You available right now?"

"Yeah, sure."

"And what's your temperature like?" he asked cautiously.

"Did I make you nervous on Friday, Frank?"

"Absolutely," he deadpanned.

"Look, I'm fine. He caught me off guard and he hurt my feelings. I do have them, you know." Alex shrugged. "I didn't like feeling unappreciated or being treated that way by someone I respect. And—if I'm being honest—it also hurt that you didn't stand up for me. That I had to defend myself."

Frank stood up. "You're right, Alex. I'm sorry. I should have spoken up."

Alex smiled, accepting his apology. "It's fine, Frank. I'm good now. It's behind me."

"Okay, then. Let's go see him." Frank gestured at his door and she led the way across the hall. Alex knocked on Jeff's open door, then walked in when he waved them in and pointed to the two chairs in front of his desk. He finished signing the paper his assistant had in front of him, handed it back to her, waiting until she left before speaking.

Jeff nodded at Frank, then turned to Alex. "Alex, before we go any further, I want to express my sincere apologies again for my actions on Friday. I discussed this with my wife and she gave me a thorough talking-to. Apparently, I am an idiot."

Alex's eyes twinkled at the idea of someone lecturing

Jeff Davis and putting him in his place. And she had to admit that him needing to bounce the situation off his wife mollified her sense of outrage over the exchange.

"Aside from being a 'sexist pig,'" he continued, making air quotes with his fingers, "I also owe you an apology for dismissing the hard work you've put into this initiative, as well as your ability to handle it. I'm sorry. I know you are more than capable of getting this off the ground."

"Thank you," she responded. "We're good."

Jeff regarded her for a few seconds, then clapped his hands together. "Alright. Let me tell you what I'm thinking. I want to structure this PMO under Frank's purview, focusing on financial and IT projects, which is right in your wheelhouse. But," he paused dramatically, looking back and forth between them, "after we prove the concept, I want to move it. My vision is to have a PMO office that oversees *all* projects, including engineering and operations. The biggest projects under operations involve setting up new locations. As you know, we've had several that have not gone smoothly in the past."

"Holy shit!" she exclaimed, blushing bright red at her outburst. "I'm sorry, I—"

Jeff waved off her interruption and asked. "How long do you think we need for the proof of concept before we implement it at a broader level?"

Alex froze in her seat, attempting to squash the immediate refusal that sprang to mind along with the fear and misgivings that accompanied it and focused on the question at hand.

"If by 'proof of concept,' you mean having all the processes and systems in place and acclimating the company to using the methodology..." She paused, waiting for his nod of confirmation before continuing, "I'd say two years minimum. We could have manual processes in place within the first year, but we would need to purchase and implement any software before we went wide like you're proposing."

Upon seeing his frown, she explained, "We'd need a project management tool to track projects and resources company-wide. In addition, we'd want an official document-storing application. Those are two major software implementations, so you're easily looking at two years to establish the necessary tools and processes."

Jeff looked at Frank, then at the calendar hanging on his wall. "I hadn't thought about new systems. We'll need to adjust the capital budget. Alex, can you get a quote on these systems before Friday and work it into your budget?"

Alex made a note on her phone. "I'll get with IT. Jackie may have ideas we can explore. We'll see what we can pull together."

Jeff nodded. "Okay, make it so. Frank, anything else?"

"I'm fully behind this effort, but I want to make sure we don't lose Alex's support team in the rush to launch the PMO. They're already engaged in our projects and will be suitable candidates for the new department, but our financial users around the world depend heavily on them for support at month end."

"Agreed," Jeff said and looked back at Alex.

"Yeah, I have some thoughts about that," she began. "I'm not sure everyone on my team wants to be a project manager. I haven't discussed it with you, Frank, but I'm considering leaving the GFS team intact and promoting Grace to manage it. It's still a bunch of vague ideas floating around in my head, but I can follow up with you later. You're right, we are intricately involved with month end close and don't want to cause issues there."

"Good." Jeff stood. "Let's get those plans fleshed out, yes? I'd like an update by Wednesday afternoon."

As they left Jeff's office, Alex asked Frank if he needed her further. When he dismissed her, she trotted back to her office. She burst with pride that Jeff had embraced her ideas and wanted to incorporate them beyond her original proposal. At the same time, she trembled at the thought of failing, which was a real possibility given the expedited timeline and broader scope he was proposing.

She couldn't believe this was happening so fast. Her heart raced at the thought. Just last night she'd been contemplating being overloaded for the next three months, and now her estimated workload had tripled within the same timeframe.

She lifted her phone. She needed Eddie to feed Felix tonight while she worked late.

FIN WOKE early on Monday and went for a run in Alex's neighborhood. The giant oak trees shadowing the manicured lawns made the neighborhood beautiful. He understood why she loved it.

Invigorated by his run, Fin spent the morning taking care of personal business. His accountant handled most of his financial obligations, but he preferred to manage the finances for his farm in Aberdeen personally as a way to stay connected to the world outside of show business.

He finished answering emails and made a quick post on social media about the fantastic weather in Houston this time of year. He learned long ago that posting occasional tweets about regular activities kept fans engaged and let them see you as human. Conversely, staying vague about your exact location in those postings kept them from mobbing you. He felt an obligation to his fans to a certain limit. His fame was due to their devotion, and he would always make time for fans. But he loved acting and would do it in some form, regardless of whether anyone knew or cared who he was. Contrary to what Ms. Cole had suggested, he did not feel like he owed *everything* to them.

When his stomach growled around lunch time, Fin fixed himself a sandwich and texted Mac asking him to call when he was free. Thirty minutes later, his phone rang. They exchanged pleasantries, then got down to business.

Fin shared his ideas about the production company he and Addie wanted to form and the film he had in mind for their maiden project.

"Before we get too deep into the details," Fin said, "do you remember Adelina Perez? She's been my business partner for many years now. She sat at our table at the Hollywood Charity Ball for the Homeless we attended a few years ago."

"Yes, I know of her. I didn't remember meeting her before—I don't think she and I talked much that night—but I have heard good things about her around town."

"She and I have discussed it for years, enough to refine the things we do and don't want to do with the company, but I recently got serious about moving forward. This new script I'm looking at, along with some other things going on in my life, has finally prompted me to pull the trigger. I told her I was reaching out to you and would get back to her afterward."

"Sounds like you and I both have been heading this direction separately for a long time. Given how like-minded we are, it makes sense to do it together." Mac listed several past projects he had worked on with different friends. Fin was familiar with a few, and they discussed the ups and downs of the projects.

"Let's get our people involved next week in LA. If the three of us feel good, we'll put together a business plan to go forward. You want to send me the script you're previewing? Or wait until we have an agreement?"

"I'll send the manuscript over today. It may help you think of other things we need to discuss next week," Fin told him.

"Sounds good. Hey, how's your chickie?"

"Pardon?" Fin asked, confused at the word.

"Your lady friend. Alice? No, that doesn't sound right."

Fin laughed. "Alex."

"That's right... Alex. You guys look good together. Is she in the business?"

"No, she's in the oilfield industry. A project manager I met on the way to Houston last week. She's not starstruck at all by me." He chuckled.

"Sounds like a keeper to me. Okay, send over the script and any ideas for the production company you already have. I'll review them both. When did you say you'll be in LA?" Mac asked.

"I'm flying in Friday, but Tuesday will be the earliest we can get together. In fact, let me ask Addie to arrange a meeting for the three of us. That way we can confirm that we're all on the same page before rushing forward."

Fin confirmed Mac's email address and ended the call. Then he emailed Addie with the information, asking her to coordinate the meeting.

Feeling productive with the day's accomplishments, he decided now was a good time to play tourist and go explore the Galleria shopping mall Alex had mentioned earlier in the week. He texted Blake to see how soon the hired driver was available and went to change his clothes.

Fin walked out of the store with his latest purchase in hand. He could hardly wait to see the look on Alex's face when she opened the box. He tucked the smaller bag with Alex's surprise into the larger bag holding the miscellaneous clothes he'd bought for himself.

Other than one brief interaction with a few fans, he'd been able to explore the three-story mall as he pleased over the last two hours. He spied a coffee shop across the way and decided an iced coffee was exactly what he needed.

A few minutes later, as he tore the paper off his straw, someone called his name. His skin crawled, and the hairs stood up on the back of his neck as he recognized a voice he would know anywhere. He hastily ran through his options as he poked the straw through the hole in his cup lid and turned around to face her.

Miranda Cole jeered at him as the man standing next to her snapped his picture. A new photographer, Fin noted, not the one who grabbed Alex.

"Hello, Ms. Cole," he acknowledged her greeting.

"What brings you to the Galleria today, Finley? Shopping for your lady love?" She nodded toward the packages he held.

"Occasionally I need new clothes," he quipped. "Don't you ever buy anything new?" Fin hadn't meant it as an insult, but when Miranda narrowed her eyes at him, he realized she wore the same blouse she had on at the press junket. He gave her his most pleasant smile.

"Not everyone has money to burn, Finley. Why are you

still in Houston? Don't you have another press junket in LA in a few days?"

"Why are *you* still in Houston?" he shot back, disturbed she knew so much about his schedule. "I thought you'd be back in Hollywood with the other blood-suckers, I mean *entertainment reporters.*" He shouldn't be baiting her, but she brought out the worst in him.

By then, a crowd had gathered and more cameras appeared. Fin took another slow, deep breath, trying to maintain his cool. He hoped that from afar, their interaction looked like a calm, collected exchange. On the inside, he felt anything but calm.

"Oh, I'm working on the story of the year. The 'Hottest Man Ever' playing with the locals before disappearing into the sunset." She held up her thumb and forefinger about an inch apart. "I'm this close to knowing her name. I'd be further along if someone hadn't got their knickers in a twist and shut down my photographer." She scowled at him. "You're a celebrity, McAlister. You're only famous because of people like me, and you should be grateful. Instead, you act like you're a god and ignore your fans. They don't deserve you."

"People like you?" Fin growled and stepped closer to her, lowering his voice so only she could hear. "People like you killed my fiancée and child. You think I should be *grateful* for that?" He scoffed. "I don't owe you a damn thing."

The color drained from Miranda's face. "Th-that wasn't my fault," she stammered. "The review cleared me of any wrongdoing."

How dare she act innocent! Fin's rage soared and his voice went deadly quiet. "It absolutely was your fault. And if you don't stop hounding me, your photographer won't be the only one I put the screws to. We're done here, Ms. Cole." Fin stepped backed from her, then turned and walked away, waving at the crowd as he left.

"WHAT DID HE SAY TO YOU?"

Miranda watched the Scottish actor walk away from her, trying to calm her erratic heartbeat.

"Ms. Cole? Miranda?"

"What?" she snapped.

"What did he say to you? You look upset."

"Just worry about your job. Did you get any photos?" She knew she shouldn't lash out at the poor guy, but she couldn't afford to look weak.

"Um, yeah, a few. I'll email them to you."

"Good. I'll catch up with you later." Miranda dismissed the replacement photographer and looked for a quiet place to sit down. Her knees wobbled from the bombardment of memories brought up by McAlister's raw accusation.

She found a bench and sat, her mind going back to the early days, when she'd noticed the young actor while doing a review of a stage production. Miranda had known at once he was going to be big someday, and had kept her eye on him.

On the day in question, she'd been excited to find a personal connection to the up-and-coming star. Miranda had tracked down his fiancée and knew the woman would open up if she could get a minute of her time. When Fiona McDonald got in her car and drove away, Miranda followed, intending to try again at her destination. More often than not, you could wear them down with persistence. She'd never imagined the tragedy that played out that day.

The inquisition had ruled it an accident, determining the driver had lost control of the car. When Miranda drove around the corner and spotted the overturned vehicle, she'd called the police like any good citizen would. McAlister had raised a stink afterwards, blaming Miranda, but the investigation cleared her of any misdeeds, proving it wasn't her fault. She was just doing her job and bad things happened.

Miranda's thoughts shifted to the present and his scathing retort a few minutes ago. Finley McAlister sure didn't seem to think it was an accident. Was he still caught up in the events from that day? He'd racked up award after award and his career had skyrocketed, so no, he wasn't mired in the past. This was definitely some personal problem specifically with her. Perhaps he was afraid she'd uncover whatever he was hiding. They were always hiding something. And a man that perfect coupled with such a strong aversion to the press set off all her reporter's instincts.

Miranda squared her shoulders. It was time to take back her power. She'd let McAlister influence her career for far too long by barring her from events she had every right to attend. She resolved to dig out whatever ugly truth he was hiding and expose it for the world to see.

She had an inside lead to where he might be this Thursday night and she was going to follow through. She had a story to write and his local fling was the key feature. The headlines were already writing themselves in her head. "Too Good to be True" was her favorite at the moment.

Miranda stood and straightened her jacket. She didn't have time for all this self-reflection. Celebrity scoops were happening everywhere and if she didn't serve them up, someone else would. She'd rather see her name on the byline.

As Blake dropped him off, Fin spotted Eddie exiting Alex's apartment with Felix in hand. Fin set his packages down and walked closer. Felix greeted him with a loud meow, and Eddie grinned.

"How's the apartment working for you?" Eddie asked.

"It's perfect. It's a lovely place. Do you usually lease it or does it serve as a place for people to crash?"

"I prefer to have the place rented, but when I'm between tenants, it turns into a crash pad."

"That's handy." Fin eyeballed the cat. "So, you've got Felix for the evening?"

"Yes, Alex called earlier. Her boss moved up a timeline and she's working late, so we're cat-sitting tonight. Felix seems to take it in stride. I sometimes wonder if we need to install a doggy-door between the two bungalows so he can go back and forth. Or should I say a kitty-door?" Eddie chuckled.

Fin smiled and scratched the cat's head. "Well, I'll let you go then. Thank you again for the use of your apartment. I wanted to remind you I'll be vacating it on Friday."

"Do you have plans for dinner tonight?" Eddie asked.

"No, I haven't thought that far ahead," Fin answered.

"Come over and eat with us. We're having Cajun tonight. Have you had Cajun yet? Never mind, whatever you've eaten won't be as good as Gabe's. Dinner will be ready at six thirty. See you then." Eddie waved and walked away, not giving Fin a chance to accept or decline the invitation.

"See you then," Fin uttered as he headed back to his temporary home above the garage.

Fin worked on the business proposal he planned to

pitch next week to Addie and Mac until it was time to join Eddie and Gabe.

While they ate, Fin learned how the two had met, the trials they'd seen as a gay couple, and listened to a few bawdy tales of their adventures over the years. When Gabe told the emotional story of losing his first love, Fin broke down and shared the story of Fiona's car crash. The two men were so empathetic that Fin understood completely why Alex regarded them as family.

"You guys have made a lovely little family here with Alex. Do you see her as a sister? Or a daughter?"

Eddie answered, "It's a good question. I think she's too independent for either of us to feel like a protective daddy. She comes and goes as she pleases and doesn't give a care what you think about it." Gabe laughed at this, making Fin think the comment had a story behind it. "But, yes, she does feel like a little sister." He looked at Gabe.

Gabe nodded. "She's an interesting combination of strength and vulnerability."

Fin snorted. "And she's completely unaware of the effect she has on others. She's quite contradictory, isn't she? Confident, intimidating, and yet oblivious and kind all in one package. I've spent the last week trying to decipher the puzzle of Alex."

"Mmm, I don't think you can pigeon-hole her."

"Agreed. Just when I think I've gotten her figured out, she surprises me. Here's to strong women." Fin raised his wineglass.

Eddie and Gabe raised their glasses as Eddie added, "And men."

"Cheers!"

The evening continued with the couple entertaining Fin with stories about their adventures with Alex over the years. Their love for her showed through, and he was thankful she had such caring friends in her life. Midnight approached when Fin finally made his way back to his place, noting the empty spot where Alex's car was usually parked.

Chapter 18

Wednesday Dinner

ALEX FINISHED her shower after work and hurried to get ready for her Wednesday dinner date with Fin. She had worked late both nights so far this week, even missing volleyball on Tuesday, and was looking forward to seeing him. She dressed comfortably with minimal makeup. As she got ready, she reflected on the last three days.

What a nightmare. She'd worked with Jackie in IT to compile a list of software packages they wanted and put in requests for quotes with their vendors. All but one had responded, and she'd updated the project budget accordingly. She'd pushed back her CEO's requested update while waiting on this final estimate, but if she didn't get that quote early tomorrow, she would either have to fudge the number or omit the software from this year's budget.

Her team was in shock at the speed they were moving with the plan for splitting the PMO from their financial support team. As she suspected, when given the option, neither Grace nor Sam were interested in changing, but Natalie was all in. While she was enthusiastic, Natalie wasn't qualified to be a project manager, but her skill at identifying unspoken requirements definitely showed her potential as a business analyst.

Alex had spoken privately to Grace yesterday about taking over as manager for the GFS support team. Grace had been stunned, flattered, and a little overwhelmed, so Alex left her thinking about the offer with the promise to circle back on Thursday.

As she finished applying her lip gloss, Alex checked her watch. Time to go. She closed her eyes and stood still for a moment, willing her body to let go of the run-run-run mode she'd been in for three straight days. In that short time, she'd accomplished an enormous amount, and fatigue pulled at her as if she were recovering from running a marathon. Tonight, she could relax and be stress-free. She hoped. She hadn't seen Fin since Sunday, when she'd asked him for some space. They'd talked over the phone and exchanged texts here and there, but the topics were light or a simple matter of passing information to each other. The butterflies in her stomach reminded her the discussion tonight would be deeper.

Alex squared her shoulders, added her phone and lip gloss into her clutch, retrieved the bottle of wine she'd picked up on the way home, and walked to Fin's apartment. She knocked three times and entered when he answered from inside.

The savory smell that greeted her immediately took her back to meal time at the ranch and her mom's home cooking. "Oh wow, it smells wonderful in here."

"Alexis... come on in." He kissed her cheek as he took the wine from her. "Let's open this so it can breathe, aye?" He deftly opened the bottle and set it aside, then turned back to her.

"Hi," Alex said.

"Hi, yourself," Fin answered as he pulled her into his arms. "I've missed you." He didn't give her time to answer before covering her mouth with his. The heat rushed up from her toes as she pressed against him. Her arms wrapped around his neck and pulled him closer.

Fin pulled back. "I see you've missed me too, *mo leannan*. And as tempted as I am to explore that, I need to finish our dinner so it doesn't burn." He smiled down at her.

Alex cleared her throat. "Right." She grinned. "Let's not burn down Eddie's garage." She moved toward the stove. "What smells so delicious?"

"Ah, let me show you. We're having grilled pork chops, grilled asparagus, and twice-baked potatoes. Gabe let me borrow that stupendous grill by his backdoor—which is fantastic, by the way. I took down the make and model so I could get one for my place back home."

Alex grinned at the enthusiasm that showed on his face as he described Gabe's grill. He acted like a little boy discovering a new toy. She set the table and poured the wine while he pulled the potatoes out of the oven.

The food was delicious. As they ate, Alex apologized for missing volleyball on Tuesday and told Fin how her bosses had taken her idea and run with it, making things crazy at the office.

"I mean, talk about taking it to the next level," she said in between bites. "Wanting this first effort to be the basis for a bigger operation later means I have to get there faster than I had originally planned. I thought we'd be growing the department slowly as the demand for our services increased. Now they want everything up and running by January. This vision? It's like they took my already accelerated time frame and demanded hyper-speed. Ugh, I'm exhausted just thinking about it."

"But you're excited about it, right?" Fin asked.

"Thrilled! But, ya know... exhausted too. It's like how you feel on a roller coaster. Terrified and holding on for dear life in between screaming with joy."

They grinned at each other, and Fin raised a toast to her success.

She sipped her wine, then asked, "So how was volleyball?"

Fin updated her on the latest gossip with her friends. Apparently, Andy had a new girlfriend and people weren't sure how they felt about her. Fin had played a few matches, filling in for missing teammates, and they'd all sang happy birthday to Alex's new teammate, Julie.

Alex laughed at the stories Fin told, and the meal passed pleasantly. Once finished, Alex moved to pick up their plates, but Fin stopped her. "Nope, sit down." He took the dishes from her and moved back to the kitchen area. She tried to see what he was doing, but he actively blocked her view with his body.

He returned carrying two bowls and set one on the table in front of her. It held angel food cake covered with strawberries, some kind of red liquid sauce, and a dab of whipped cream.

"Dessert!" he proclaimed. "Gabe told me this was your favorite, and I missed your birthday earlier this month. Happy birthday!" he declared with a flourish.

"Yum." She rubbed her hands together in anticipation. "Yeah, my birthday was the week I was in England, a few days before we met. My coworkers took me out pub-crawling where we danced our hearts out. This is way better though." She bit a generous portion and moaned in appreciation.

Fin leaned forward and wiped at her mouth with his

thumb, showing her the whipped cream he'd collected. She licked her lips to get any leftover cream. She watched him swallow and his lips part. Warmth poured through her body like liquid magma.

"Eh, okay." Fin cleared his throat. "Let's finish our dessert before it becomes inedible."

Agreed, Alex thought. They needed to talk about things, and it wouldn't happen if they wound up in bed too soon. She grinned to herself that ending up in bed was definitely on the menu—it was simply a question of when.

Fin told her about his exchanges with Addie and Mac and how they'd be meeting in Los Angeles next week. As they finished dessert and cleared the table, Fin talked about his schedule for the weekend and some obligations he had coming up over the next few weeks related to the film. Luckily, they were nearing the end of the promotional campaign, so the activity was winding down, with only a few events remaining.

Alex realized he was setting the tone for discussing the future. They moved to the living area where Fin turned on the stereo system. She smiled as soft jazz filled the air, comforting and relaxing. He was attempting to make it easy for her. She appreciated it.

"Okay, I'm ready to talk," she said as he settled in next to her on the couch.

"Okay."

"First of all, I've enjoyed our time together. It's been fun. And I've specifically enjoyed your company. To the point where the thought of not seeing you again makes me sad, which is a surprising development because I wasn't expecting that. I assumed from the beginning this was a tryst that I'd tell my grandchildren about one day. You know, I hung out with that really famous actor for about a week and had a blast. Then we went back to the real world."

Fin nodded and she continued. "My friend—you know Melissa—made some observations that gave me pause. I have issues with relationships and control. When I was still a kid, I swore I would never let romance derail me from what I wanted to do with my life... I would never sacrifice myself for a man. Melissa brought it to my attention that I have always controlled any relationships I had. *I* decided if there would be a relationship and *I* was the one to break it off. She also astutely pointed out that I intentionally picked men who had no chance with me because it made it easier to walk away when I was done."

She paused to take another sip of wine and watched Fin over the rim of her glass. He lifted his glass as well and stared back at her, not saying anything. His warm gaze was encouraging, not judging, and gave her courage to go on.

"Now mind you, I can count the number of boyfriends I've had on one hand. And to be honest, those were more like casual, someone-to-do-stuff-with type things. Mostly, I don't have the time or energy for it. I'm busy." She shrugged.

"Aye, you are a rising star in your company and have ambitious plans," he agreed.

Alex narrowed her eyes, searching his face for any hint of sarcasm. Not finding any, she continued, "I have lots of male friends. Men who stimulate me intellectually, but nothing physically. And I've met a few men who got me all hot and bothered physically, but I swear had the IQ of a black-eyed pea."

He barked a laugh at her description.

"Fin, you're the only guy I've ever met who does both." Alex glanced at him before lowering her eyes and studied the glass in her hands. The smooth sound of a saxophone playing in the background filled the conversation void, and her face warmed with embarrassment as she ran out of steam. The sofa dipped as he moved closer. His hand came into her field of vision and he raised her chin up so she could see his eyes. She could feel tears gathering in her eyes.

"Alexis," he murmured, "I ken what you mean, lass. You spoke of the intellectual connection. Obviously, we have that. And the chemistry is off the charts. For me, there's another important factor... trust. I immediately trusted you. And I'm not one to do so lightly."

"Yes." She nodded. "I trusted you straight away as well. And that's uncharacteristic of me, too. I have lots of friends, but only a few who get the whole me. Most people only get pieces of me. Do you know what I mean?"

"Aye. I've seen it. You are good at compartmentalizing. You have your volleyball friends who get the athlete. Your adopted family," he nodded toward Eddie and Gabe's house, "who get the emotional vulnerability of you. And your lovers, who get the sexy, confident siren that you are. I do the same. For me, it's survival in an unrelenting industry. Why is it that way for you?"

Alex huffed. "Probably the same. Male-dominated field in a male-dominated industry. You get protective of your inner sanctum when you realize no one treasures it like you do. And you build a tough outer shell to protect yourself. Even in college, I could see the differences in how professors treated me versus my fellow male students, and it changed how I dealt with the world. It's like I've been fighting my entire career."

Alex waved her hand. "Anyway, all that was to tell you I agree with you. We have something worth pursuing. But also to warn you: I'm not easy and I have hang-ups. I suspect I'm a pain in the ass. On top of all that, next year will be nuts for me. This week's insane pace is my new normal for the next couple of months. And it'll be only slightly less intense for the six months after that. I have no idea how we will manage a relationship with the schedules you and I have."

She raised her hand and shrugged in a helpless gesture.

"Come here, *mo chridhe*." He pulled her in for a hug. "We'll work it out. Other busy couples do this all the time."

"What does 'mo-kree-eh' mean?" she whispered, cringing at how she butchered the word.

"My heart," he answered, his warm breath brushing her ear.

"Oh, my god. Panty-melter."

"What?" Fin asked as he pushed her back and gazed at her face, his eyebrows raised.

Alex burst out laughing. "Your accent, your breathtaking Scottish sayings, calling me 'your heart,' and freaking Simply Red playing in the background," she said as she pointed to the sound system. "Definitely a panty-melter of a moment."

She watched him try not to laugh, but he couldn't contain it.

"Come here, lassie. I'll melt those panties right off of you," he growled.

She squealed and made to get away, but wasn't fast enough. Fin caught her and did exactly as he'd promised.

HOURS LATER, Alex drew lazy circles on Fin's chest, admiring the volleyball-themed charms dangling from the silver bracelet he'd placed on her wrist earlier. His thoughtfulness took her back to their earlier conversation. "You talked about trust being a major concern for you. Did that come with fame? Or was it because of something beforehand? Did someone hurt you, Fin?"

His hand on her hip tightened for a split second before relaxing. "My trust issues developed after I started my career. I had been in a few films and was starting to draw attention, especially around Scotland, but in general the reporters and paparazzi didnae bother with me too much then. They focused on my more famous costars. Except for this one."

Fin went quiet and Alex raised her head off his shoulder and propped her chin on her hand, watching his face as he stared at the ceiling.

"To be fair," he continued, "I have to give her credit for knowing her stuff. She latched on to me when I was a nobody. And now I'm not. So, she's good at spotting potential, I guess."

Alex continued lazily stroking his chest as the story of Fiona and Rodney spilled from him. When tears formed in his eyes, she wanted to pull him to her and kiss them away but held back. She sensed his need to tell the story in his own way, so she continued to listen and offer her touch as comfort.

As he concluded, Fin rubbed his eyes and rolled to face her. "And that's why I've become so protective of my private life over the years. I'm afraid I've developed a reputation for being aloof or standoffish, but it's damn near necessary to protect my family and those I love."

Alex laid her head back on his shoulder and hugged him tight. "Just so you know, as a previously ignorant fan, I always had the impression you were simply private and mysterious. It never seemed to me that you were unfriendly or cold. But I'm probably biased because I also crave my privacy and likely have a slanted view toward the paparazzi."

A thought occurred to Alex and she raised her head to look at him. "So, wait... is the reporter who caused Fiona's accident the same one from the press junket *and* the one who ripped my dress?"

Fin nodded.

"Jesus, Fin. She's stalking you. Miranda Cole, you said?" At his nod, she continued, "Just let her show her face around me. I'll teach that heifer some manners."

Fin laughed and pulled her on top of him. "You and Addie are fierce women. My protectors." He punctuated his sentences with kisses. "Addie has her legal team on it. Now, let's talk about more pleasant things."

Fin rolled her over and tried to tickle her. "Surprise!" Alex beamed. "I'm not ticklish. But you are."

Alex attacked his ribs with her fingers, and Fin squirmed like a fish. A wrestling match ensued that ended with Alex on bottom, her arms stretched above her, grasped firmly in Fin's hands.

"Och, you're a strong one. Not ticklish, eh? That's unnatural. What's wrong with you, woman? Aye, then we'll have to find something else to make you wiggle." And he proceeded to do so.

Chapter 19

Last Day

Last night, Alex had purposely set her alarm early enough to allow time for them to say a proper goodbye this morning before she headed to her apartment to prepare for work.

As she slipped on her shoes, she addressed Fin. "Tonight's your last night."

"Aye. My plane leaves mid-morning tomorrow."

"Volleyball tonight or no?"

"I'm content either way, Alex. Spending time with you makes me happy, whether it's with your friends or you alone."

Alex sighed. "I feel torn. I want you all to myself and yet, I feel an obligation to my team, especially given that I missed Tuesday. Ugh."

Fin pulled her into his arms. "Let's do volleyball then. We have time, *mo leannan*. It's just a matter of scheduling."

"Okay." She kissed him goodbye and told him she'd text later about sharing rides after work. Then she was out the door and running to her place to get ready for the day. She hoped work would take her mind off the growing heaviness in her heart.

FIN SPENT the morning packing his bag and cleaning up Eddie's apartment. Before leaving, Alex suggested he stay at her place tonight, so he didn't have to worry about closing up the apartment tomorrow morning before his flight. He appreciated her foresight and recognized that planning for unexpected issues was a skill she exercised daily. *You've got to love a woman with a brain*, he thought.

No one answered his knock at Eddie's place, so Fin made his way to Alex's back door, which he found unlocked. Fin used the magnetic notepad Alex kept on her refrigerator to write a thank you note to Eddie for the use of his apartment. He preferred to thank him in person, but left the note on the kitchen counter for Alex to deliver in case Fin didn't see him before he left.

With his immediate chores taken care of, Fin made himself comfortable on Alex's couch and opened his laptop to work on his to-do list. Felix hopped up on the couch and situated himself next to Fin, meowing until he reached over to pet him.

He penned a quick email to Alex asking if she wanted to join him in Los Angeles the second week in November. He would be too busy next week, but he had a break the following week before traveling back to Scotland.

Fifteen minutes later, an email notification dinged and he switched over to read Alex's response. She wasn't available as she had training in Dallas that week for a new software they were implementing. And she couldn't take any time off through the end of the year. They would have to find weekends where they could both get away.

Fin sat back, frustrated. His past relationships had mirrored Alex's in that they were casual. However, most of the women he dated were in show business, where both of their careers centered on events rather than weekdays. Coordinating around openings, award shows, and other industry happenings made spending time together easy. He realized Alex was right—synchronizing their schedules was more difficult than he'd first thought. But they could figure it out.

Fin put those thoughts aside and focused on the manuscript he and Addie were reviewing. She had reviewed his ideas on the script and sent her remarks yesterday. He was almost finished going through her revision notes. Fin loved the way she took his comments and expanded them, nailing down what he was after even when he couldn't find the right words. An hour later, he received a second email from Alex.

She had set up a shared calendar where they could each record their travel plans. The link he clicked on showed several blocks of dates marked with her upcoming trips. They contained her name and the location where she would be. Fin's first reaction was excitement. Having each other's travel itinerary would make coordination easier. His second response was wariness. An online tool that could be hacked or shared was dangerous for celebrities. He needed to run this by Addie before doing anything that might leave him exposed to the public. Fin liked the idea, but he needed to make sure his personal information was safe. He forwarded the email to Addie, asking for her opinion, and returned to his manuscript.

Just as Fin broke for lunch, Alex called. "Hello, lass. How's it going?" he greeted her.

"Awesome. I submitted my final budget for the new department. The last quote I was waiting on showed up just as I was fixin' to flay someone over it."

"Congratulations. You must feel relieved to have all your fixing done," he teased.

"Smartass." Alex laughed. "Yes, I'm glad that's done. Now it's hurry-up-and-wait time. We can't move forward until it's approved, but at least I've completed the proposal. Anyway, I'm calling to tell you a cold front is coming in this afternoon, so it will be nippy at volleyball tonight. Do you have warmer workout clothes to wear? And a thick pair of socks you don't mind ruining? The sand gets chilly this time of year. I have special shoes I use. When I pick you up, I'll grab my shoes then."

"Hmm, I need to see what I packed. I didn't bring many athletic socks with me this trip. What type of shoes do you have?"

"I'll send you a link," she said.

"Sounds good. What time do I need to be ready?"

"We have the early game tonight, so we should leave my house by five-thirty. I'll text you when I'm on my way."

"That works. Okay, I got your link. I'll do some shopping this afternoon and see if I can find a pair of these shoes."

Fin waited when Alex paused.

"You'd go buy new shoes for just one night?"

"Aye, since I plan on playing with you again, they will be an investment I'll use repeatedly."

"Oh, okay. I didn't think that far ahead." She changed gears. "What did you think about the shared travel calendar?"

"I like the idea. I need to vet it first because I don't want my schedule to wind up in the public's eye. Hackers love exposing celebrity private data. I'm having Addie review the application before I add anything."

"Oh, sorry, that never occurred to me. I'm still getting used to having the public-at-large interested in our activities."

"Nae bother. It looks like a perfect way to coordinate. Once she approves, I'll upload my itinerary so we can suss out when we can see each other again."

A voice in the background asked Alex if she were ready and she muffled the phone for a moment. Then she was back. "Okay, I've gotta run. See you later."

"Later, love." She giggled before disconnecting and he smiled to himself. He texted Blake and asked if he wanted to grab a bite to eat. While Fin waited for his reply, he looked up the link Alex had sent on the sand shoes. He located a place in town that carried them and decided he would pick up a pair after lunch.

While Fin was out, Addie had answered his inquiry about the shared calendar, suggesting he use an alias when he set up his profile. Blake dropped him off afterwards, confirming the early-morning pickup to the airport, and Fin settled in on Alex's couch to enter his upcoming travel events to their shared calendar.

Thirty minutes later, he sat glowering at his screen. He accepted that Alex had to work during the week, but he thought they'd be able to sneak in a weekend here and there. However, all her free weekends matched up to when he was out of the country. The ten-hour flights to meet up would use a sizable chunk of their limited time together for a weekend rendezvous. And—based on her schedule the last couple of days—even if he flew in for the week, they would have little time together.

Fin leaned back and exhaled in frustration, staring off into space. After two weeks of nonstop togetherness, it seemed the next leg in this journey would be from a distance. Based on their mutual calendars, phone calls and virtual meetings were on the menu for the next three months. Even their holiday schedules were at odds with each other.

He closed the app and pushed his frustrations aside as an email from Mac arrived. Mac had called him yesterday, excited about the script. He'd told Fin his team would draw up the papers ahead of time using a fill-in-the-blank format so they wouldn't have to waste time with a bunch of legal mumbo jumbo next week and could get to work straight away. The email contained the legal papers needed to set up their joint venture. He spent the afternoon reviewing and communicating with Addie and Mac on their new company, MPM Productions.

Mac had surprised him by wanting a minority share. His argument was he had fingers in too many pies and didn't want that much responsibility. While there was probably some truth to that, Fin believed Mac enjoyed playing support roles both off the screen and on. As it stood, he and Addie would each own forty percent, with Mac holding the last twenty percent of ownership. By the time they met next week in Los Angeles, attorneys from both sides will have reviewed everything and they would sign the final papers, making it official.

When his phone pinged with a text from Alex saying she was on her way home, he put everything away in his satchel and got dressed for the evening.

WHEN ALEX ARRIVED HOME, she found Fin dressed and ready to go. She slipped off her work clothes and donned her workout gear for cold weather. She stuffed her sand shoes in her workout bag and met Fin back in the living room.

"It's getting cold outside, and the temperature is supposed to drop even further in a few hours. Do you have a jacket you could bring?"

"Aye, I threw a jumper in my bag earlier."

Alex tilted her head to the right. "A jumper is a sweater, right?"

"You know your proper English, even if you dinnae use it."

"Ha! I once told someone that even though we speak the same language, I still need a translator when I travel to Great Britain. We use the same words, just differently. Funny story," she said as she fed Felix, "we once came into work on a Saturday at our London office. The local controller typically wore suits to the office, so when he showed up in casual clothes, he looked completely alien to me. I told him I liked his pants. Later over lunch, he told me I had startled him into checking to make sure his zipper was closed. That's when I learned that pants meant underwear over there and I should have said I liked his trousers."

Fin burst into laughter at her story. "I can imagine. I've had to navigate those differences before and had similar awkward moments. Not only with American versus British English, but with the additional Scottish and Gaelic sayings."

She grinned in appreciation. "Let's go."

The drive to Rally Up didn't take long, and soon they pulled into the parking lot.

"The parking lot is awfully full," Alex said, as she looked around. "It's league night so there shouldn't be any private parties or anything. I wonder what's going on."

As they retrieved their bags from the back, Fin pointed to a mob of people standing near the doors. "Danger, Will Robinson," he quoted a classic line from a 1960s TV show. "I've learned to recognize the fan mobs. You up for this? Or should we bail?"

"Great," she mumbled. "No, I really need to show up after missing Tuesday."

Someone in the group shouted Fin's name, followed by several high-pitched squeals. A mob of people rushed toward them.

"You go ahead," Fin told her, "I'll follow shortly."

"You sure?"

"Aye, let's keep this," he gestured to the approaching crowd, "out here in the car park."

"Okay. Good luck."

Alex left Fin signing autographs and walked inside.

The bar area was more full tonight, and only one of the giant garage doors was open. October signaled the coming of the cold season, and this was the last league until the weather warmed up again.

Alex supposed the drop in the temperature was what had driven everyone inside. She looked for her tribe and spotted a few of them at a corner table by the dartboard. As she walked their direction, Alex noticed a woman approaching. Her skinny jeans, silk blouse, and stylish heels marked her as not a regular. The woman was older than Alex and had an *haute couture* look about her that highlighted how out of place she was amongst the casual crowd.

"Yes? Can I help you?" Alex asked as the stranger stopped before her.

The woman pointed her phone at Alex, a large red button and the word "recording" on the screen. "Ms. Tanner, my name is Miranda Cole and I'm doing a story on Finley McAlister for the..."

Shit, shit, shit, Alex thought as the woman's words faded into the background. *Why didn't I wait for Fin?*

"I'm sorry, who did you say you were?" Alex stalled for time to think.

"Miranda Cole with *Celebrity News*. You've heard of the show?"

Alex studied the woman. She was cool and confident. Her mouth displayed a pleasant smile, but her eyes held a gleam in them that didn't match the friendly vibe she attempted to project.

"Yes, I know of it."

Alex returned the woman's stare as the reporter sized her up. Before she could ask another question, someone from the table shouted, "Alex! Come on, we're up and we need to warm up."

"Be right there, Jules," Alex shouted over her shoulder while maintaining eye contact with the woman. "Sorry, I need to go. Catch you later?"

Alex walked away before she could respond. She threw her stuff on the table and unlocked her phone to text Fin. *Miranda Cole inside. Can avoid via side gate. Goes straight to courts.*

She locked her phone and tucked it away into her bag before moving it next to Melissa. "Hey, can you keep an eye on this? There's a reporter here and from what I've heard, she wouldn't be above going through my stuff or trying to look through my phone."

Melissa's eyes opened wide. "Sure, I'll throw your stuff back here with mine and Scott's."

"Thanks. Gotta run, we're up."

Alex ran off to join her team on court five. At some point during the match, Fin appeared on the sidelines and cheered her on. She noticed he still had his bag, so he must have taken her advice to avoid the bar area.

After Rick spiked the winning point on the last game, the team congratulated each other as they headed back to the seating area. Her teammates chattered comfortably with Fin, and Alex appreciated how easily they had accepted him into their inner circle.

She asked Fin if he had seen the reporter yet and he shook his head no. "Okay then. Looks like we'll face that beast together. Do we need a strategy?"

"No. Just answer as you wish. I find brief answers with no details work best. And a simple yes or no works nicely as well."

As they neared the building, Fin took her hand in his. *He's making a statement,* Alex thought.

More people had packed into their corner. Melissa waved to them, revealing the seats she saved. Alex was relieved they were on the side near the wall, making access to Fin more difficult for the relentless reporter. She looked around and spotted the woman seated at the bar, watching them. How creepy was that?

As the conversation ebbed and flowed, the news that this was Fin's last night in town came up, and the group peppered them both with questions. What was he doing next? When would he be back? Was Alex joining him in Los Angeles? They answered with what they knew and redirected when they could.

Someone asked Fin to substitute and he headed to the

courts. Alex ordered them something to eat, then made her way to the ladies' room. As she washed her hands, Miranda Cole sauntered in.

"So, you're McAlister's new love interest. How are you finding the Hollywood lifestyle so far?"

Alex took her time drying her hands, then flicked her gaze at the women in the mirror before turning to face her. "I don't know anything about the Hollywood lifestyle. The unexpected media attention has been a surprise though."

Miranda's eyes widened then narrowed, as if the direct answer surprised her and she didn't quite trust the honesty of it.

"You guys have been rather tight these two weeks. Did you know each other previously?"

"Are you interviewing me, Ms. Cole?" Alex asked, politely waiting for a response.

Again, the woman hesitated. "I suppose I am. He's very popular, you know. Despite his habit of hiding from the press and not sharing his life with his fans."

Alex pondered the statement before asking, "And you believe he should be an open book with them?"

"They made him what he is. He owes them."

"But if he's popular without sharing, doesn't that prove his fans don't require him to do so?" Alex continued before Miranda could respond. "Forgive me for my ignorance. This is my first experience with a celebrity and how the whole fame situation works." She smiled to take the edge off.

Thinking to gain some insight into the reporter, Alex decided to answer her original question. "We met on the plane. He was flying to Houston and I was coming back from a business trip. We sat next to each other. Quite an engaging conversation, as you can imagine."

"What in the world did you talk about? You have nothing in common." She sounded genuinely interested.

Alex laughed. "You'd be surprised. We talked about the things normal strangers on a plane talk about... Business or pleasure? Where are you from? Those kinds of things."

"I can't imagine. He's usually stiff and cold."

"Ah, but then I was some random stranger on a plane who he never thought to see again versus someone trying to get a story on him, right? I bet anyone would be wary facing someone digging into their private life."

Miranda narrowed her eyes again at Alex. "You don't seem to be wary."

"Because we're just two women talking in the ladies' room." Alex shrugged. "There was a moment last week when I had cameras flashing in my face, people shouting at me, and one guy even ripped my dress!" Alex sighed. "I loved that dress and it's ruined now. Anyway, in that situation, I was shocked and a bit terrified. I wasn't sure what was going on."

"So are you two a couple? By the way, you're good at avoiding the question. Like a pro, in fact." Miranda smiled, and Alex realized how attractive she was. The smile failed to remove the predatory glint in her eye, but emphasized her high cheekbones and flawless skin.

"Wow, you should... Oh my god, I almost said 'you should smile more.' How sexist does that sound?" Alex laughed at herself and waved her hand in the air. "Let me rephrase. You have a wonderful smile. Your whole face lights up. I'd guess female reporters have it tough, right? Having to be a hard-ass to be taken seriously because if you're too feminine or soft, people blow you off?" Alex rolled her eyes. "Just like everywhere else."

Miranda blinked at her. "I am a hard-ass."

"Well, sure. Any woman who's spent any time in a field ruled by men is not only a hard-ass but also a badass. But that doesn't mean we want to *always* be that way. Sometimes, we want to be the softie."

Before Miranda could respond, two women walked in laughing and Alex excused herself. "It was nice to meet you, Miranda. Try the burgers here if you're hungry. They're pretty good. But maybe avoid the hot dogs."

Alex walked back to her friends thinking about the interaction she'd just had. Fin talked about the Cole woman as if she were the devil incarnate. She had been civil to Alex, not precisely nice, but not unbearable.

Alex had done some research after hearing his story from the past and agreed with his assessment that Miranda Cole had targeted him through the years. Tonight, she'd witnessed the woman's ambition firsthand, but wondered what drove the personal attention to Fin. Perhaps guilt from the resulting crash of that first encounter? Or maybe that event had caused a career setback and she had some score to settle?

"Alex, settle this argument, will you?"

Alex shrugged off the encounter with the reporter and joined her friends' latest light-hearted debate.

MIRANDA WASN'T EASILY SURPRISED, but the woman whom Finley McAlister was dating had left her speechless. Alex Tanner possessed the composure of a Hollywood veteran. The empathy she displayed for Miranda's position as a woman in an industry of men moved her in a way she hadn't expected. Miranda shook her head and walked back to her seat at the bar to observe the couple.

As the evening progressed, Finley's comfort level among this group of people—and theirs with him—became evident. In fact, everyone at this place seemed happy and at ease. No one trolled him for pictures or autographs. Indeed, this man seemed like a complete contrast to the one she usually dealt with.

Miranda considered the story she'd been piecing together on Finley McAlister. When she'd learned he would be at the Houston press junket, she had jumped at her chance to get close to him again and felt a moment of triumph when she'd secured a spot on his roster. Of course, everything had gone awry when he'd walked out of the interview, but the desertion had fueled her need to respond with an exposé. After tracking him these last two weeks and now speaking with Alex Tanner, she had an overwhelming suspicion that her reporter's instinct might have been off on this one.

She caught the couple looking at each other and held her breath. She had been certain she was chasing a major story and maybe she'd gotten that part right. Perhaps she had misinterpreted the type of story. After this evening, she suspected her "expose the bad guy" story might in fact be a "dream come true" story.

Waving to the bartender for her check, Miranda pulled out her wallet to settle her tab. She had more research to do.

Later that evening, Fin said his goodbyes and they headed home. Some of her friends acted like they would never see him again, and others treated him like he'd be back next week. Fin must have been thinking along similar lines, because he brought it up in the car. They talked about the group of friends and who Fin would miss the most as they headed back to her duplex.

That night, they made love slowly and quietly. Nothing was rushed. They savored every touch, every sigh. *We're saying goodbye*, Alex thought.

"Man, I don't want you to go," she told him as she lay snuggled in his arms, her hands against his chest. "I'm not ready for this vacation to end."

"Are we *ever* ready for the vacation to end?" She could feel him smiling into her hair.

"These last two weeks have been a roller coaster ride of emotions for me. Don't ask me how, given my current crazy workload, but these have been the best two weeks I've had in a long time. I'll miss having you around." She bit his ear playfully. "And you're hot."

Fin growled at her and rolled her onto her back so he could look down at her. He brushed her hair out of her eyes, his face all seriousness. "Best two weeks for me too, lass. But it's just the beginning. Once we get our schedules sorted, it will only get better."

"Do you really think so? I'm having difficulty imagining it."

He kissed her forehead. "We'll get there. Have faith." He peppered kisses along her nose, making his way to her mouth, where his kiss deepened. The heat built between them, and they didn't talk again for a long time.

Chapter 20

Scheduling Problems

Beep. "Hey, Fin. Sorry I missed your call. My meeting ran long. I'll try to catch you tonight."

.

Beep. "Hello, Alexis. Thought I could catch you before you boarded your plane, but looks like I missed you. I'll be tied up with an event when you're landing, so I'll have to try you again tomorrow."

.

Ding. Got your text, you naughty boy. So uncool to send me shirtless pics of you when I'm in a meeting with my boss! LOL

.

Beep. "I can't believe we keep missing each other. I'm going to send you a meeting invite and block out some time for a freaking phone call! It's inconceivable that I have to schedule my love life like I schedule my projects."

.

Beep. "Last night was lovely. I've never done the phone sex thing before. Oh, shite! I hope you aren't listening on speaker! Eh, sorry about that. Let's make that a regular Wednesday thing, eh? Later, lass."

.

Ding. Sorry lass, can't talk. More interviews. Later?

.

Ding. Hey, Mr. Hollywood. I'll be free tonight if you want to talk. Or just breathe heavily at each other. LOL

.

Beep. "Good lord, Alexis. Do you always work this hard? Your calendar is completely booked."

THREE WEEKS LATER...

Fin closed the lid on his laptop and leaned back, stretching his torso and arms. He'd originally planned to be home in Scotland this week tending to his horses, but the production company had progressed quicker than anyone expected. When word spread that he and McBrewster had teamed up, congratulations—and a few offers—came pouring in from other leading actors, directors, and producers in the industry. Mac and Addie hit it off right away, and before Fin knew it, the company's offices were up and functioning with the requisite staff to manage the basics. Instead of riding his horses, he found himself mired in the new business.

His caretaker, who lived on-site at the farm, was a top-notch ranch hand, but Fin liked to visit quarterly, if not monthly, to see things for himself. Worried about the extended time away, he'd asked his brother to check in at his Aberdeen property on his behalf. Ethan treated visits to Fin's ranch as a vacation and reassured Fin that he was excited to spend a weekend at the farm with his family. The horses would get plenty of attention from Ethan's daughters.

Fin considered the pile of messages in his inbox. Juggling so many projects, all hurling at him with urgent deadlines, he now understood the stress Alex was under back in October. The movie script he'd been playing with in Houston was now in its final revision, and the hiring call for actors was out to various agencies. Mac was in talks with a director about the film, while Fin and Addie worked on building their production team. The response had been overwhelming. He had no idea Hollywood would receive his debut project with such enthusiasm. He hoped the momentum kept going.

While his career was suddenly taking off in new directions, his love life appeared stuck in neutral. He and Alex touched base every night. Sometimes only in passing via text message or voicemail exchanges. When they could connect, they were often either too busy or too exhausted to have any deep, meaningful discussions. They still talked about important topics, but the time available didn't allow that same connection they had when in person. And he missed holding her. His growing dissatisfaction with the long-distance relationship wore on him. He understood now why showbiz people dated and married other showbiz people. Who knew schedule coordination was a real consideration for selecting a proper mate?

He stood and stretched the rest of his body, hoping to work out the stiffness from sitting at a desk most of the day. His thoughts strayed to Alex again. Phone sex was something he'd never engaged in before, but Fin discovered it had its place. And Alex excelled at it. The woman both frustrated and delighted him. As he remembered last night's call, he glared at his wall calendar, then moved into the first of his tai chi forms meant to calm his mind.

"Hey, boss... hello... anyone home?" His new assistant's voice broke through his daydreaming and brought him back to the present.

"Yes, Kathy?" Fin stopped mid-movement and turned to her.

"Wow, you were miles away. Must be a great meditation technique." She grinned at him. "You have a call on line one. Alex?"

"Right. Thank you." The muscle in his jaw clenched as he strode toward his desk.

Chapter 21

Insight

ALEX HUNG up the phone and sat back on her couch, rubbing Felix as he lounged in her lap. She'd always seen the calm, considerate, and fun side of Fin, with occasional glimpses of quiet anger when dealing with the press. This was the first time she'd caused his frustration.

His life had become as busy as hers. The ideas lingering in his mind for years were now living, breathing things that had taken off all at once. She knew from experience his head was spinning with the unexpected fast pace of everything happening in unison.

But what she got from the phone call wasn't stress from his world spinning faster. From everything she could tell, he thrummed with renewed energy toward his career. No, what she sensed on the call was aggravation with her and their circumstances.

One of Fin's primary objectives when he'd left Houston in October was to find time for them. With her world running at full-throttle and his ramping up, the time he sought was an elusive thing that slipped away when you looked for it.

Alex stretched out on the couch, making herself more comfortable, and pondered her current situation. Until last month, everything in her life had revolved around her career. She'd even organized her personal life to accommodate her work schedule. She played volleyball and gathered with friends when she wasn't working. As recently brought to her attention, she chose the men she dated by how well they fit into her work life, and discarded any who wanted more than she wanted to give.

Felix bumped her hand to signal her neglect of her rubbing duties. Alex scratched him in his favorite spots as she considered those two weeks with Fin.

Fin had blown in like a hurricane, completely disrupting her life and making her reconsider what was important. But once he'd left town, she'd fallen back into her regular patterns, focusing her time on her career rather than her personal life.

And she missed him. Oh man, did she miss him. They talked or texted every day, but those interactions didn't contain the same intensity as having him here. She had told him she was all in and she would try, but had she really been trying? No, she'd been drifting along the same way she did before he came into her life. She decided his annoyance was justified. She wasn't holding up her part of the bargain.

With that conclusion, she moved Felix to the side and stood. Time for her to become part of the couple, not just give it lip service. She fixed a quick salad and poured a glass of wine, then sat down with her laptop to study their shared calendar.

After seeing what Fin noted, that their schedules showed them traveling in opposite directions for the next six months, she changed tactics and looked for opportunities to meet up during their travels, rather than taking complete breaks in their calendars. On the fourth sweep, she found a potential candidate and dialed Fin's cell number.

"Hey, lass. I'm sorry about earlier—" he began.

"No, you were right to be frustrated. I haven't been pulling my weight in this, leaving you to worry about our personal stuff. But I have an idea. The first week in December, when you fly to Los Angeles, you entered your actual itinerary rather than a destination. Can you get all your itineraries entered this way?"

"Aye, but why?"

"Well, from the flight details you entered, I can see that you have connecting flights in New York City. I'm flying to London that weekend. If I route through New York with a layover and you rearrange your flights, we could squeeze in a short weekend together."

"Truly? That's brilliant!"

"Right? I'm thinking if we enter our itinerary information in this calendar, we may find more moments like this."

"I'll begin straight away." He paused, then asked, "Are you okay if I give my assistant access to the calendar? She can update it with the travel details and keep it updated in the future."

"Um, do you trust her?"

"Aye."

"Yeah, okay. If you trust her, then I will too. And Fin... I'm sorry for not committing fully. I see that now. I slipped back into my former pattern of putting my job first and let you carry the load on our relationship. If I do that again, give me a nudge, okay?"

"Dinnae be too hard on yourself. This is unfamiliar territory for both of us. We'll get it straight. And if I have to bash you over your stubborn Texas head, I'll be happy to do so."

She laughed and started to say more, but hesitated when she heard someone talking to him in the background.

"Ah, *mo leannan*, I need to go. Talk later?"

"Yep. Later, Hollywood." She hung up, feeling much better.

Alex spent the evening adding travel details to her own calendar entries. Hopefully Fin would spot an opportunity she didn't.

Alex finished her notes on the resume she'd been reviewing and stood up to stretch. The Houston office was quiet this week because of the Thanksgiving holidays. While the U.S. offices closed for the two-day holiday—and many used saved vacation days to take the entire week off— the global users supported by her team were still working. Her team took turns alternating who was off each holiday, so someone was always available. Alex had volunteered months ago to cover this week, and appreciated the quiet time it gave her to develop her plans for the new department.

She picked up the next resume. Both Alex and Frank were excited at the number of responses to her internal job posting for positions in the new PMO. When a company could promote from within, things generally worked well for all parties. Valued resources stayed within the company, and employees loved having new opportunities in a known environment. A direct bonus for her was that the most qualified applicants were spread out, giving them the desired geographical coverage for the PMO office.

The downside was she would spend a large part of her time in the next few months traveling for interviews. She was calling it her "world tour," and the company travel department was already working on an itinerary. Alex expected to have something back from them in the next two days.

Her cell phone rang, interrupting her thoughts. She smiled when Eddie's name popped up on the screen.

"Hey, Eddie. What's up?"

"Alex, your mother just showed up at your house. Were you expecting her? I ask because you normally give me a heads up and tell me it's okay to allow people in your place."

"*What?* Um, no, I wasn't expecting her. And yes, please let her inside. I'll call her and see what's going on. Thanks for letting me know. I appreciate you looking out for me."

"No problem, kiddo. Talk soon."

Alex disconnected with Eddie, but hesitated before calling her mother. Her parents lived 500 miles away, which meant either a nine-hour drive or an hour-plus airplane ride. Aside from that, Debra Tanner never showed up unannounced. She considered it rude and bad manners. Something was definitely up.

Alex reviewed her agenda for the day. She had no meetings scheduled, and everything on the to do list was waiting on someone else. She blocked off her calendar and forwarded her desk phone to her cell in case anything urgent arose, then gathered her stuff and left.

She arrived home in record time. *If only everyday traffic was as minimal as holiday traffic*, she thought as she pulled her laptop bag from the car. She took a steadying breath and mentally prepared as she walked toward her back door.

"Mom?" she called as she walked in the door.

"In the kitchen, dear."

Alex set her stuff on the desk in her living room, then

walked to the kitchen to give her mother a quick peck on the cheek. "What are you doing here? Is everything okay? Is Dad okay?"

"Yes, yes, everything's fine back home. I'm making tamales for dinner. Do you want red sauce or green?"

"Red. I didn't see your car in the carport. Did you fly in this morning? Also, you don't have to cook for me."

"I understand I don't have to cook, but I enjoy doing it. I flew in and took one of those rideshare thingies where they pick you up and drive you. A nice young man gave me a ride. I tipped him generously. He's in college and driving is how he pays for his tuition and books."

Alex laughed. While she couldn't believe her mom actually knew what ridesharing was, much less had used the service, it did not surprise her at all that her mother had learned everything about the driver during the ride.

"Mom, why are you here? And are you staying for Thanksgiving? What about Dad?"

Debra squared her shoulders and placed the wooden spoon she held in the spoon rest on the counter. "I'm working with our county agent this year and offered to meet with the Houston Livestock Show and Rodeo committee for our 4-H group, so that gave me an excuse to fly to Houston. I met with them this morning before driving here, by the way." She paused and cleared her throat before continuing, "But the reason I came in person instead of meeting them over the phone is to see you. I've been *reading* about you more than I've been talking to you on the phone. I decided that was crap and I needed to fix it."

Alex ducked her head and shifted her weight from one foot to the other. "Mom, I'm sorry. You're right, I haven't called as often as I should. It's been crazy at work—"

"No," Debra interrupted her, "I didn't say that to make

you feel guilty. I was explaining why I came. I want to have some mother-daughter time so we can enjoy each other and get to know each other again. We never talk like we used to, and I miss it." She picked up the spoon again and stirred the sauce. "I hope I didn't come at a bad time. I would have called, but I was afraid you'd blow me off again." Debra stared intently into the pan, her posture rigid as she waited for Alex's response.

Alex took in her mother's body language and sighed. "That's fair. I probably would have told you I'm too busy. But the truth is, now is a good time since the office is slow this week. And my friends have recently pointed out that I don't make enough time for me or the people in my life. So, yeah, you've come at a good time and I'm glad you're here."

Debra laid the spoon on the counter and pulled Alex in for a hug. She gripped her tight and Alex returned the hug, holding on until Debra moved away, wiping her eyes.

"Those onions get me every time."

They laughed together. Alex slipped off her jacket. "Let me go change and I'll help."

The two of them spent the afternoon getting caught up on everything they'd missed since they'd last talked. Debra shared the local town gossip and updates on various family members while Alex shared news from her friends whom Debra knew.

Alex explained the coming changes at her job with the new global department. Debra asked questions and commented on how impressed she was that Alex was in charge of such a large endeavor. Alex felt like her mom was listening to her for the first time when she talked about her career.

As Alex set the table for dinner that evening, Debra asked, "And what's going on with Mr. 'Hottest Man Ever?'"

Alex tightened her grip to avoid dropping the plate she held and swung around, her mouth agape.

"What?" Debra asked. "I told you I've read more about you than I've talked to you. What did you think I meant?"

"Right. Um, well, we're kind of dating. It's weird."

"Weird in what way?" Debra placed the tamale dish on the hot pad in the middle of the dining table.

They sat at the table and filled their plates while Alex contemplated the question. "He was flying to Houston for two weeks for business and I was flying home. We started talking and just hit it off. He's down-to-earth, intelligent, and funny. We hung out while he was in town. I like him."

Alex bit into a tamale and swallowed a drink of iced tea before continuing. "He's at a different place in his life than I am. His career is established, and he's looking to settle down. I'm still climbing my career ladder and have never considered a committed relationship."

"Why is that?" her mom interrupted her speech just as Alex warmed to the topic.

"Because I have things I want to accomplish."

"Why can't you do them with someone by your side?"

Alex stared at her for a second before answering. "Because they take too much away from you."

Debra's eyes narrowed. "What do you mean by that?"

Alex swallowed. "I don't want to give up my dreams to follow someone else's. I have my own dreams, and I refuse to give those up just to become someone's wife."

She lowered her gaze to the napkin she fiddled with in her lap and waited.

"Alex, look at me," her mom commanded.

Alex raised her eyes to meet Debra's gaze.

"Do you think that's what I did? Gave up my dream to follow your dad?"

"Yes. You wanted to be an artist, and you were—no, you *are* really good. But when you met Dad, you just quit. Threw everything away and became what he needed." Alex reached over and took her mom's hand. "I don't want to lose myself in someone else. I'm happy where I am."

"Oh, sweetie. I didn't give up my dreams. They morphed into something bigger. When I met your dad, my world expanded beyond the canvas. Instead of *painting* about things I wanted to see and do, I got to live those things. Running the ranch gave a purpose to my life that painting never did. Yes, I loved to paint, both then and now. But painting was always a hobby for me, not a life goal. I love my life. I'm in charge of the ranch, directing the menu, managing the help, keeping records of our stock. And I get to do all that with the man I love."

Alex watched her mom's expression soften as she spoke of her husband. "I always assumed you'd given up your dreams. That you'd put yourself aside to focus on Dad's vision."

Her mom snorted. "You think your dad came up with all those new ideas on how to promote the ranch? Or save money by contracting with local butchers? Your dad thinks like a scientist. He's all about crop rotation and breeding charts. He couldn't balance a budget if his life depended on it." Debra pointed her fork at Alex. "You got your business sense from me, young lady. And your flair for color." She waved the fork in a circle, indicating the living area.

Alex burst out laughing. She'd never thought of her mom as a businessperson. Debra smirked at her mirth. How was it that, with all her experience reading people, she'd completely misread her mom all these years?

"So, back to the movie star...?"

Alex cleared her throat. "Um, yeah. He wants a serious relationship."

"And you don't?"

"Well, I wasn't expecting it right now. And, geez, I can't see it working for so many reasons. First off, it's terrible timing. I'm ridiculously busy at work right now trying to get this department off the ground. And I'm fixin' to be traveling every month for the next year. I'll have so many miles racked up, the airlines will give me a parade when I enter the airport. They'll set up a room for me because I'll live there." Alex rolled her eyes toward the ceiling.

Her mom snorted as Alex intended with her overly dramatic delivery.

"Second, he's a movie star. What the hell do I know about show business? It's such a different world that I have nothing to relate it to. Mom, they follow him everywhere. Any privacy he has, he ferociously guards. So far, I've only encountered it a few times, but according to Fin, it's been light. The whole thing is bizarre."

"And? What else?" her mother asked.

"Aren't those enough? We can't even coordinate times to meet up because we are both so busy."

"How do you feel about him?" Debra asked, her tone soft and speculative.

Alex blew out a breath. "I like him. He's different from most men I've dated. Fin has a brain and uses it. He's compassionate and caring about people. And funny. He makes me laugh all the time. You know, the man does not have a celebrity-sized ego as you'd expect. He doesn't crave the spotlight. In fact, he runs from it. I would never have expected that from a movie star. I thought they were all attention-craving ego maniacs."

"And the sex?"

Alex sputtered and choked on the drink she had just taken. "What the hell, Mom?"

Her mother shrugged. "Answer the question," she ordered, before taking another bite.

Alex's mouth fell open as she regarded her mother. They never discussed these kinds of things. Ever. People always recounted that awkward moment when their parents tried to give them the sex talk. Alex had never had that moment. She'd grown up on a cattle ranch, where breeding techniques were part of the nightly dinner conversation. Tonight, in her twenty-ninth year of life, was the first time her mother had ever discussed sex with her. *Okay*, she thought, *you asked for it. Here we go.*

"Mom, the men I have had in my life have been one of two kinds: they stimulate my mind, or they stimulate my body. It's either one or the other. Fin does both." Alex nodded. "He's a panty-melter."

Alex watched her mother swallow hard. Triumph warred with guilt inside her.

"Well, okay then. And for the record, I knew he was a… a panty-melter." Debra's cheeks reddened. "But being good-looking and smooth with the ladies doesn't equate to mutual chemistry. You didn't like that Brad character your dad tried to hook you up with a while back, and he was pretty."

"Well, no, I'm not usually attracted to dim-witted assholes."

Her mom smirked. "He was a bit of an asshole, wasn't he? But he was good-looking."

"Yeah, ya know… it's not about the looks. Some of the most attractive men I've ever met have been average-looking, but the way they command the room and the confidence they have really catches my interest. Apparently, I'm intimidating, so a man has to be able to hold his own against me." Alex shrugged her shoulders.

"Don't I know it," her mom muttered.

"What?"

"You scared all the boys away when you were in high school, too. For a while we thought you were gay, but you were equally standoffish with girls. It took time for us to realize you were more interested in your activities than other people. I was afraid you'd be lonely, but you always had plenty of friends and seemed to be popular. Eventually we quit worrying about you."

"I never knew you did."

"I'm your mom. Parents always worry about their kids. They try not to let it show because they don't want their kids to worry. So, what are you doing about... what did you call him? Fin?"

Alex nodded. "We've created a shared travel calendar and are trying to find times where our paths cross and we can catch a moment together. It hasn't been easy, but we've found a weekend in December that looks promising. We're trying to coordinate a meetup in New York City."

"Oh, that sounds wonderful."

Alex told her mom stories from when Fin was in town while they finished dinner and cleaned up the table. It surprised her to learn her mom was an avid reader of the Hollywood tabloids and followed several celebrities online.

As the evening wore on, Alex's view of her mom changed. Instead of a mother bound to her husband and his path, she perceived her as a woman satisfied with her life. With this new insight, it was as if she was hanging out with a friend rather than a parent, and she relished the new take on their relationship.

Chapter 22

New York

ALEX FOLLOWED a fellow passenger down the jetway to the terminal. Their New York weekend was finally here. This was the first time she was actually visiting New York City rather than just passing through. She could hardly wait to see Fin. His landing time was earlier than hers, and he had arranged for someone to meet and escort her to their rendezvous point. As she passed through the doors to the terminal, she spotted a man in a suit holding a sign with "Alexis" on it. She grinned at the use of her full name and threaded through the crowd toward him.

Ted, as the man introduced himself, took her carry-on bag and led her across the terminal to a side door she never would have noticed on her own. Stepping through the door, they followed a long hallway, their steps muted on the plush carpeting. Eventually, Ted led her into an elegant room with various seating areas scattered throughout, and several ornate doors spaced along the walls. She assumed these led to the private suites Fin had mentioned.

Alex recognized Fin's figure from across the room. He handed over paperwork to the man standing near him and looked about the room. Fin's smile lit up as he noticed her coming his way. A calm warmth settled over her as she approached.

"Hi," she said as she came within talking distance.

"Hi, yourself." He wrapped his arms around her and lifted her off the ground in a giant hug. He pulled back and kissed her thoroughly, while letting her body slide down his until her feet touched the floor again.

She broke off the kiss with a laugh. "Miss me much?"

"Aye, lassie." Fin held on with one arm and took her bag from the porter with the other. "Thanks, Ted. Appreciate your help with fetching *mo ghràdh*."

"Hey, I can carry that." Alex reached for her bag.

"Och, no. I've got it. They'll be bringing your luggage along shortly, so you may need your hands for those."

Alex spotted two large suitcases beside him and raised an eyebrow. "No traveling light for you this time?"

Fin followed her gaze. "No, I'm leaving most of this stuff in Los Angeles. I didnae expect to be there this much, but since everything exploded, I need a semi-permanent place to stay. Addie has a cabana in her back-yard similar to Eddie's garage apartment, so I'm staying there for now." He shrugged. "Would you like to sit while we wait for your bags? I have a car service on standby, and we can walk straight from here to the car park without being seen. It's a similar setup to the one at Heathrow."

"Ms. Tanner?" a voice behind her spoke. Alex turned to find a uniformed woman standing with her suitcase beside her.

"Goodness, that was quick."

The woman smiled and nodded. "We aim to please."

Fin stepped up beside Alex and the woman stared, her

mouth dropping open. "Thanks, lass," he said and handed her a tip.

"Thank you, sir!" she responded crisply. Then broke all professional decorum by giggling and spinning away.

Alex and Fin looked at each other and laughed. "Seems like they'd be accustomed to coming in contact with celebrities," Alex observed.

"Aye. Perhaps she's new. Ready to go?"

"Absolutely!" she exclaimed. She couldn't stop grinning.

Half an hour later, they followed a porter to their suite on the fifty-fourth floor of the Mandarin Oriental Hotel. Alex walked in first and stopped, taking in the room's luxury. The focal point of the room was where the two floor-to-ceiling windows overlooking Central Park joined in the corner. A semi-circle couch faced the stunning view.

Fin gently nudged her further into the room, allowing the porter access to the bedroom off to their left, where he deposited their luggage. Alex followed and marveled at the second floor-to-ceiling view overlooking downtown Manhattan, while Fin thanked and tipped the man. As the door shut behind him, leaving them alone, she pivoted from the window to face Fin.

"My god, Fin, the view is breathtaking. When you told me you would arrange our accommodations, I didn't give it much thought, but... Is this how you usually travel?"

"Hardly. I go more subtle than this. We're only here for two nights, so I thought we'd indulge. I take it you like it?"

"It's fantastic. I've never seen anything like this." Alex wandered into the bath area and then back to the front room, inspecting the suite. "I've never stayed in a hotel room equipped with a guest bathroom. That's hilarious."

"Aye. I did some research, and many celebrities stay

here. I imagine they take meetings in the living area and the guest toilet allows them to host others in their room without compromising their private area."

"Oh. Well, that makes sense. We didn't really need a suite, though, did we?"

"No, but I thought we might spend lots of time here and the suites have a cozy dining area. That allows us the option to wander around like tourists or stay put the entire time and never leave."

"Nice. Who knew you were such a meticulous planner?" Alex walked back to Fin and ran her hands up his chest and around his neck. "I've missed you."

He bent his head and kissed her softly. "Aye, lass. It's been difficult. Those first two weeks with each other spoiled me, I suppose."

Alex's stomach picked that moment to rumble, and Fin laughed. "Hold that thought. We should get something to eat, aye? I'm hungry too. Do you wish to go out or order room service?"

"Let's go out. After sitting on a plane for hours, my legs could use a good stretch. I'm sure the concierge could direct us to a wonderful eating establishment around here."

"Sounds good."

Alex stuck her room card in her purse and slung it over her shoulder as they left the suite. They discovered the hotel was part of a large complex containing a variety of places to eat, and they didn't have to walk far at all.

While they ate, Fin told her what he'd read about the hotel and its amenities. When he mentioned the swimming pool, Alex was glad she had packed her swimsuit.

"So the spa is supposed to be top-notch. They have this treatment called a couple's escape where we could get special baths, then side-by-side massages and several other spa treatments. I was ready to sign us up for that until I real-ized it lasted for four hours."

"Wow. Four hours is a large dose of hands-on treat-ment." Alex smirked at her play on words.

"Bah-dump-bum." Fin mimicked the standard drum noise to acknowledge the joke. "Agreed. With our limited time here, it sounded a bit much. But," he emphasized, "we can get a couple's massage for an hour or ninety minutes if we want. And I believe they will do it in your room if you ask."

"Mmm, that sounds good. I love massages, and doing it that way doesn't bite in to our 'together time.' What else have you been scheduling for us?"

"That's it. I knew you liked massages, and frankly, I do too. And I assumed we'd be spending most of our time in the room, so I didn't really look for outside entertainment." He waggled his eyebrows at her, and she giggled.

"I've never come here as an ultimate destination. It's usually just a pass-through on my way to somewhere else. Honestly, Fin, I'm up for doing anything as long as we're doing it together."

He smiled and reached for her hand. "Aye, lass, me too."

As Fin predicted, they spent most of the weekend in their room. On the handful of occasions they left the premises, they encountered a few fans, but nothing resem-bling the frightful mob in Houston.

They discussed Fin's new movie, and he explained the overall process to her. She found it fascinating how much happened behind the scenes of a two-hour movie, and had many questions for him.

In return, Fin asked Alex about her progress with the new department. This extended trip to London was to interview potential candidates for the newly created project manager positions. She told him about the prospective candidates, their locations, and the variety of expertise they brought. She hoped to promote from within, but needed to make sure they all shared the same vision.

As Sunday morning dawned, their time together came to a close. As much as they wanted every possible minute together, they both had long flights waiting for them, and neither wanted to be too tired to function on Monday. While they packed, they discussed the immediate future.

"So I've rearranged my schedule for Christmas and am hoping we can wrangle some time together that week," Alex said as she zipped up her suitcase.

"That's fantastic." Fin grinned at her as he slipped on his shoes. "Why didn't you say anything earlier?"

"I was waiting for confirmation on one meeting reschedule and didn't want to jinx anything. I still need to coordinate with your assistant and make sure you're available."

He pulled her into an embrace. "Oh, I'll be available, love. Kathy knows you are a priority on my schedule."

He kissed her thoroughly, stopping when his phone vibrated. He glanced at it and the smile slid off his face. "Our car is here. It's time to go." She nodded and grabbed her bags.

The trip to the airport was quiet. They sat in the back-seat holding hands, each lost in their own thoughts. They arrived at the VIP lounge, completed the boarding process, then found an intimate corner where they could spend their last moments together in private.

As the time for Alex's flight grew nearer, her heart grew heavier. "I don't want to leave," she whispered.

"Neither do I. This weekend's been lovely. I look forward to when we don't have to be apart like this."

Alex met his eyes. "Do you imagine we'll ever reach that point? Neither of our schedules looks to slow down much over the next year." She slumped back in her seat, crossing her arms and harshly releasing the air in her lungs. "Times like this, it sounds impossible."

Fin reached over and pulled her arm toward him, moving his hand down until it clasped hers. "Hey. Aye, right now feels wretched. But the past two days have been incredible. Much higher on the good scale than on the bad scale, right?" He looked at Alex, waiting for a response. "Right?"

Alex nodded her head.

"Okay, that's what you have to remember. The highs. They make up for these lows. And we have video chat and phone calls, which help. Can you imagine living hundreds of years ago when none of this technology was available? People said goodbye to their loved ones forever, just for moving to another country. Or state, if you're American."

"Or to another town, if your state is the size of Texas." She smiled begrudgingly.

"Exactly. We'll be okay, *mo leannan*." Fin brought her hand to his lips and kissed it.

"I don't think you've ever told me what that one means."

"We will be okay, my sweetheart," Fin reiterated.

Alex leaned over and kissed him properly. He pulled her close, deepening the kiss. A polite cough interrupted them, and Alex pulled away, straightening her shirt. She glanced at the uniformed gentleman standing in front of them, and her cheeks heated at his knowing expression.

"Madam, your flight is boarding now. May I escort you to the gate?"

"Of course. I'm sorry."

"No need to apologize, miss. That's what I'm here for."

Fin stood with her and hugged her tight one last time. "Be safe," he whispered in her ear, "call me when you land."

She gave him a hard kiss goodbye, hoisted her carry-on over her shoulder, and followed the porter without looking back.

Chapter 23

The Story Breaks

T WO WEEKS LATER...

Fin halted in the middle of a sit-up, wiped the sweat from his brow, and answered his cell phone. Addie rarely called this early in the morning, so seeing her name pop up on the display was a surprise.

"Morning," he greeted her.

"Heads up, Fin. Cole's story published today."

"Is it bad?"

When she hesitated, he prompted, "How bad, Addie?"

"It really depends on your viewpoint. It's surprisingly flattering. Instead of an ugly exposé as we expected, the article reads more like a love story. It chronicles your life from university to today." Fin waited while Addie paused, drinking what he assumed was her morning coffee. "She talks about Fiona and Rodney."

Fin dragged a hand through his hair, then rubbed his neck. "And Alex?"

Addie continued, "Oh, yeah, she's in there. There's a surprising amount of personal information about her. Cole did her homework. Did you know Alex was a barrel-racing champion when she was twelve years old?"

"Jesus."

"Something else… It's not in her usual rag. It's in *The New York Times*. And she included photos of you two in both Houston and New York… lovey-dovey kind of photos."

"*Feckin' bawbags.*" Fin rubbed his face with his towel. "Send me the link? I want to read it, then warn Alex. She'll go *aff her heid.*" He growled as another thought occurred to him. "Shit, *The New York Times* means wider distribution, right?"

"Yes. This will get international coverage. There. I just sent it," Addie said, as his phone pinged. "Fin, aside from the personal stuff, it's not a bad article. She painted you in a rather positive light. It's… well, it's weird."

"I think that's Alex's doing."

"Explain."

"Cole cornered Alex in the toilets one night. Alex relayed the exchange to me. Apparently, they discussed the challenges of women working in a man's world. When she told me, I dismissed it as something Alex misinterpreted. But, based on what you're saying, I'm wondering… Alex has a way with people. I've seen it. She could calm a rabid dog. Anyway, let me read the article and call her, then I'll get back to you."

"Sounds good."

"Addie," Fin caught her before she hung up, "thanks for the heads up. I appreciate you."

"No problem, Fin-Fin. Now go."

Fin disconnected and pulled up the article to read it. Addie was right. The story portrayed him favorably. And was unexpectedly factual, unlike other pieces published by Miranda Cole. He'd never seen her outright lie about him,

but she often hinted, suggested, and speculated in her arti-
cles. This one didn't. It appeared to be more biographical in
nature. She even mentioned the reporter chasing Fiona and
the investigation that had followed, although she didn't
reveal that *she* was the reporter involved.

The details concerning Alex bothered him, though. He
read through, learning things about his lover she hadn't
shared. It gave information about her hometown and the
names of her parents. Fin cringed. He imagined her reaction would be volatile, at minimum.

They had carved out time for the upcoming holidays,
and she planned to fly to Los Angeles to spend time with
him next week. If Cole had waited one week to publish, he
and Alex would have been together when the story broke.

He bookmarked the link and called Alex's number. He
wanted to give her the heads up that Addie gave him.

Alex's phone vibrated in her pocket as she made a note
on the candidate's resume. She absently switched off the
ringer as she moved to the next question on her list.

This was her last individual interview. Afterward, she
had a group meeting scheduled for a roundtable discussion
with all the candidates about their expectations for the
PMO. Then she was done.

The trip had gone well so far, which was encouraging.
At Frank's suggestion, rather than flying all over to meet
everyone, she'd arranged for the applicants to come to the
centrally located London office. By doing so, her trip was
condensed into two weeks, instead of months as she'd originally planned. Most of those she met were excellent
prospects for the new team. The guy from the Asian sales

group surprised her, and the one from the Norwegian office seemed a bit too superior in his attitude. She would know more about how well they played together after the upcoming group meeting.

Alex wrapped up the interview and headed to the break room. She had a fifteen-minute break to use the restroom, refresh her drink, and situate herself in the larger conference room. Her phone showed a missed call from Fin. Alex intended to call him back, but when she walked into the conference room, everyone was already gathered and waiting for her. She sent him a quick text that she was in a meeting and would call later.

"Okay, thanks everyone." Alex addressed both the people in the room and those on the big screen whom she'd met with last week. "I appreciate y'all taking time from your schedule to fly over and meet with me. I'm excited to work on the plans. The feedback from the past two weeks will help tremendously. The next step is to coordinate with management on rounding out the team. With the holidays coming up, you probably won't hear back from me until after the break. Safe travels." Alex wrapped up the meeting and gathered up her things.

"Alex." She looked up at Troy, the area sales manager from the Asia/Pacific region. "I wanted to thank you again for giving me a chance. My boss didn't understand, and I was afraid I'd be given the boot before I could apply."

"No problem, Troy. I will admit that a resume coming from the sales division surprised me, but your experience is unique, and you certainly have solid ideas around setting up new offices. That's an area that needs attention. You flying home tonight?"

He nodded and extended his hand. "Yes, I need to get back and it's a long flight. Apologies for missing dinner later. Talk to you soon?"

"Definitely." She shook his hand and followed him out of the room.

As she walked back through the building to the visitor's office, she noticed the quiet buzz going around. Every person whose gaze she met looked away as soon as she made eye contact. Okay, something was up.

She found Ben and Paul, her primary contacts in the London office, waiting in her temporary work space. "Hello, boys. What's up?" she asked as she laid her stuff down.

Ben took the lead. "So, Alex... you're entirely circumspect regarding your personal life. So guarded in fact, that no one here knew you even had a personal life. We just assumed you worked all the time. And now we learn that you're dating Scotland's own superstar."

Alex froze. "Wh-what are you talking about?"

"Finley McAlister, of course. Your fiancé?" Paul added.

"No, it didn't say he was her fiancé, just that they were madly in love," Ben chided as he scrolled on his tablet.

"What. Are. You. Talking. About," Alex repeated through clenched teeth.

"Oh, you haven't seen it? *The New York Times* published an article about you and the 'Hottest Man Ever.' Page one of the entertainment section." Ben handed her the tablet.

Alex read the title and groaned. "Scotland's Favored Son Finds Love" was displayed in large text on the screen. She scanned through the feature, stopping short when she read her name.

"Oh, my god." The article listed details about her parents, her hometown, and even her place of work. "Oh, come on."

Ben and Paul perked up. "You mean it's true?" Ben's voice squeaked on the last word.

Alex ignored him and kept reading. Everything was out there. Even the time they'd spent in Galveston. She sank into the chair behind her desk.

Paul commented to Ben, "They have pictures, don't they?"

"I assumed they doctored them."

"Shut up," Alex told them. They did indeed have pictures. Some she'd seen, but a few new ones were mixed in. She thought they'd been inconspicuous in New York. Ben's excited voice finally penetrated Alex's absorption in the article, and she looked up to find several folks crammed around her doorway, all eyes focused on her.

She handed Ben's tablet back to him and asked him to please send her the link to the article. She clamped her lips together and puffed out her cheeks as she gazed back at the people looking expectantly toward her.

"Well, shit. Okay, yes, I'm dating Finley McAlister. Happy?"

Alex covered her ears at the loud cheers that rose around the office. "Seriously, guys?"

The cheering died down as the barrage of questions hit her: What's he like? How long have you been seeing him? Are you getting married?

She made a motion with her hands for them to quiet down. "Guys, let me finish up here and then let's get a drink. We were planning on dinner tonight. Should we meet at the pub earlier than we planned?"

"Excellent idea," an authoritative voice from the back

called out. Everyone scrambled back to their desks as the director of finance for the eastern hemisphere walked into her office with a pink newspaper tucked up under his arm.

"Oh my god, don't tell me it's in the *Financial Times* as well."

One side of Matthew's mouth rose. "It's never dull when you're in town, Alex. Usually it's because you're bringing me extra work or happy results of extra work. This is the first time it's ever been your personal life that's spicing things up." He laid down the paper and flipped to the life and arts section, where the British-based paper referenced and summarized the article from the U.S. paper.

Alex put her head down on her desk. Not only was Matthew Richards the second highest ranking man in the financial department, he was also a perfect representation of the polite English gentleman. And *he* was giving her grief over this! Her colleagues at home would be ten times worse. They weren't so polite.

"Oh, come now. Just taking the piss." She raised her head to see Matthew examining her desk. "Are you done for the day?"

"Well, I'd planned to write up some summary thoughts, but there's no way I'll be able to focus after this. Are you ready to leave?"

Matthew had been giving her a lift every day since he lived close to her hotel. He typically worked late, which worked fine for her, but the briefcase in his hand signaled he was ready to depart early today.

"Originally, I had assumed we would stay later this evening because of the planned goodbye dinner. However, I expect after this," he nodded at the newspaper, "you're ready to head to the pub."

Alex laughed and nodded vigorously. "Yes, I am. If you're ready, I am too. Meet you up front in five minutes?"

"Lovely." Matthew looked out the window behind her. "Lucky for us, the pub is so close. We should enjoy it while we can." Before Alex could ask what he meant, he continued, "I imagine our guest count for the pub just went up considerably. Still planning to pick up the tab?"

Alex groaned and rolled her neck. "I guess I better put a limit on drinks. But we booked a reservation at the restaurant. We should enforce that limit."

"Agree. I'll let Ben know. See you in the car park in five."

"Yep."

She snatched Matthew's paper from the desk and shoved it into her bag, along with her laptop and other personal items. Talk about a roller coaster ride of emotions. From top of the world, can't do anything wrong, to what the hell just happened? She'd worked so hard to change the way men in this company viewed her... to forget she was a tall, leggy blonde and see her as a colleague who was strictly business. All her efforts over the years to make her personal life invisible had just exploded with one headline, making her feel completely exposed and vulnerable.

Alex picked up her phone and listened to Fin's voicemail warning her about Cole's feature. She shook her head, glad she hadn't seen the article prior to her last meeting, because she wasn't sure she could have concentrated otherwise. She was no longer looking forward to tonight's get together.

Chapter 24

Madness

ALEX TRUDGED THROUGH THE AIRPORT, still wearing her sunglasses. She'd also altered her appearance by wrapping her neck scarf higher on her face, rather than loose around her neck as she usually did.

A window display caught her eye and she paused. She'd never been a hat person, but the hats reminded her of Fin's efforts to go unnoticed. She entered the fashion store with a mission. After yesterday's events, another layer of protection wouldn't hurt.

The previous evening had been both relaxing and exhausting. Her coworkers had accepted the celebrity status of her relationship with aplomb. They'd given her a hard time and made jokes about her fame while still talking to her as if nothing had changed. If she were honest with herself, the evening had been a great relationship-building experience and provided her with an opportunity to learn more about her potential new team members far better than any stilted company dinner would have. But despite the camaraderie, she was still reeling from the deep dive into her personal life. It felt so invasive.

This morning had been worse. Upon exiting the taxi, a mob of reporters had bombarded her with cameras flashing and an onslaught of questions. They ranged from her life in Texas to intimate questions about her relationship with Fin, which embarrassed her immensely. She knew without a doubt she looked like a startled fish with her eyes wide and mouth agape.

She sensed someone approaching as she perused the different models of hats and stiffened at the notion of facing another reporter.

"Are you looking for anything in particular?"

Alex relaxed as she considered the saleslady. *I'm already paranoid and this is only the beginning*, she thought.

"Yes, thank you. I need something that hides my face." Alex stopped short as she realized how blunt that sounded. "I find myself suddenly in the spotlight and am seeking a deterrent," she offered as an explanation. "Or better yet, a shield." She shrugged at the woman.

"Ah, yes. You may be surprised at how many people stop in here for precisely that reason. How about this one? It's a trilby. You can pull the brim down as needed. And this model is collapsible for traveling." She reached for a dark gray hat that resembled a fedora, except with a smaller brim. "It's versatile and you can wear it with both casual and more formal outfits. This style will look good with your hair."

Alex tried on the hat and examined herself in the mirror. The style was cute, and she could see wearing it around town, but the brim didn't seem to cover her face as much as she wanted. She put her sunglasses back on.

"Oh, that's better," she said, surprised by the difference they made together. Alex removed her glasses and turned to the saleswoman.

"Okay, I like this one. What is that one called?" She

pointed to a hat that reminded her of movies set in the 1920s.

"That's a cloche," the woman said as she reached for it. "This color will look lovely on you. This one also collapses for travel."

Alex exchanged the trilby for the cloche, then donned the purplish-blue hat that fit close to her head. The style wasn't one she would normally consider, but something about the cloche appealed to her.

"Ooh, that one really brings out your eyes."

Alex frowned. "I'm trying to disappear, not attract attention." She donned her shades again and rotated her head back and forth. "Better."

She handed the second hat to the woman. "I'll take both. And I don't need a bag. I'll wear the cloche and put the trilby in my carry-on. Can you remove the tags for me, please?"

Having made her purchases and now outfitted with a better disguise, Alex made her way through the airport to her gate. No one made a fuss over her, so either her disguise worked, or she had overreacted by dressing up all cloak-and-dagger like. Once she boarded the plane, she removed her accessories and settled down for the long flight home.

ALEX TURNED her phone on once the plane landed in Houston. She had several missed calls, a few texts, and several voicemails from her mother and father. While the plane taxied to the gate, she listened to the frantic messages. The press had found her family. Alex groaned and buried her face in her hand.

"Is everything okay?" the lady next to her asked.

Alex reassured the woman she was fine, just beleaguered by things piling up while her phone was off. Once the doors opened, she collected her things and made her way into the terminal, looking for a quiet corner to call her parents.

Her mom answered on the first ring, her voice shaking, yet abrupt at the same time. "Alex, are you okay?"

Alex's brow furrowed in confusion. She couldn't tell if her mother was scared or angry. "I'm fine. Are you okay? What's going on?"

"Oh, we're fine, but these overbearing reporters won't leave us alone. We figured out afterward what was going on, but we were confused and upset when they first mobbed us."

The speaker overhead announced the boarding status for a flight in the terminal.

"Alexis, where are you? The background is noisy."

"I'm in an airport. I've been on a plane for ten hours and just landed. What happened?" Alex closed her eyes and pinched the bridge of her nose with her free hand.

Debra inhaled sharply. "Okay, let me start over. A reporter approached your dad in town asking a bunch of questions about you, and Dad reacted as you'd expect. Told him to go jump in a lake and mind his own blankety-blank business."

Alex chuckled at her mom's way of cursing and at the image of her dad in "grumpy" mode.

"Yes, well," Debra continued, "when he arrived home, more of them were on our front lawn. The nerve! I was out back in the garden, so I didn't realize they were there. They were shouting at him. He ignored them and came inside to call Bill."

"Who's Bill?" Alex interrupted her mom.

"Bill is the sheriff, dear. Anyway, your father called the sheriff who came and chased them away, but they kept coming back. Or maybe new ones showed up. Either way, Bill made them move off the property and back to the highway. Some are still there, if you can believe that. Hold on, sweetie." Shuffling noises came across the phone and her mom's next words were muffled. "I'm talking to her now, Tom." Another scraping noise came across the phone. "Okay, I'm back. Are you still there?"

"Yes. Mom, are you guys okay?"

"Yes, we're fine now. But we were so confused until we saw the news. Some breaking story came out about you and Finley. The local station picked it up and I'm fairly certain we've been on TV. What do we do?"

"What do you mean?"

"I mean, what do you want us to do? How should we handle it?"

"I have no clue. I'm barely handling it myself. Oh, and I bought a freaking hat. I am wearing a hat and sunglasses *inside* the airport." Alex shook her head and steadied her breathing. "I guess for now, keep doing what you're doing, and I'll check with Fin and his people to see if they have tips for dealing with this."

"Okay. Don't let those vultures bully you, Alex."

Alex smiled. "I never do, Mom."

"If you can get past the invasion of privacy issue, the whole thing is rather exciting. We're suddenly famous! The girls at my bridge club will be so jealous."

"Hmm, speaking of... maybe watch what you say. You never know when a stranger is listening or when someone else will pass on what they think is a juicy piece of gossip."

Her mom snorted. "It's not like you've shared much about your personal life anyway, Alex. But I take your point. You be careful too, sweetie. Oh, lord, something crashed in the garage. I better check on your dad."

"Okay. Talk later."

"Bye-bye."

Alex sat quietly for a moment, taking stock and shoring up her defenses. Hopefully, she'd made a big deal out of nothing and nobody would be waiting for her in the baggage area. *Okay, girl, you got this*, she told herself.

She did not have it. Not in any way, shape, or form. As soon as she passed through security and down to baggage claim, they hounded her. Luckily, the call to her mom had allowed enough time for her suitcase to make it to the conveyor belt. Alex seized the bag and walked away without ever slowing down. She managed to catch a crowded elevator where she aggressively blocked anyone from boarding with her luggage bag. She beamed a big fake Southern smile at the stymied photographers and was rewarded with several flashes going off in her face. Once the doors closed, she moved to the side and shrugged to her fellow passengers, who watched her with mouths open.

She walked to her car without incident and drove home, slowing down as she approached a line of cars parked along her street. Sure enough, as she neared her duplex, she saw people congregating in the driveway.

"For heaven's sake!" she exclaimed. "They found my home?"

Alex drove past and turned at the corner before parking a few blocks away and calling Eddie. She listened as he told her how they had shown up, what he and Gabe had done to discourage them, and how her next-door neighbors, also Eddie's tenants, had complained.

She relayed how her parents had called the authorities to make them leave and advised Eddie to do the same. As she talked, the queasiness in her stomach grew. She realized she hadn't eaten in a while and told him she planned to grab a bite to eat and would call back before coming home. Hopefully, the police would dispel the crowd before then and food would settle her stomach. She disconnected the call and drove to her favorite diner for some home style cooking. Nothing like comfort food to settle a nervous stomach.

By the time she pulled into the carport an hour later, most of the reporters had left. The few who remained sat in their cars or vans along the street and off the property. Eddie came out and helped her carry everything in. Alex set the carryout containers of chicken and dumplings she'd brought home for him and Gabe on the counter and kicked off her shoes. She walked to the living area and fell backwards onto her couch.

"How bad was it? Am I in trouble?"

"Well, the last two days were definitely atypical. And, no, you're not in trouble. However, I suggest you close your curtains tonight as a few of those vultures are still there." Eddie walked to each window as he spoke, pulling her blinds closed. "And double-check your doors just to be safe."

"Really? I mean, I always lock them, but you think a reporter would be so bold?"

"You never know. And why take that chance?" Eddie perched in the side chair. "How are you holding up?"

"I'm freaking out. I'm not sure all this is worth it. Does that make me a horrible person?"

"No, it makes you a normal person. Finley's had years to become used to this. You've had days. They will disappear once there's a new lead story. Just you watch."

"Can it come soon?" Felix jumped up on the couch and rubbed his head against her, demanding attention.

Eddie made soothing noises and made his way to the kitchen. "Listen, you take the rest of the day to recuperate. Take a nap, soak in the tub, drink wine, read... whatever you normally do to destress. No TV and no social media." He shook his finger at her before grabbing the doggy bags from the counter. "Thanks for this, darling. Never tell him I said this because I love Gabe's hoity-toity cuisine, but sometimes you need the basics."

He gave her an air kiss and disappeared down the hallway. The click of the lock being engaged echoed back to her and Alex silently thanked him for locking her in. She lay where she was and pet Felix until she drifted to sleep.

ALEX DROVE to work bleary-eyed on Monday morning. She and Fin had played phone tag all weekend, leaving voice mails and short "I'll get back to you" texts. It was as if the universe had conspired against them. Eventually, she gave up and spent most of her time doing exactly what Eddie told her not to do, hunkered inside reading and watching the entertainment news. She and Fin were everywhere. New photos of him in Los Angeles had popped up, plus a couple of her at the London airport, but nothing else afterward. The reporters at her house had thinned, appearing to give up on catching her.

She couldn't express the violation she felt at having her life displayed like that. As much as she enjoyed being with Fin, she wasn't sure anything was worth this upheaval. She would weigh it heavily this week when she visited him in Los Angeles. She had been looking forward to meeting Fin's older brother and his family, but none of that seemed important anymore. All the positivity she'd felt about the ability to have an actual relationship seemed to have evaporated over one weekend.

As she pulled into the garage at work, the number of cars in the parking lot surprised her. She'd expected the number of people at the office to be low, with everyone using vacation time this week to supplement the time off for the Christmas holidays. Alex shrugged it off. Perhaps the other companies in the building weren't as lenient with their holiday schedules.

She grabbed her computer bag and headed up the back stairwell. Constant travel made it hard to maintain a regular workout schedule, and one way she stayed in shape was to take the stairs to her ninth-floor office. The stairwell from the garage conveniently opened in the hallway close to where her team was located. She used her keycard to exit the stairwell and walked toward her office.

"Alex!"

Alex had been reviewing her to-do list in her head and failed to notice the crowd of people outside her office door. Sam's call brought even more people into the hallway.

"Hey, Sam. What's up?"

"You came in the back way?" he asked, nodding at the stairwell behind her.

"Yeah, same as I always do." She raised an eyebrow at him. He was acting weird. They all were. Then it hit her. They'd seen the story. Alex sighed. "You read the article."

"Well, yes, but more to the point, I waded through the reporters in the front lobby."

Alex stopped walking. "What? You're kidding me."

The crowd standing in the hallway all shook their heads no.

She hung her head and closed her eyes, collecting herself. "Okay. Let me set down my stuff and I'll find out what's happening and what I can do about it."

After dumping her things on her desk, she extracted the folder with all the HR paperwork for Frank to review. Might as well deliver it before she freaked out on everyone.

Alex stepped into her boss' office. "Frank, I completed the paperwork needed to fill the PMO positions. I've also typed up my thoughts on each candidate and why they do or do not meet our requirements. You can let me know if you disagree with anything."

"Alex. Hello to you too. Have you seen our lobby?"

Alex grimaced. "Sorry. Sam told me what was going on and I'm headed there next. Has anyone called security yet? Because that's my next step if I can't get them to leave with a simple request."

"I don't know. It's not quite 8 a.m., so most folks aren't here yet. How did you miss them coming in?"

"I take the stairs."

Frank gaped at her. "Every day?"

"Yes, it helps me stay in shape."

Frank raised his eyebrows but didn't comment further on the topic. "Okay. Do you want help?"

Alex shook her head no. Frank was an authority figure at their company but was definitely a conflict avoider type of guy. As much as she appreciated his offer, he wouldn't be much help if things got ugly.

"No, I'll handle it. Thanks, though."

Alex strode to the IT section of the office and found who she wanted. Jack was a quiet, unassuming man packaged in a professional football player's body. She needed his size and fierce looks.

"Jack, can you walk with me? I need to address a

problem in the lobby and could use your brawn standing behind me."

The systems admin sat back from his keyboard. "Are you expecting trouble?"

"No, but I prefer having the threat of an ass-kicking looming behind me when I tell them all to go to hell." She grinned at him, knowing he would love the bluff.

"I'm in. Need anyone else? I think the server team came in early today."

"Nah, we should be okay. I'm calling security before we talk to them."

"Well, okay then. Let's do it." Alex winced as Jack rubbed his hands together in eager anticipation.

She used his desk phone to call building security and brief them on the situation. The man who answered informed her someone had called earlier about the problem and they were already on their way up. She thanked him and hung up.

"Here we go." She turned toward the lobby. Alex clenched her fists to hide her shaking hands as she walked down the hallway, Jack following close behind. She was normally calm as ice during a crisis and had handled emotional situations similar to this before. But those were never about her. She was a neutral party in those circumstances, and this felt distinctly different.

She stopped in her tracks at the sheer number of people packed into their lobby. Floor-to-ceiling glass walls separated the lobby from the interior of the office, and the glass doors required a key card to open. The space was a temporary waiting area for visitors and had room to accommodate up to seven or eight people comfortably. Right now, reporters, camera crews, and photographers packed the anteroom. Alex looked at Jack, whose mouth hung open.

"There must be twenty people jammed in that room!" she said.

"Maybe thirty," Jack added.

"For fuck's sake," she muttered before she could help herself. She cringed and mouthed an apology to Jack for her unprofessional language. "Thank goodness for the key cards to keep them corralled." Alex squared her shoulders and marched forward.

A barrage of flashes went off as she and Jack entered the lobby and several people shouted her name.

Alex stood silently, her hands folded in front of her, until they quieted. She looked every person in the face before speaking.

"This is a place of business. This is not an entertainment venue or a Hollywood premiere. Kindly leave the premises on your own or we will have you escorted out by security. Failing that, we will call the police and have you arrested for trespassing. Thank you."

The crowd fired off questions, and Alex crossed her arms refusing to speak. As if she'd planned it, one of the two elevators dinged, and two security officers stepped off. Once the security team had things under control, she and Jack left the lobby and walked back inside.

"Thank you, Jack. Sorry for using you like that, but sometimes your menacing linebacker look comes in handy."

Jack chuckled, but put a hand on her arm to stop her. "Hey, if you want me to escort you to your car when you leave, give me a call, okay?"

She patted his hand and thanked him for the offer. They separated at the corner and she headed to the executive wing. She found Frank in Jeff's office where he was updating the CEO on the lobby situation. Jeff typically arrived early, so he'd likely missed the spectacle.

Normally, she would have flopped in one of the visitor's chairs and boldly asked why the hell they were talking about her behind her back, but not today. Right now, she felt like a fragile dandelion that would break apart and drift away at the slightest breeze.

"You okay?" Jeff asked.

"To be determined," she replied, then addressed Frank, "I'm scheduled to be off this week starting tomorrow, but I'm thinking of bailing now, if that's okay. I intended to meet with you today to discuss the interviews, but I'm not sure my head's in the right place at the moment. Can you look over what I gave you and email me?"

They both looked at her with such concern that tears threatened. She glanced away. *Get it together, Alex.*

"Of course. I'll send you my thoughts before I leave today, and we can compare notes via email throughout the week as planned."

She tried to answer, but her voice cracked. She cleared her throat. "Okay. I'm gonna grab my stuff and bail. Thanks."

Jeff stopped her. "Let's get you an escort in case those assholes didn't leave." He picked up his phone to call someone.

"No, really, it's okay. I came in from the garage stairwell and wasn't aware they were here until Sam told me. I'll leave the same way."

Jeff opened his mouth to speak, but Alex cut him off. "Really, Jeff. I... I don't want to lose my cool in front of anyone. Please. I'll sneak out the back and be fine."

"If you're sure..." He reluctantly put the handset back in its cradle.

"I am. And thanks. See you guys after the break." Alex bolted.

She updated her team and left as fast as possible. The tears began once she got in her car and she couldn't stop them. She noticed a security guard observing her and realized Jeff had sent someone to check on her despite her protests. That only made her cry harder.

As she drove home, all she could think about was the media besieging her place of work. This was the second time within a matter of days that her professional environment had been disrupted by personal matters. For her entire career, she'd fought to keep those two aspects of her life separate in order to prove she could do the job. Now, her personal life was spinning out of control and taking everything else with it. Her carefully constructed walls separating the two worlds were crumbling.

I can't do this, she thought.

ONCE HOME, Alex stripped off her work clothes, washed her face, and changed into her favorite pair of jeans and a soft, long-sleeved tee. She clicked on the TV in the living room for background noise while packing her bag for the trip to Los Angeles. As she threw a couple of outfits on the bed, she caught her name mentioned in the other room and wandered out to listen. Footage from this morning in her office filled the screen as the local news anchor described the scene.

"C'mon! *Really?* Freakin' vultures." Alex couldn't believe they had the story on the air so quickly. "Why is this news?"

She sat down hard and reviewed the past month in her head. She could think of half a dozen times where she'd left work early or rearranged meetings to accommodate her relationship with Fin. How many meetings had she been late for or unprepared for because she'd spent a little too long on the phone with him? She'd begged off a few gatherings with friends because she'd scheduled a phone call with him. She must be starstruck. That's the only excuse for letting her life derail like this.

This is bullshit, she told herself, anger replacing the helplessness she'd been fighting all day. After all these years of telling herself that she would not sacrifice her career or her goals for a man, she had done exactly that. Before Fin, she never would have been sloppy with meetings, let deadlines slide, or rearranged her schedule for some private time with a man. She was done with this.

Alex opened her laptop and looked up flights for West Texas. She found a flight later this afternoon that would put her at her parents' house before supper. She purchased the ticket, then called her mom to tell her she was coming home for the holidays after all. Eddie and Gabe had already planned to care for Felix while she was away, so she let them know the cat needed their attention a day earlier.

Her next call needed to be to Fin. She set a kettle on to make a cup of tea and went to repack. Christmas in West Texas required a vastly different wardrobe than sunny Los Angeles. After adjusting her packed items and settling down with her cup of tea, Alex punched in his number.

Fin set down his phone in shock. Alex wasn't coming.

They had been so excited they were able to find time together over the holidays. Fin had invited his family to join them. His parents couldn't make the trip, but Fin's brother had taken him up on the offer and his family would arrive tomorrow. Fin could hardly wait to introduce Ethan to Alex.

But she wasn't coming. Not only was she not coming, she didn't want to see him anymore. She wasn't up for "all this madness." According to Alex, his life was a madhouse and didn't fit in with her life plans. She needed to focus on her career and "the Hollywood bullshit" didn't work for her.

He sat still, replaying the conversation in his head, letting her words wash over him.

Sometime later, Fin realized he was sitting in the dark. The sun had set. He stood up, stiff from sitting still for so long, and moved toward the bar, where he had a bottle of superb Scottish whisky waiting for him.

Chapter 25

Licking Wounds

FIN HAD ARRANGED for a car to pick up Ethan and his family at the airport while he worked on tidying up and getting the bungalow ready for overnight guests. Addie referred to it as her cabana, but in actuality, the building was a small house complete with two bedrooms, two baths, a modern kitchen, and a roomy living area. Earlier that morning, Fin put fresh sheets on both the sofa bed in the living room and the bed in the second bedroom. He assumed Ethan and his wife, Moira, would take the bedroom and the two girls would sleep on the sofa bed, but he would leave the sleeping arrangements up to them.

The intercom chimed as Fin put away the last of the groceries he'd purchased for the week. He confirmed the visitors were his family and hit the button to open the front gate. On his way to greet them, he picked up the garbage bag sitting on the porch, the empty bottles inside clinking together, reminding him of last night's binge. Fin dropped it in Addie's bins as he walked to the front of her house. They didn't need to see evidence of the hot mess he'd been last night.

Fin came around the corner as his brother and his sister-in-law attended to his nieces in the backseat. The two little girls exploded from the car as soon as their parents unbuckled them from their seats and raced to him. "Uncle Fin! Uncle Fin!" they cried. He grunted as they almost barreled him over with their hugs. He squatted to their eye-level and gave them the once-over. Shaylee, the oldest at seven years, was a miniature version of her mother, her sky-blue eyes framed by long, dark lashes that matched her hair. Tara, the five-year-old, had the coloring of her father. She had the same blue eyes, but her hair was a light sandy color somewhere between brown and blond.

"Who are these wee lasses you've brought, Ethan? They are far too grown up to be my nieces!" As expected, the girls burst into giggles and shouted their names to him.

The driver finished unloading their bags, and Fin pulled out his wallet to tip the guy. "Och, you don't have to do that, lad. I can take care of it," Ethan protested.

"Let me. I've been holing up my money for so long, I'm delighted to spend it on my family." Fin shrugged him off and thanked the driver.

He hugged Moira and kissed her cheek, then hugged his brother. Ethan thumped him on the back a few times for good measure.

"It's fantastic to see you all, Ethan." Fin's eyes filled with tears and he was thankful for the girls clamoring at his feet, drawing attention away from his emotional state. "Let's get everyone settled inside."

Moira looked up at Addie's house. "Is this yer house, Finley?"

Fin followed her gaze to Addie's spacious Spanish-style home. "No, it belongs to a friend. It's far too extravagant for me. She has a guest house around back where we'll be staying. If it's too tight for your comfort, there's a decent hotel I can put you up at not too far from here."

He selected the largest suitcase and walked them around back. When the girls caught sight of the large pool, they bounced up and down, talking over each other, asking Fin if they could swim. He reassured them that swimming was on the schedule this week. This winter was warmer than normal, so the water wasn't too cold. Although, he suspected they would have braved cooler temperatures regardless of the weather.

While Moira busied herself with unpacking their suitcases, Shaylee and Tara investigated everything in the cottage. After declaring the place acceptable, the girls settled down at the kitchen bar after Ethan set them up with juice and a snack.

"So...?" Ethan eyeballed him over the water bottle he held. Fin raised a hand and stopped him before he could speak and pointed at the girls.

"Right, then. Topic for later."

"Thanks." Fin rubbed the back of his neck and looked away. "Plans changed without warning, so it's only us. We'll talk later. Are you guys tired?"

"Not yet, but I'm sure it's coming. We encouraged the lasses to sleep on the flight, but they were too excited. None of us got much rest." He watched his daughters comparing their juice boxes. "I suspect the crash will come within the hour."

When Moira joined them, Fin ushered them toward the living room where they could sit and visit. The couple brought him up to date on family happenings and he answered their questions about his life. They astutely avoided questions concerning Alex, although he knew they had to be bursting with curiosity, especially since he had made such a big deal about them meeting her.

Soon after getting comfortable on the couch, the girls' eyes drooped. Moira interrupted the conversation, saying they all needed a nap and ushered them into the bedroom, closing the door behind her.

Once the girls left, Fin asked Ethan if he wanted to go sit outside. He expected his brother would enjoy the balmy eighty-degree weather compared to the forty-five degrees he'd just come from. Fin pulled two beers from the refrigerator and led the way.

"The grounds are beautiful. Kind of posh too," Ethan observed.

"Yes, Addie entertains often and enjoys having a space for people to move around and feel comfortable."

"Addie is your agent?"

"Aye. And my best friend."

"I could nae believe it when you told me to pack swimsuits."

Fin laughed. "I ken how odd that must have sounded. But it's a heated pool, so even if the weather turns cooler, swimming is still an option."

"Nice." Ethan tipped his beer back for a long pull. "So... We read the article about you and Alex. I expected her to be here before us?"

Fin slumped further into his seat. "Aye. She canceled at the last minute."

When Fin offered nothing further, Ethan prompted, "Something work-related came up?"

"No. She canceled me." Fin stood up and paced. "In all fairness, she's only seen a glimpse of the Hollywood life. With this article, she got a full dose of what it's like to be a celebrity. She was half a world away and completely caught off-guard. If they had waited one more week, she would have been with me and I could have helped her navigate it."

Fin rubbed his face, then dragged a hand through his hair before sitting down again beside his brother.

"She got scared and ran like a rabbit? Seems a bit drastic. Was there more to it?"

"From what I understand, the paparazzi harassed her parents in their hometown, then a crowd of reporters showed up at her office, which is sacred to her. The disruption at her place of work was the last straw."

They sat in silence for a few minutes, enjoying the late afternoon before Ethan spoke. "From everything you told me about the lass, she sounded special. And strong enough to handle you and everything you bring with you. Running without explanation doesn't fit the woman you've described. Ye sure it's just the stardom thing?"

"Ah dinnae ken. I'm still reeling from it." Fin turned his head to Ethan and met his gaze. "But I'm putting it aside for now to enjoy my family."

The men clinked their bottles together and drank.

Later, while trying to fall asleep, Fin considered what Ethan had said. Alex *was* an intelligent woman, and it seemed unlike her to run from trouble. But he knew better than anyone else what unwanted attention could lead to, and he wouldn't place that burden on anyone. Perhaps Alex was right... you couldn't have everything. You were either successful at work or successful in relationships. He curled up on his side and wondered how long his heart would ache this time.

～

Fᴜɴ sᴘᴇɴᴛ the week swimming with his nieces and sight-seeing with his brother's family. The reporters and photographers who followed him around fascinated Ethan's clan, and they stood by politely when he signed autographs for fans.

Normally, Addie held a large Christmas party at her house, but with Fin's family in town, she had elected to attend Mac's holiday party instead. Her over-the-top explanation of giving Fin private time with his family made Fin suspect more than just business was going on between his two business partners, and he was happy for them both.

They spent Christmas Eve decorating the tree and remembering past Christmases. As bedtime approached, Moira shuffled the girls off to the guest bedroom, declaring that Santa didn't come when children were still awake. After an hour full of "I'm thirsty" and "I need to potty" routines, the girls finally settled in and fell asleep, giving the adults a chance to arrange Christmas gifts under the tree. Fin poured everyone a glass of wine and settled in on the couch to admire their handiwork.

"This is nice," Fin said. "I don't remember the last time I decorated a Christmas tree. I'm either away on location or some assistant puts up a small, pre-decorated tree for me. Kids make Christmas more fun, don't they?"

Ethan smiled and Moira agreed. "Aye. Their excitement is contagious."

"Fin." Ethan got his attention. "It's been educational watching you in your world. You get loads of attention, and yet you roll along as if it were everyday stuff. Like I might handle a horse needing a new shoe."

Moira laughed. "Or how I might handle getting our wee lasses dressed or cleaning up their messes."

Fin chuckled, recalling the spilled juice incident earlier

in the week and how upset Tara had been when she'd thought she'd ruined Uncle Fin's bonnie rug. Moira had handled it like a champ, and removed the stain before he could call someone to manage it.

Ethan continued, "You've had over a decade to get to that point. It's something Alex hasn't dealt with before. Mayhap you should call her and talk it through."

Fin sighed and tilted his head back, not wanting to deal with his broken heart right now.

Ethan quickly added, "No pressure. I'm just thinking about how I would react if I found myself thrust into the limelight." Then he changed the subject. "So, did you see Manhattan United have a new goalkeeper?"

The conversation flowed to the upcoming football season, and the brothers fell into familiar habits of disagreeing with the other's opinions of who had the best strategies. Before too long, their yawns convinced them to turn in before the girls woke up looking for evidence of Santa's visit.

FRIENDS AND RELATIVES crowded the house and spilled into the backyard. Alex had exchanged gifts earlier with her parents, then helped her mother prepare for the traditional Christmas luncheon hosted every year at the ranch. The Tanner family extended invitations to friends, ranch hands, and anyone else associated with the ranch or her family. It always surprised Alex how many people came every year. She'd mentioned it to her mother earlier, speculating about why they weren't spending the holiday with their own family. Debra had shrugged and said they either had no remaining family, couldn't afford to travel, or preferred this family to the one they had.

Her parents always had the event catered, so no one had to worry about cleaning up. This year, they'd hired a local group whose specialty was mesquite brisket to supply the meal, and everyone else had brought drinks, desserts, or any specialized food they wanted.

Alex's father had set up the outdoor games for anyone willing to brave the brisk winter temperatures. Lawn darts and cornhole were favorites, but they'd also dug out the basketball and added a fresh net to the rim so the kids could shoot some hoops if they wanted. A little cold weather never stopped the rugged West Texas folks from enjoying themselves. Alex had played a cutthroat game of horse with some ten-year-old boys until their frozen fingers drove them inside for some hot cocoa in front of the warm fire.

Having so many people around reminded her of Fin. While he only had two siblings, he treated his cousins like brothers and sisters, making his family stories sound like he belonged to a large, boisterous family. And from what he had shared, they had the same sense of community as her parents. If she hadn't canceled, she would be in LA sharing Christmas with his brother, sister-in-law, and their two girls. Fin had been thrilled she would get to meet them.

"Alex, can you come help me reach this?" her mother called from the kitchen.

Alex wiped the moisture from her eyes and went to help her height-challenged mother reach whatever bowl was too high. She had always teased her mom about having to buy a kitchen stool once Alex left for college because her "reacher" was no longer available. When Alex came back home, the stool sat in the corner, unused.

The last guest left around six. Their closest neighbor

had stuck around, helping her father pick up the outdoor furniture and put away the games. Alex and Debra had finished cleaning up the inside and sat at the kitchen table drinking iced tea when her dad came in the back door.

"Well, another wonderful party this year," he concluded. "Looks like it might snow later."

"The forecast said snow was possible," her mother reminded him as she poured him a glass.

"Eh, I didn't believe them. But the clouds are building, and they look heavy."

"I hope it won't cause problems for me getting to the airport tomorrow," Alex said.

Her father shrugged. "Shouldn't. It rarely snows enough to do harm. It's the ice you have to watch out for. And your flight is later. The ice will have burned off by then."

"Right." Houston's weather differed so greatly from West Texas, it was hard to believe they were in the same state. Houston was humid and subtropical, the temperature ranging from the mid-nineties in summer to the mid-forties in winter. By contrast, the Oil Patch, where her family lived was on the edge of the Chihuahuan Desert extending out of Mexico. Summers were dry and hot, with temperatures regularly reaching over a hundred degrees. Winters were much colder, frequently dipping down into freezing temperatures. It sometimes snowed, but mostly just froze, and black ice was a danger to many drivers during those cold months.

Alex wondered what the weather was like in Los Angeles right now.

"Alex!"

She jumped and looked up to find both of her parents staring at her. Her mom must have called her name more than once.

"Sorry, I was miles away."

They shared a look, and her dad excused himself to go finish something in the garage. Once he left, her mother arranged herself more comfortably in her seat.

"Alex, you've been dismal since you arrived. I know something happened with you and Fin. Please tell me. Just saying it out loud will relieve you of the burden you carry."

Alex sighed and leaned back in the chair. She yawned and stretched her arms, giving herself time to put on her game face. Her mom was right. She needed to talk about it. Otherwise, the stress was like a festering sore.

"I didn't handle the publicity well. I told you guys about the mob of reporters showing up at my work?" At her mother's nod, Alex continued, "Afterward, I kept thinking about all the ways Fin's fame has interfered with my life. It's like... out of nowhere, everything pivoted on a dime. There I was, heading down the path I meticulously planned, checking off my goals one by one, and just when everything was smoothly sliding into place, a sharp left turn appeared without warning and everything derailed. Because of Fin."

"You're still proceeding with the big department, right?" her mom asked sharply.

"Yeah, it's still on track."

"So what derailed exactly?"

Silent tears ran down her cheeks, and she got up to grab the tissue box. She dabbed at her eyes and considered the question.

"I've been completely stressed out. Like this constant pressure sitting on my chest. Normally, I would relish the challenge and not stress about it at all, but the last few months, I've had trouble concentrating and been completely off my game." Alex listed examples where she'd been late or unprepared for meetings and where she'd rearranged or put off work to spend time with him. She told her mom how off-kilter and out of her element she'd felt every time her personal life had barged into her work space. "I think the most humiliating thing about it all is how hard I've worked over the years to gain the respect of my colleagues, and now they all see me as some kind of sex object hanging on the arm of a celebrity."

"Oh, honey, do they really see you that way? Or are you being overly sensitive? You do good work. You've told us before that your bosses are happy with you and keep expanding your responsibilities. Has that really changed just because they know more about your love life than they did before?"

Alex lifted one shoulder in a half-shrug and blew her nose again as her mom continued.

"Here's something I don't understand... you've dated in the past and didn't have issues with your career, right? So it's just the fame thing?" her mother asked.

"No, it's him too. The other men I've dated were... convenient. They didn't interfere with my work, and if a conflict arose, work came first. Every time. I... um, I never cared enough about them to rearrange work. Those relationships were shallow and meaningless and Fin's not."

And then the water works began. Alex covered her face and sobbed into her hands. Her mother got up and sat beside her, wrapping her up in a warm hug.

"I miss him so much, Mom. I've never cared about anyone like this before, and I think I made a giant mistake. I think I approached my love life with a risk management attitude and spent a lot of effort mitigating risks and avoiding complications. I'm pretty sure that makes me a shallow bitch."

"Shh, it's okay."

Her mom was practically rocking her like a baby. She felt like one. She'd been so miserable since she'd left Houston. Alex had never understood what musicians meant when they sang about heartache, but this week that feeling had become crystal clear. Her chest ached and the constant lump in her throat made her miserable.

"Have you talked to him since you left?" her mom asked.

"N-no. The cell phone coverage here is crap. And—if I'm being honest—I'm too ashamed of how I ditched and ran."

"Cell phone coverage is no excuse. We still have a land-line here and you're welcome to use it. You should call him."

"You think so?" Alex sniffed and sat up to grab another tissue.

"Yes. He told you he cared about you. Right now, he's probably just as confused about what happened as you are. You need to talk to him and tell him what you just told me."

Alex stared at her mom.

"What?" Debra asked.

"You sound so wise."

"Yes, well, I wouldn't go that far. I just know any time your father and I got angry with each other, we'd talk it out. More often than not, we'd realize one of us had misunderstood the other, and our entire argument was over something silly." Debra stood up and smoothed non-existent wrinkles out of her jeans. "I'm going down to the barn to collect some eggs for breakfast while you call your man."

Alex blew her nose and sat up straight, pulling her shoulders back as her mom walked away. She shook her head and assumed her "go get 'em, tiger" pose, the one she often used to buck up her confidence before entering any difficult meetings.

She checked her phone, and seeing she had three bars of coverage, dialed Fin. With each ring, her spirits sank. Knowing Fin usually answered within two rings, she disconnected after the fifth ring before his voicemail answered. *He doesn't want to talk to me. I've really messed up,* she thought.

Alex dropped her laptop bag on the couch and went straight to her bedroom to change from her work clothes into something more comfortable. The week following Christmas was often as slow as the holiday week, but she used the time to catch up and organize.

Last week's news story of Finley McAlister's love interest had disappeared, and she had seen no reporters since she'd gotten back over the weekend. The quietness of it all reaffirmed her suspicion that she may have overreacted.

She changed into her usual jeans and t-shirt outfit, dug her tennis racket out of the back of her closet, and headed next door for her weekly dinner with the guys. Though the distance to Eddie's was less than ten yards, the weight of her fatigue dragged at her like she was walking up a large hill.

"Hey, Eddie," she said as soon as the door opened.

Eddie greeted her with a hug and a kiss on the cheek. "Come on in, sugar. Gabe's in the kitchen." He followed Alex through the house. "What is this?" he asked as he spied the gift she'd brought.

"You mentioned taking up tennis last month and I remembered I had this racket. It's practically brand new."

She handed it to him for inspection. "When I first moved to Houston, I joined a social club to meet people, and tennis was something they did. It didn't really suit me, but I never got rid of the racket, so it's yours if you want it. I don't need it anymore."

Eddie swung it back and forth. "This is much nicer than the one my sister had."

Alex shrugged. "I don't know a lot about tennis gear, but my buddy insisted this is a quality brand. I know the racket wasn't cheap, so if price correlates to quality, then..." She raised her hands and shrugged her shoulders again.

"What do I owe you?"

Alex waved him away. "Absolutely nothing. It's been collecting dust in my closet and would have wound up in the donation pile, eventually." She moved next to Gabe and gave him a side hug. "What smells so good?"

"Hey, Lexi Bear. New recipe. I'm trying a chicken and rice dish with my own special flavoring."

"Well, it smells yummy. How can I help?"

Gabe nodded toward the wine bottle on the counter. "Pour yourself a glass. We already have ours."

"Tell us about Finley. You guys seemed so happy. What happened?" Eddie asked as he pulled plates from the cupboard.

Alex groaned as she sat in a chair at the large island in Gabe's kitchen. "Wasn't meant to be, I guess. Two separate worlds that don't mesh well together." Why did her chest ache when she said that?

"Really? Because in the two weeks that boy was around, you were lighter and freer than I've ever seen you."

"What do you mean?" She leaned back in her chair, unsure if she wanted to know.

"I mean, as long as Gabe and I have known you, you've

always been such a serious girl. Work, work, work. Even when you are home, you work."

"That's not true. I play volleyball—"

Eddie cut her off. "Yes, yes, you play volleyball when it doesn't conflict with your work schedule." He eyeballed her, daring her to argue. "And you treat your men the same way. You keep them around as long as they aren't interfering with your work."

Alex sensed a theme with her friends and loved ones and was tired of talking about it. She snapped, "What's wrong with being ambitious? With having strong goals and striving towards them?"

"Nothing, my dear. Absolutely nothing. But you also have to live, or else what's the point in having those goals? The reporters and photographers concerned us at first, but they seemed to have moved on. And you know the whole 'no pain, no gain' mantra you're always spouting when you're nagging us to exercise more? Seems to me there's a parable in there somewhere."

Gabe chuckled at the stove. "Eddie whines more than a proper Southern lady about messing up his hair or his muscles aching or sweat in his eyes."

Alex slumped in her seat and gazed out the window. "You know, the last week or so, I've gotten tons of never-before-heard feedback from my friends on how they perceive me. I sound like some career-focused, man-eater bitch. Even Melissa said everyone perceives me as cool and aloof, which is completely opposite of how I see myself. I think I'm charming and warm." Her attempt at humor fell flat.

This time, Gabe spoke. "You are charming and warm. You're a lovely person. You treat the little guy the same as you treat the big guy, and people love that about you. You're successful because you radiate warmth outward. The problem is, it's all one-way."

"What does that mean?"

"Most people are a two-way street. They project themselves out and let people in. You only do one-way. You project out, but let few people in." He used the wooden spoon in his hand to point to Eddie and back to himself. "We are a member of an elite club."

"I have lots of friends," Alex argued, crossing her arms.

"Name the people who have spent time in your house. And I'm not talking about a 'come in while I grab my coat' situation. Really hung out, spent quality time with you in your inner sanctum. Name them."

Alex scowled. "You guys, Melissa, my mom..." Her voice failed as she tried to come up with names.

"Finley," Eddie helped.

Alex rolled her eyes at him. "Fin. Um... Oh!" She snapped her fingers and pointed at Gabe. "Grace from work came over once and we worked from here." Prompted by the look Gabe threw over his shoulder at her, she continued, "I'm counting her because I *never* let people from work into my sanctuary, so that means she is in the elite group." She stuck her tongue out at both of them.

"I'll allow it based on your persuasive argument," Gabe conceded. "Is that it?"

"I always thought I had lots of friends." Alex leaned forward to cross her arms on the table and buried her face in them.

"You have many people whom you know. Tons of acquaintances. Only a few real friends," Eddie chimed in. "The point Gabriella is making," he smiled as Alex smirked at the nickname, "is that you allowed Fin into your private domain immediately. None of that 'try before you buy' nonsense. You and he were tight as soon as you met. That's rare, girl. And inquiring minds want to know why you ended it before it could take off and go anywhere."

Alex sat up. "Who said *I* ended it?"

Eddie lowered his chin and pierced her with his gaze.

She dismissed the argument and considered his point while Gabe plated the food. As they moved to the dining table, she commented, "It was kind of like insta-trust, wasn't it?"

Alex sighed and recounted the events from the past two weeks, starting with how she'd learned about the article and everything that had followed. She told them she'd already concluded she might have acted in haste and beaten herself up over it.

"Why haven't you called him?" Eddie asked.

"I did. Several times. He never answered. He's avoiding my calls."

Gabe's brow furrowed. "Did you call him when you were at your parents' place?"

"Yeah, why?"

"They get shit reception. Remember when Felix got sick and we couldn't reach you because your phone never rang?"

"But this wasn't the same. My calls went through. The phone rang on the other end."

Eddie jumped in, "But did they?" He sipped his wine before adding, "I think you should try again."

Alex stared at him, then decided she needed a break from the emotional barrage and changed the subject. "Anyway, what's new at the restaurant, Gabe?"

The guys, recognizing the delaying tactic, let her off the hook and moved on to what was new in their lives.

Later, as she lay in bed cuddling Felix, she went over all

the feedback she'd gotten from her loved ones. She had definitely screwed up. She needed to make it up to Fin and figure out how to fix things between them. Obviously, she cared more for this man than she'd realized. Alex grew drowsy, and memories of happier times carried her off to sleep.

Chapter 26

Hope

JANUARY

Fin stretched his neck left, then right. They had signed the deal for the production studio in Glasgow last week and had finished the first walk-through this morning. He was on his way to a meeting with the production team in their temporary office, where they would discuss getting everything set up in the new building. This was the first time Fin had worked in the back end of filmmaking to this degree, and he wavered between excited and drained at the work involved.

On top of keeping busy, he wasn't sleeping. Every night, he tossed and turned, tormented by memories of Alex and their near-perfect time together. Following Ethan's advice, he'd called her over the holidays, but his calls went straight to voicemail and she never returned them. Fin got the message loud and clear. She wasn't interested. He rubbed the back of his neck and tucked his thoughts away as his driver approached their stop.

As he stepped out of the car, a familiar face greeted him

along with her film crew. She aimed the microphone at him like a weapon as she spoke.

"Finley McAlister, how's the new production company going?" Miranda Cole asked.

Was she being a tad more civil than usual? Or was Fin simply so exhausted she no longer riled him?

"Good morning, Ms. Cole. Your resourcefulness never fails to amaze," he replied.

"Finley, you've been occupied with your new production company. Does this mean you're giving up acting? Is your future now behind the lens?"

Fin stopped and considered the question. "My long-term business partner and I have teamed up with Mac McBrewster to create MPM Productions. Our first film under the new label is in production. I'm wearing two hats on this project, both executive producer and lead actor. To answer your question, I'm expanding my playbook to work both in front of and behind the camera."

"And what about Alex Tanner? You guys were hot and heavy for a while, but we haven't seen much of her lately."

Fin raised his eyebrows at the reporter's soft tone. The inquiry came across as a sincere question rather than an accusation, as they had always sounded in the past.

"As always, my private life is private. Now if you'll excuse me." He made to push through when suddenly, the weight of the last few weeks pulled at him. He turned back to the camera. "That's wrong. My private life has never been private, thanks to those in your profession. Regardless of how fiercely I work to protect myself and my loved ones from public scrutiny, I can't win. I've now lost two women I loved because of the news media. It makes me question whether any of this is worth it. If you find me disappearing behind the lens, as you say, it's because I'm not interested in living in a fish-bowl any more. If I must work behind the scenes to avoid the scrutiny and interference, I will. Good day to you, Ms. Cole."

He spun around and walked into the building, feeling both lighter and heavier. The grief of a broken heart weighing him down, alongside the relief of unloading a burden lifting him up. He climbed the stairs to the third floor and greeted the team waiting for him.

A week after that dinner of hard truths with Eddie and Gabe, Alex still wasn't getting any sleep at night. She availed herself to the fully stocked company break room, adding creamer and two packets of sugar substitute to her coffee cup, in an effort to wake herself up with a jolt of caffeine.

"Coffee, Alex? I didn't think you did coffee." Sam asked her as he refilled his cup.

"I'm fairly certain it doesn't qualify as coffee by the time I've added all the other stuff."

Sam laughed at her joke as he leaned on the counter next to her. "Seriously, though... you doing okay?" He waited for her to look at him before continuing, "I know you're a private person and we don't get into each other's personal business, but... you look tired. And you're not as energetic as you normally are. So I'm asking. Is it the PMO project? Or...?"

Alex held up a hand, acknowledging his thoughtfulness. "Thanks for asking, Sam. I'm just dealing with all kinds of... stuff... right now. The escalated timeline for the PMO is a substantial energy suck. I've pretty much abandoned the planning system project to you and Natalie because of it.

And, yeah... some of it's personal. Thanks for asking." She finished stirring her coffee before adding, "Did you hear we're talking about shutting down the London office?"

"Why?"

"When the lease came up for renewal, the new monthly rate was thirty percent higher. They weren't expecting it, and, man, were they pissed. Anyway, basing the European PMO branch within that office is no longer an option." Alex threw the used stir stick in the trash. "We'll discuss it in this morning's meeting, so bring some ideas with you." Her gaze swung up to the clock on the wall. "Yikes! Is that the time? I gotta run if I'm want to catch Frank beforehand. See you then."

"Yep, later."

Thirty minutes later, she and her team sat with Frank and Jeff discussing the new department and brainstorming ideas for viable locations.

"Alex, weren't two of your candidates in Scotland? Close to the new Glasgow office, right?" Sam asked.

"Oh, you're right. I met with several people in London and think of them as coming from all over, but, yeah, two of them lived near Glasgow. One of them came with the October acquisition."

Grace asked, "Have you been to the Glasgow office, Alex?"

"I haven't, but Frank has." Alex directed her question to Frank, "Would they have room to house our European PMO office?"

"Actually, that's a solid idea." He paused and peered at Jeff.

Jeff cleared his throat. "This is not to leave this room." He waited until everyone responded. "The local management team is aware, but we haven't made a general announcement yet. We plan to move the Glasgow tooling operation to the England plant, so the offices used by that department will be available."

The team was quiet as they contemplated the ramifications of this announcement.

"How many offices are available at the Glasgow facility? Do you know?" Alex asked.

"Not the exact number, but roughly half the building. I like this idea." Jeff leaned back and folded his hands on top of his head as he considered it.

Frank added, "Don't forget the regional sales guys." He explained to the group, "Since we'll have the space, we're thinking about consolidating the U.K. sales teams and eliminating the smaller offices scattered throughout the area."

Jeff sat up from his laid-back position in the chair, checked his watch, and made a note on his pad. "Yep, let's do that. Alex, give Susan in HR a call tomorrow and ask for the office layout and all the details. When we're finished here, I'll send over an email telling her to expect your inquiry."

"Can we state the PMO gets priority on seating since the sales guys already have bolt holes in the wild?"

Jeff grinned at her. "Yes, ma'am. You get first rights. Now make it happen." With that, he rose from his seat and walked out, Frank following close behind.

"Okay, any updates from the other projects we're involved with before we break for lunch?" Alex asked. Her phone pinged three times and a quick glance confirmed three different text messages.

Before she could read them, Sam caught her attention. "Yeah, the sales team requested a meeting with me and Nat this afternoon over the planning system project. I'd like you to sit in if you can. I have a sour feeling in my gut, like they're getting ready to lob something unexpected at us."

"Trouble?" Alex asked.

"Maybe. Natalie and I both think they're getting ready to come back with additional requirements outside of the original statement of work. Now whether they will be show-stoppers or minor adjustments remains to be seen. I'd like to have you in there, ready to steer the ship in case it's an iceberg."

"Yeah, okay. Forward me an invite. I'll rearrange if I have to."

"Thanks."

By the time Alex made it back to her office, she'd received several more texts and missed one phone call. She sat down and scanned through the texts, then listened to her mother's voicemail. They were all talking about a video with Fin going viral, insisting she needed to see it.

She opened up her browser and found the interview. It opened with a prelude from Miranda Cole. *Of course it's her,* thought Alex.

"Apparently, not all fairy tales end in happily ever after. Finley McAlister, last year's 'Hottest Man Ever,' seemed to have it all. An established position as one of Hollywood's A-list movie stars, a burgeoning career as a producer, and a new love in his life. But now, barely one month later, not every-thing is idyllic as it appears."

"According to Finley himself, he's lost the love of his life and is considering retiring from public life. Here's what he had to say."

Alex's heart thumped louder in her chest as Fin's face replaced Miranda's in the video. She listened as the woman interviewed him.

"... I've now lost two women I loved because of..."

"Wait, what? He loves me?" Alex asked aloud. She clicked the rewind button to listen again, then watched the rest of the video. She stopped at the point where Miranda began speculating about the price of fame.

Alex sat back and absorbed what she'd heard. Warmth spread throughout her body at the revelation that perhaps she wasn't too late. Maybe she still had a chance to make things right.

Energy flowed through her as she devised her checklist. Time to "man up" as her roughneck coworkers would say. First up, she needed to find Fin. *Where are you this week, Mr. McAlister?* she thought.

She sat forward and opened the travel calendar they had set up in October. The recent entries showed Fin's assistant was still updating it. Alex reviewed his itinerary for this week. He was in Glasgow through tomorrow, then in Aberdeen at his parents' house through next week. She opened the Aberdeen entry and was surprised to see their home address. *Bless you, Kathy, for that. Risky, but helpful.*

Her next task was arranging travel. She'd need a day or two to get her schedule sorted, so Friday was the earliest she could travel. She dialed the in-house travel agent's number.

"Jake speaking."

"Jake, it's Alex. I have an emergency trip I need to make. Um, and it needs to go on my personal account."

"Hey, Alex. Okay. Personal account. Trip details?"

"I need to get to Aberdeen, Scotland. And I'd like to leave Friday night or Saturday morning. I'll need at least one night in a hotel room, possibly more, depending on how it goes. I have no clue how long I'm staying. It may be a week or I might get right back on the plane and come home." She paused. "Am I asking you to do something impossible?"

Jake laughed. "Nah, I'm always up for a challenge. We've had to book stuff like this before with soft end dates. We'll figure something out. What about a car?"

"Um, I'm assuming I can grab a cab or ride share, but I'm not familiar with Aberdeen. Can you confirm that's an option?"

"Yep, let me get on it. And, Alex?"

"Yeah?"

"I'm rooting for you."

Alex froze, then relaxed. She was still getting used to people knowing her business. "Thanks, Jake."

"Yep. I'll hit you back if I have questions. Later."

Alex hung up the phone and pulled up her calendar. She spent the next two hours moving things around and pushing meetings back. She'd just sent a request to move a budget meeting forward to Friday morning when Sam walked in.

"You declined the planning system meeting?"

"Yes. You don't need me there. You know what our goals are and can handle those guys just fine. I'll be unavailable next week."

Sam's grin covered his entire face. "Okay, boss. Have a nice trip."

Alex shook her head. *Everyone is ahead of me on this one*, she thought.

Her next stop was Frank's office. She waited outside for him to finish the call he was on, then tapped on his door and asked if he had a minute.

"Sure, come on in," he said, pointing to the empty chair. "What's up?"

"I'm going to be out next week. I'm taking a vacation."

Frank sat up straighter in his seat. "Kind of a busy time to take off, isn't it?"

"Yes, but sometimes you have to prioritize your life."

He raised an eyebrow and waited.

Alex rolled her eyes. "Okay, I've already begun clearing my schedule and delegating tasks where I can. Tomorrow, I'll have all the official offer letters completed and delivered to our PMO candidates and by Friday, I'll have the initial list of projects we intend to tackle for the year. Grace and the team have the support tasks covered for year-end close. Happy?"

Frank grinned, but said nothing.

"It's been over a year since I took any vacation time. I need to use it. Even when I got the flu last year, I continued to work from home. Life can't be all work, ya know?"

"You don't have to convince me, Alex. Take your vacation. Things will be fine here. Safe travels."

Alex blew out her breath. "Okay, then. Thanks."

She stood and walked out. Her stomach fluttered. Telling Frank she was taking time off was the point of no return. It hadn't felt real until now.

FIN SAT in the back seat of his parents' car and watched the scenery go by as his mother discussed the Sunday sermon with his father. He'd arrived yesterday morning and planned to stay for the week. His sister, Caitriona, was due later today, and Ethan would show up tomorrow with his crew.

It seemed an odd time to have a family get together so soon after the holiday break, but Fin's great-grandfather had passed this week several decades ago, and they had unconsciously adopted a new family tradition to gather to celebrate and remember.

"Who's that?" His mother's words cut into his reverie.

Fin followed her gaze to the front porch of their house and sucked in his breath. The blond woman sitting on the steps reminded him of Alex.

"Fin? A reporter?" his father asked.

"No." His answer was barely above a whisper. "But I know her."

Alex stood up as Fin's father parked the car. Fin got out before his parents and tread slowly toward her, his eyes searching hers for an explanation.

"Hi," she said, then chewed on her bottom lip as she watched him. He'd never seen her look so unsure.

"Hi, yourself." He stepped closer and held his arms open to her.

Alex sobbed and rushed in to hug him. Fin wrapped her up in a tight embrace. He could feel the convulsions rack her body as she cried. He looked back over his shoulder at his parents. They hadn't questioned him over his love life when he'd shown up this weekend, and they continued their quiet support by slipping toward the back. He waved at his mom in thanks, and she acknowledged with a nod.

"I'm so s-s-sorry, Fin. I had this entire speech planned where I planned to talk to you calmly... to tell you how wrong I was and ask for a second chance. But then you opened your arms and... Now I'm a blubbering mess. Damn it."

Fin smiled. How like Alex to get mad at herself for not being the tough girl she projected to the world.

"Shh. It's okay, lass." He stroked her hair and kissed the top of her head.

Alex pulled away and he let her go. She scrubbed her eyes, then looked around. "I seem to have scared away your family."

"They went in through the back."

"Oh."

"Tell me why you're here, Alexis."

Alex shuddered and looked up at him. "I'm an idiot. I ran like a coward when the reporters came. And when you didn't return my calls, I just gave up. I've never given up on anything, Fin. Anything! Any time I've run into opposition, I've dug in and fought harder. So why did I run, Fin?"

"Back up. You called me? When?"

Alex went still. "Um, the week following the hubbub. I called a few times, but you never answered."

"I never got your calls, Alexis. Why didn't you leave a voicemail?"

She grimaced. "The first time, I was too chicken. The couple of times after that, the call never went to voicemail, just kept ringing and ringing."

"That's odd." He paused. "I tried to call you too. You never answered my calls. I believed the press had completely ruined my chances with you."

"I didn't receive your calls either. The same week?" Her brow furrowed as he nodded. Alex turned her head and her eyes grew distant. "Gabe was right."

"Right about what?"

"I was at my parents' ranch that week, and cell reception is terrible there. I assumed that if it rang, the call went through." She looked back at him. "Shit, Fin. We both tried to contact each other and were defeated by technology. Ugh, what a hot mess."

Fin reached for her hand and led her to the bench on

the porch. "So, you freaked out, but got over it, then gave up again when you couldn't reach me?"

Alex rolled her eyes. "It sounds so juvenile when you say it like that. But, yes, I ran home like a scared little kid. When you didn't answer my calls, I assumed you were done with me because I couldn't handle your fame." She shrugged. "So I gave up."

She stood and paced back and forth in front of him. "Fin, I've never felt this way before. I've never been in a relationship like this before. I've always been the one to leave so, when I didn't want to, I wasn't sure what to do. Everyone told me I screwed up, but I didn't believe them. Then the longer I went without you, the more I realized how empty my life seemed. The things I used to think were most important no longer seemed important at all." She gulped. "Then I watched your interview with Miranda Cole." She stopped pacing and looked shyly at him. "The one where you said you loved me. Knowing you felt the same way as me... I knew then I had thrown away something wonderful. Can you forgive me?"

Fin reached out and dragged her into his lap. He gripped the back of her neck and pulled her into a fierce kiss. She stiffened, then relaxed. Her arms came up around his neck and she deepened the kiss.

Fin pulled back. "What about your work? Your new position?"

"I took a break. I'm on vacation with strict instructions not to be disturbed. I needed time to get my priorities right." She searched his eyes. "Can you forgive me?"

"Aye, *mo ghràdh*, if you can forgive me as well."

"Forgive you for what? I'm the one who was '*aff ma heid*.'"

Fin burst into laughter at her terrible attempt at a Scottish brogue. "No, lass. I shouldn't have given up so easily, either. I ken how brutal the media can be. But I also know how strong you are, and I should have given you the benefit of a doubt."

He noticed her luggage beside the steps. "How did you find me?"

"Oh. Um, your assistant is still updating our travel calendar," she said as she ducked her head and looked down for a split second before raising her eyes. "You should probably tell her not to enter personal information like your parents' address. It's not like you don't know it, right?" The twinkle in her eyes made him grin.

"Right. I'll mention it to her."

"Ahem." The quiet voice from the front lawn had Alex scrambling out of his lap and adjusting her clothes. "Giving the neighborhood a show, big brother?"

"Cat." Fin grinned at the tall, dark-headed woman nonchalantly observing them from the sidewalk. "Let me introduce you to Alex, sister mine."

Chapter 27

Beginnings

Two months later...

Alex sat back in the first-class seat and closed her eyes. Her new department was gaining traction. She would split her time between the two base offices in Glasgow and Houston. Last month, she'd flown over to organize setting up the Glasgow office. While there, she'd moved in with Fin and now shared his upscale apartment. This trip marked her first stint in Glasgow, which would last three months until she traveled back to Houston for the mid-year budgeting process. *Today is the beginning of the rest of your life*, she thought as she smiled to herself.

"Excuse me, miss?" a deep, soft-spoken voice with a lovely Scottish accent spoke next to her. "That is my seat."

Alex's smile grew bigger as she opened her eyes to stare up into a pair of dazzling blue eyes looking back at her. "Oh, I'm sorry. Am I in the wrong seat?" She batted her eyelashes up at him.

Fin kissed her before sliding into the window seat beside her. "No, *mo chridhe*, you are right where you belong."

"When you texted me your connecting flight was running late, I worried you'd miss this one. I'm happy to see you made it on the plane."

He buckled his seatbelt and reached over to hold her hand. "I can move fast when motivated. Remind me to thank my assistant for finding coordinating flights, allowing us to fly this leg together." Fin grinned. "We're finally doing this. I thought the day would never come."

"Right? I'm so excited I can't sit still. What a journey!"

"Aye, lass."

The captain came on overhead, making sure everyone was settled so they could close the cabin door and be on their way.

She didn't believe in fate, but that left turn she'd once described to her mother had somehow melded their two worlds into one. On matters of fate and destiny, it made one wonder.

She lifted Fin's hand in hers and kissed the back of it. "I love you," she said.

"Aye, *mo ghràdh*, and I you."

IF YOU ENJOYED *LEFT TURN*, I would love for you to let your friends know so they can experience the relationship between Alex and Fin as well. Reviews help authors sell more books—not to mention, pay more bills—and the feedback helps us improve our craft. Please leave a review for *Left Turn* on the site from which you purchased the book, Goodreads, or other book review places. I would love to read it.

You can stay up-to-date on upcoming releases and sales

by visiting the Reader's Corner page of my website (https://lancymccall.com) or joining my newsletter, also found on that page.

Acknowledgments

Thank you so much to everyone who helped on this book. Special thanks to my husband, who told me to write my own book, and my sister-in-law, who was my first alpha reader and encouraged me to keep going.

Also, thanks to my editors, who were great with helping a newbie author find her way: Megan Records and Julie Mianecki. And a super fun thanks to fellow author, Chloe Archer, who helped me play with blurbs. (*Why are those so difficult?*)

Final shout out to another fellow author, Michael Aspen, who helped me muddle through some of the unknowns as I reached the end.

About the Author

Lancy McCall is a native Texan who grew up riding horses and rounding up cattle. Ranch life provided a wealth of experiences to share, including a few scary tales involving coyotes and rattlesnakes.

Her love of reading and storytelling developed early. Since she was able, she always had a book in hand. This habit filled her personal library with genres ranging from romance to horror to autobiographies, with fantasy and sci-fi holding a special place in her heart.

After a successful corporate career as a global project manager, she's now found a new calling to turn those experiences into stories for others to read.

Lancy is active on these social platforms:

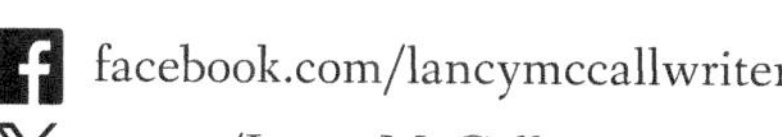

facebook.com/lancymccallwriter

x.com/LancyMcCall

instagram.com/lancymccall

pinterest.com/lancymccall